THE
HONEYMOON

A Second-Chance Romance

ANNE TROWBRIDGE

THE
HONEYMOON

A Second-Chance Romance

ANNE TROWBRIDGE

ISBN: 979-8-9865072-2-4

For my daughter, Madelyn.

*You're independent, fierce, funny,
and filled with a strong sense of self.*

Keep dreaming big dreams.

Other Books by Anne Trowbridge

The Curveball Incident Series

Curveball: A Love Story (Book 1)

Curveball: A Wedding Novella (Book 1.5)

Out of the Park: A Romance (Book 2)

Ticket to Love Series

The Honeymoon: A Second-Chance Romance (Book 1)

The Bridesmaid: An Insta-Love Romance (Book 2)
(coming soon, but available now in Kindle Vella)

Cruz Into Love Series

The Distance Between Us:
A Hidden-Identity Romance (Book 1)
(coming soon, but available now in Kindle Vella)

The Friendship Divide:
A Friends-to-Lovers Romance (Book 2)
(coming soon, but available now in Kindle Vella)

What Separates Us:
An Enemies-to-Lovers Romance (Book 3)
(coming soon, but available now in Kindle Vella)

Prologue

"OLIVIA, I'M WORRIED about you, girl," Donna said as she leaned back to sip her wine, her brown eyes narrowing over the top of the glass. "I don't even understand what's going on with you, and you won't tell me anything. You're not yourself, you're not eating, you're being super emotional and mysterious. And, oh yeah, no one's seen your husband since your wedding day."

Donna's words floated through Olivia's mind as she dragged her fork through her salad, searching among the leaves of lettuce as though they would hold all the answers if she only dug through them fervently enough. What words could she even assemble that could begin to ease her friend's worries? She could fill an ocean with all her problems right now. Which one would Donna even want to hear about first?

But honestly, none of that mattered anyway, because the truth was that she just couldn't bring herself to confide in anyone right now—she didn't even want to try. If her tears started, they might never stop....

"Hello? Olivia? Are you in there?" Donna persisted, setting her wine glass down before leaning back, crossing her arms, and narrowing her gaze even further. "Did you even hear me? I was worried before, but now? Now I'm working my way up the ladder to atomic-level freak out."

"No, Don, really, I'm okay," Olivia said with a sigh as she abandoned her fork on her plate and sat back, too. Then, finally, she drew her eyes up to meet her friend's steely, assessing gaze. "I just have to get through this year. That's it. I'm simply slogging through one day and then the next. If I can make it to my anniversary…well, things are going to get better. You'll see."

"Your anniversary?" Donna asked, not looking relieved or pacified one bit by Olivia's attempt at an explanation. "The one that's months and months away? *That* anniversary? That makes absolutely no sense."

Olivia knew she was being maddeningly vague, but how could she ever truly explain what had happened? No one could possibly begin to comprehend—or even believe—what she'd been through since her ill-fated wedding day. Even if she wanted to find the words, there just weren't any that could accurately summarize it all.

"Why would your anniversary be so very magical when your wedding day was such a complete horror show?" Donna asked, cutting through her inner turmoil again.

"Oh, come on, now. You say that like it's a bad thing. You know how much I love horror shows." Olivia's weak attempt to make Donna smile fell flat. Nevertheless, she plowed ahead with the joke—"It's like a dream that I got to star in one of my very own."

"Okay, sure…sad attempts at humor," Donna said, her head nodding as though she were making an exciting breakthrough. "I get it. So tell me, did you murder your husband on your honeymoon? Was that how your horror movie ended? Because I know I've said this before, but no one's seen John since you two flew off to Paris. Where'd you hide the body?"

"As far as I know, he's alive and well," Olivia mumbled, trying to ignore the lurch of fluttering nerves and worries that the mention of John's name elicited inside her.

"As far as you know? *As far as you know?*" Donna parroted, looking flabbergasted now. "You don't know where he *is,* either?"

"No." The misery in Olivia's voice matched the pain in her heart. "But that's going to change. Like I said, I just have to make it to my anniversary, and then everything will be better."

Donna sighed. "Okay, I'll bite. What's going to happen on your anniversary?"

"I'm going back to Paris," Olivia said with a hint of a smile as she watched the confusion play across her best friend's face.

"Would you just spit this story out already?" Donna asked, looking even more frustrated with her now. "*Why* are you going back to Paris on your anniversary?"

Olivia took a deep breath. And then, with a rapid exhale, the words tumbled out of her as though she couldn't hold them back if she tried.

"I *have* to go to Paris. It holds the key to everything," she said fervently. "And I'm going on my honeymoon."

Chapter 1

Cold Feet

Two Months Earlier....

THE WOMAN staring back at Olivia in the full-length mirror looked exactly like a happy, beautiful bride should look on her long-awaited wedding day. An elegant, ivory dress swept down her tall, thin figure, its silk barely brushing the tops of the dainty ivory shoes. Her thick hair was gathered loosely on her head in a mass of black curls dotted with sparkling diamond-and-pearl pins. A simple pearl necklace and earrings—gifts from her father—completed the sophisticated look.

Definitely beautiful. Definitely a bride. Definitely her wedding day...but definitely *not* happy.

A small tear formed in Olivia's eye, but she gingerly blotted it away with annoyance. After what she'd paid for this makeup job, she'd die before she'd let it get ruined over a stupid thing like regrets. It was simply too late for those. Her family, her business associates, and all her friends were out there waiting for her, not to mention John's family and friends and colleagues. And, of course, John himself. He was out there, too.

John.... Sweet, kind, funny, loving John. And boring John—let's not forget that part. He would soon be waiting for her at the altar. It would never occur to him to *not* show up. He would never experience any kind of last-minute waffling. Because John was utterly and completely in love with her. No, she'd certainly never have to worry about infidelity or a lack of devotion from him.

The funny thing was that Olivia really did love him back. He was a great guy, after all. He was smart, handsome, polite to a fault, kind to animals and old ladies....

She let the laundry list of his do-gooder qualities trail off in her mind. Who was she trying to convince? Herself? And if so, why was she doing this? Why did she doubt this decision she'd made, this commitment she had thought she was ready to enter?

She could try to fool herself, but she already knew the answer to those questions. Because at forty years old, she couldn't help but wonder if she'd panicked and settled. Had she hit the end of her thirties and just grabbed the first unattached man who walked past without drooling or dragging his knuckles? She was pretty sure some of her friends thought so, probably because Olivia hadn't gone through that giddy, sparkling, isn't-he-so-wonderful "madly-in-love" stage that most people seemed to go through when they find The One. Nope, John had just fit into her life comfortably, like an old, worn-out shoe. No sparks, no fireworks, no fights, no problems. Comfortable.

Maybe it was because she was older and more mature than most first-time brides when she'd met her husband-to-be. Perhaps, under the same exact set of circumstances, only at the age of, say, twenty, Olivia would have been swept off her feet by this man, and the electricity would have knocked her over. Maybe.... Regardless, that hadn't happened.

She took a deep breath and exhaled it slowly, still gazing at, yet still not seeing, her reflection in the mirror. It was true. She loved John, but she wasn't *in* love with him. And that was only part of her problem. The other part was that she had waited to admit this to herself until about thirty minutes before she should be making her gleeful entrance into the church, down the aisle, and into his arms forever.

"I couldn't have acknowledged these feelings twenty thousand dollars ago?" she muttered to herself as she straightened a spaghetti strap on the gown and centered it on her shoulder. Olivia and John had paid for the wedding and honeymoon themselves. Both in their forties, neither even considered asking their parents for help—or accepting help when it was offered. That would have been ridiculous. They had tried to keep things simple, with about a hundred or so guests who would soon be converging on her father's backyard in northern New Jersey under the tents that the caterers had set up. The caterers were the big expense, of course. That and the honeymoon. She smiled dreamily as she thought about the trip. Two weeks in Paris, which meant the Eiffel Tower, tours into wine country, strolls along the Seine River, afternoons exploring the *Louvre* and the *Musee d'Orsay*.

She laughed out loud because she was more excited about the trip than she was about the ceremony. Or the marriage. Or the groom. Then the laughing smile on her face turned into a scowl. She was a smart, successful, extremely independent lawyer. If she had wanted to visit Paris, she could have gone at any point in the past twenty years. So she surely wasn't using John as her ticket there! No, she refused to believe she was that shallow and needy. She had plenty of girlfriends who would have been thrilled to go wrap their credit cards around the City of Lights. This could *not* have been about the lure of the honeymoon.

So, if it wasn't the honeymoon, then what was it?

Perhaps the enticement of the automatic date at every work function? Or a talisman to ward off a lonely, multiple-cat-owning future? A way to finally convince her father that she wasn't deliberately trying to destroy his life by not producing grandchildren? Whatever her motives, she was now stuck with the consequences of her actions, bad decisions, and terrible timing.

Poor John, she thought. He really didn't deserve a half-hearted bride or a disappointed wife. Of course, he also didn't deserve to get stood up at the altar. Which was worse? Maybe a quiet divorce later would be kinder than a scandalous jilting now. *Or would it...?* Olivia sighed. Was she *really* considering jilting him? Or leaving him right after they got back from France? Had it really come to this?

She sat down in the rocking chair, leaned her head back, and closed her eyes. The church provided this small, private room off the bathroom so brides could get ready. There was the full-length mirror, the chair, and a narrow wooden table for critical items like makeup, hairpins, and curling irons.

She was extremely glad the room was so small; it made a convenient excuse for being alone right now. Of course, there wasn't exactly a crowd of women out there, beating on the door trying to get a glimpse of the bride. Her mother had died not long after Olivia was born, and she had no sisters with whom to share the day. Or to talk over her feelings of regret and panic. She had friends, of course, but they were already seated in the church. In the interest of keeping things simple, they had decided not to have any attendants. So there really was no one.

Gently rocking the chair with one foot, she tried to make herself relax by letting her mind wander. Peaceful thoughts; calm, serene, happy thoughts. Flowers. Children. Puppies. *John.* Yes, she tried to focus on him again. *John.* Even his name was dull. A smile flitted across her face as she remembered the first time she met him and learned his dull-as-dishwater name.

"Olivia, I don't think you've met John yet. He's one of Acadia's top-secret weapons," her boss, Elliot, had said in his usual full-schmooze way before he oozed off across the room. Acadia was the accounting firm that her company, A&I Electronics, had hired, and John was a CPA there. A&I made airplane parts, and they were going through an accounting review in preparation for a bid on a big government contract. Olivia was on the legal team reviewing all aspects of their bid process, making sure no red tape blocked their way. The party they had both attended that night was just a little celebration of the forthcoming happy partnership.

"Hello, I'm Olivia Conte," she said, reaching out her hand. John met it with his own, and she remembered being impressed by his firm, warm shake, plus the fact that he looked directly into her eyes when he spoke.

"John Daux," he said, his voice rich and deep.

"Doe? D-o-e? John Doe?" Olivia asked, a confused smirk stealing across her face as she assessed him. "Fine, don't tell me your name."

He was tall, muscular, and handsome in a non-threatening kind of way, she decided. His hair was short and brown, and it was showing signs of thinning on top. His eyes, which she could only describe as "kind," were green. All in all, he just looked like a nice person.

And a nice person with no wedding ring, she noticed idly.

"No, D-a-u-x," he said with a self-deprecating smile. "And yes, before you say it, I've heard more unidentified cadaver jokes than you can imagine."

"Your name really is John Daux?" Olivia teased, judging John to be a guy who could take the ribbing. She had felt comfortable with him instantly. "Nope. Sorry, but I just don't believe it. That's got to be an assumed name. You're CIA, right? Or, no! You're a mob informant in the Witness Protection Program, right? Your real name is Lefty Petracelli, but your friends call you 'The Knife'? Why don't I just call you 'Alias' and cover all the bases?"

"Sure, that's right," John said with a laugh. "I'm a man of mystery and possible mob ties. But you can call me whatever you'd like, Livvie." He reached for two glasses of white wine from a tray as a waiter walked by.

"Oh no you don't," she said, reaching for the glass he was offering and taking a sip before continuing. "No one calls me anything other than Olivia."

"That's a beautiful name, Liv," he said, a playful sparkle in his eye.

She narrowed her dark brown eyes and made a face at him. "Thanks, Alias."

And so the relationship had begun. They spent the rest of the party together, and that continued pretty much up to this moment. They met, and then they simply *were*.

Olivia opened her eyes and sighed again. She wasn't at that party now, and she wasn't sipping wine and meeting the actually not-so-mysterious John Daux for the first time.

No....

No, it was one year later, and she was about to marry him.

Maybe.

Or maybe not....

She had fifteen minutes to make up her mind.

Chapter 2

No Doubts

John tried again to stab the silver body of the link—a wedding present from Olivia—through the tiny holes in his right sleeve. Being righthanded wasn't helping his struggle, either. Too bad she hadn't wanted attendants, because he could sure use a best man about now. After a few more minutes of effort, he swore under his breath, palmed the errant link, and shoved it in his pocket. Surely someone would drop by to see him before it was time to take his place in the front of the church.

As the cufflink dropped, he heard a tiny clink, and that brought a smile to his face. *The ring.* Livvie's ring. A simple, platinum band to match the solitaire she'd picked out. John reached down and felt for it. The metal felt smooth and warm and solid in his fingers. He continued to roll it around, his eyes staring unseeing in front of him. The ring. The wedding. Today! It was finally here. The day he was going to marry gorgeous Olivia Conte. Amazing.

He remembered the day they met. Her sleazy boss had introduced them at some party launching a project between their two companies. The details were fuzzy, but one thing was vividly clear in his mind: how beautiful she looked that night.

She'd teased him about his name—face it, who didn't?—but there was a kindness behind the banter.

She was obviously sizing him up, seeing if he could take a joke. He'd tried to maintain his end of the conversation, hoping he was hitting more of a James Bond vibe than, say, a Mr. Bean tone. He must have said something right, because he remembered her laughing, her eyes sparkling as she sipped the wine that he'd handed her.

And easy, too. Yes, with her it had just been so easy, right from the start. He knew he had to ask her out, he *had* to see her again. So, he did, and she said yes. From then on, they had been a part of each other's lives. No growing pains or gradual upping of the commitment. No drama or fights. They were just together. And now they were making that commitment permanent. They were so in sync with each other that he'd never even formally proposed. They'd just wandered into a jewelry store one day, and John had encouraged her to pick a ring out. Then they started making wedding plans. So natural and...

Easy.

How had he gotten so lucky? He'd spent his whole adult life in and out of relationships, some good and some bad, some hot and some cold. He'd even made a couple of them permanent—today marked John's third trip down the aisle. But it was going to be his last; he knew that beyond any doubt. Past mistakes had been washed away and the slate was clean because Olivia was The One. Their personalities and their lives had melded seamlessly. It had been that simple and that comfortable. It was just right.

A lot of that had to do with Olivia herself. She was so completely accepting of him. Nothing in the past seemed to matter to her. John wasn't even sure if she knew he'd been married before. None of the baggage that's usually dragged into relationships had been packed and brought into theirs. And when he was with her, nothing else seemed to matter anyway. It hadn't even occurred to him to talk about his past failures with her. He'd never really thought about why, but again—when he was with her, nothing and no one else mattered. Past loves not only weren't on his mind, it was like they never existed in the first place. Olivia was his everything. She never questioned him about the past, grilled him about his belief in this or his stance on that. She loved him. *Him.* Not his beliefs or his stances or his history or his exes.

It was so amazing. *She* was so amazing.

And this smart, sophisticated, sexy, elegant woman had agreed to be his wife. Because she felt it, too. Their love was one of a kind. John was sure about all of this, and they had their whole lives to get to know the other little details about each other. Those silly little things that make people so unique and make relationships so interesting. That comfortable love flowing between them was enough to make John know beyond any doubt that this was right. This was *it*.

He blinked a few times and shook his head, trying to clear the foggy daydreams away. He turned toward the mirror and silently assessed himself. His jacket was on, and his tie was knotted in a perfect bow. Other than the stubborn cufflink, he was ready.

Fifteen minutes to go.

Chapter 3

The Warning

"JOHN, YOU TAKE my breath away, you handsome devil," his sister said, peeking around the door of the room the church had provided. It was in a small office by the altar.

"Katie!" John said, smiling at her in the reflection of the mirror. "Hey, come on in!"

"Can I hug you, or will you wrinkle?" she asked, affection lighting her face.

"Never too wrinkle-free for you," he replied, turning to open his arms as she moved in with a tight squeeze.

"Hey, what's wrong?" he asked, noticing tears in her green eyes—which were so much like his own—as he pulled back from the hug.

"No, it's nothing," she said, grabbing a tissue off a nearby desk.

"It's not *nothing* if you're upset, so spit it out. I've got a wedding today, you know," he said, a quizzical half-smile on his face.

"Oh yes, I *know*," Kate replied with a sniff as she balled up the tissue and threw it in the trashcan with a little too much vengeance for the situation.

"Is that what you're upset about? That I'm getting married? I'm forty-two, Katie, not four. It's okay for your brother to make big adult decisions, you know." There was a sarcastic edge to his voice, mainly because he was starting to get a little impatient with her.

"Yes, of course. But…." Kate's voice trailed off.

"Kate, really, I don't have time to play animal, vegetable, or mineral with you. What's wrong? Speak now, or forever hold your peace." He was completely confused about what could possibly be upsetting her. This day was about happiness, love, and celebration, not tears.

Either his words or his tone worked, because the reluctance to speak seemed to melt away as Kate suddenly spun around to stare at him, her gaze sizzling with intensity. "John, honey, are you *sure?*"

"Sure about what? That I don't have time for guessing games?" He was trying to rein in his frustration at this point.

"No. Sure about *this*," Kate said, her arms gesturing wildly around her. "About getting married today. About marrying *Olivia?*"

"*Of course* I'm sure. She's not dragging me down the aisle or tricking me into this. I'm crazy about her, Katie." He cocked his head to the side like a curious dog. "Where is this coming from? What is this even about? You know how much I adore Olivia. I thought *you* liked her, too."

Kate inhaled deeply but didn't respond right away. She appeared to be thinking about what she should say next very carefully.

"Your time for true confessions is rapidly running out," John said, tapping his watch in reply. "If you've got something, just say it."

"John, I'm not trying to spoil this day for you, I'm really not," Kate told him, exhaling a frustrated-sounding sigh. "But for some reason I feel that something's just not right with the two of you, and I'm really worried that you're not thinking this through. It's only been a year—why jump into marriage so soon?"

"Kate, we both know I've made mistakes. And no, this isn't my first wedding day. But it really feels like it is, you know? I was a child when I married Val. And let's not even go into details on the second one. But they were both a lifetime ago. I know what I want now, and I don't need any more time to think about it."

"And you're positive it's got to be with her?" Kate asked with a pleading tone.

"Kate, if I just wanted to be married for the sake of being married, would I have waited this long? Would I have divorced the first two?" John was completely shocked he was even having to say these things to her. Couldn't his family and friends feel how strong their bond was? It was almost tangible to *him*, after all. "I love her, and I fully intend to spend the rest of my life with her. Not just a few years until the shine wears off."

"And I want that for you too, John, really I do," Kate said, still looking unconvinced. "I'm not trying to hurt you here, but, well, you're sure the feeling's mutual?"

"You're asking me if Olivia loves me in return?! Or if she wants to be married as much as I do? Kate, I have to tell you, this is really crazy. I can't believe you're asking this."

"Just hear me out, okay?" Katie said, gesturing with both hands. "Does *she* love *you?* The same way you love *her*, I mean. I want you to really think about it, though. You're positive?" Now she reached out and gripped his arms as though she were considering shaking him like a rag doll.

"Kate, I'm saying this from the bottom of my heart, okay?" he replied, reaching up to peel her hands off, then holding them together in his own. "I *know* beyond any sort of doubt that this is right. That Olivia loves me every bit as much as I love her." He glanced at his watch. "And in about ten minutes, we're going to prove it to you."

"Okay, okay," she said, leaning in for a hug. "I'm sorry, John. Steve told me to stay out of it, and I tried, I really did. But when today arrived, I…I just couldn't let you do this without saying something to you first. I couldn't live with myself."

"I know you're just trying to take care of me, and you love me. I'm not mad. Of course I'm not." He pulled back from the hug then, a smile reappearing on his face. "But hey, you *could* help me with something—a stupid cufflink." He pulled it out of his pocket and handed it to her. Kate worked it through the holes on his sleeve and then rotated it before twisting the little bar lock into place.

John gave her another hug, then turned her around so she was facing the door.

"You better get out there and find Steve and the kids," he said. As much as he loved his sister, he wanted a few minutes alone to shake off their conversation before meeting Olivia at the altar.

She started walking, then stopped to look back at him. A flicker of regret was evident in the half-smile she offered before going out, closing the door behind her.

He stared into space for a moment before turning back to the mirror to make sure he was ready. He straightened his tie once more, then finally leaned back against the desk to wait.

Where had Kate come up with those last-minute fears? he wondered silently. He and Olivia had spent time with his sister and her family, so there had been plenty of opportunity for Kate to see them together—see how happy they were—during the last year. Why was she doubting Olivia now? And why in the world had she allowed Steve to stop her before if she truly believed the things she had just said? Waiting until the last possible minute to spring these doubts on him wasn't very helpful.

But John still wasn't angry—he never was angry with her. Not for long anyway. In fact, he didn't have much of a temper at all. He'd never had cause to be mad at Olivia, either. Even Val, his first wife, and Jackie, his second wife, in the midst of their breakups and divorces, had never driven John to get really mad. He was just a laidback, relaxed guy. Life was much too short for arguments and bitterness, he often thought.

So he let the conversation with Katie fall from his mind before it could plant any seeds of doubt. And why would it? This was right, John knew it deep in his soul. Kate would see she'd been wrong about Olivia.

He took a deep breath.

Just under five minutes to go.

Chapter 4

The Options

SHE HAD FEWER than five minutes to go. *So little time left to decide the course of the rest of my life....*

Olivia could feel the panic bubbling up inside of her. Should she make a run for it? Just grab her phone and keys, race out to her car, drive away from this fiasco, and go....

Where? Paris, maybe? Treat myself to a solo honeymoon?

As soon as this thought floated through her mind, she dismissed it. Wandering alone through a honeymoon vacation sounded like the very definition of depressing. She already felt torn and confused; she didn't need abject misery too.

Well, she couldn't just go home and binge whatever might be streaming on a late Saturday afternoon, either, as though nothing had happened. John would find her there, for starters. And the last thing she wanted was to look in his eyes after he'd suffered such devastating humiliation. But she didn't have anywhere else to go or anyone else to flee to. This wasn't going to turn into a scene from *The Graduate*; she didn't have any relationships on the side ready to take John's place after rescuing her from the church. That's not what this was about.

Okay, so if there was nowhere to go and no one else in the picture, did that mean she should stay? Perhaps go out there and tell everyone thanks for taking the time, but sorry, no ceremony today? It would save

John the pain of having to do it. Of course, that was a spineless thing to do, too—tell John and the receptionist at her firm and her cousin Dora all at the same time. It seemed worse than leaving him here alone to figure it out. That scenario also ran through her imagination—the organ playing as John stood at the altar, happily looking over his shoulder waiting for her to appear. The sound of people starting to murmur as the minutes ticked by. The look on John's face when her dad showed up, very obviously alone, at the end of the aisle. And then her dad shaking his head no, followed by John's heart ripping to shreds and bleeding in front of everyone they knew as he turned around to make the announcement.

Would he cry? She'd certainly never seen him cry before. Would he be enraged? She almost laughed at the thought—nothing could make John angry. He was the epitome of Zen. Would he leave? Or would he be the eternal good guy and play host at the reception? Probably. That *was* John.

This whole scenario was painful to watch even in her mind's eye. *Okay—so what, then?* Should she go find him? Make everyone wait and wonder while she dumped him behind the scenes? There was so much to say. So much explaining she would have to do. And she barely understood these feelings herself; she wasn't sure she was ready yet to have them exposed and analyzed in a huge breakup fight. Although, again, John was an easygoing guy, so there probably wouldn't be a fight. If anything, he'd probably apologize for making her feel that way. Meanwhile, everyone would be sitting out there, waiting and guessing what was happening. Or hearing it, depending on how upset they both got.

So, what option did that leave her with? Going

through with the ceremony? Lying to God and a minister and basically everyone she knew? As dishonest and distasteful as that sounded, it seemed the fairest choice so far. It was right that she should be the one to suffer and not him. She would have to swallow her pride, get through this day with a fake smile plastered on her face, and get through the next two weeks without him suspecting something was wrong. Hopefully she was a good actress. And then, after they got back, she could let him down gently. Sometime before they started opening all those presents, preferably. The ones that would have to be returned.

Ugh, what a nightmare.

One more minute...she had one minute left before she had to make her appearance. There was still time to race out of here if she wanted to. *But should I?* What was right? What should she do?

Olivia leaned her head back against the rocking chair and squeezed her eyes tight. Her heart was racing, her breaths becoming shallower. She was going to have a full-blown panic attack if she didn't calm down.

Take a deep breath. Exhale. Take another.

She focused on her breathing, hoping she could avoid hyperventilating or even passing out.

There was a knock at the door.

"Olivia, honey," her father said. "It's time. Are you ready, darling?"

Chapter 5

Waiting at the Altar

JOHN CHECKED his watch yet again. Yes. It was finally time. He smoothed his jacket sleeve back over his wrist, took a deep breath, and opened the door.

"I was just coming to find you," said the minister, startling him as they met at the door.

"Is something wrong?" John asked.

"Nope, it's just time to get this show started. Are you ready?"

"Yep, I'm ready," John said. *Never more ready for anything in my life,* he thought as he followed the minister into the sanctuary and walked to his spot in front of the altar.

The pews were fairly full, he noted. *When two fortysomethings get married, that's eighty years' worth of family and friends to invite,* he thought idly as he glanced past all the happy, familiar faces to the end of the aisle. Where was Olivia? he wondered. He couldn't wait to catch a glimpse of her. She was sure to be absolutely stunning today.

He turned back toward the altar, trying to conjure up a mental image of how she would look in her wedding gown, with her dark Italian features and thick black hair. She was so exotic, he reminded himself for the millionth time. Well, at least compared to his Mr. Whitebread from Upper Milquetoast coloring. In fact, she stood out among his ex-wives, too. Val, his high school sweetheart, had brown hair and green eyes, both of which were remarkably similar shades as John's. All his high school buddies used to tease him that Val looked more like his sister than Kate did. *Yeah, that joke got old fast.* And Jackie was very blond—naturally blond—so she had the super light skin and blue eyes to match.

Of course, that isn't the only way Olivia stands out in that crowd, he reminded himself.

He shot a quick look over his shoulder. She was still nowhere to be seen. He checked his watch—only a few minutes past the time the ceremony was supposed to start. So he turned back to the altar. It was no big deal. Let her take all the time she wanted. He'd wait here all day for her.

The organist was playing the prelude and didn't seem concerned that the moment to segue into the march Olivia had chosen had also come and gone. It was fine. No problem.

John's mind drifted back to his first two wives. Val, his high school sweetheart—he could still remember exactly the way she'd looked the first time he'd caught sight of her his sophomore year. She had been standing in his kitchen.

Uh, hi, she'd said with a cute giggle.

Uh, hi yourself, he'd cleverly shot back, opening the fridge and pulling out the milk. *Who are you?*

Valerie. Katie's friend. You must be her brother.... And it went from there.

He used to tease her, years later, about her big opening line. "Uh, hi," he'd say in a goofy falsetto before they'd both dissolve into laughter. His relationship with Val had always been fun, and John smiled at the memory now. As one of his sister's high school friends, she was a year younger. When Katie continued to bring her around the house to hang out, John had gotten to know her. By his senior year, they were officially an item. They went to all the football games and pep rallies and dances and proms together, as inseparable as two people could be. Two people who were living with their parents, anyway.

Now thoughts of high school were inextricably wound together with thoughts of Val. The experiences were one in the same. She had been heartbroken when John headed out of state for college—how was she ever going to make it through her senior year and all its rallies and proms without him? *But the clout that went with having a boyfriend in college made up for the loss pretty nicely*, John remembered with a smile. As soon as she joined him on campus, getting married just seemed the logical next step. They practically lived in each other's dorm rooms anyway. So, before he knew it, he had his first marriage license before he earned his bachelor's degree.

Speaking of marriage licenses and bachelors....

He looked over his shoulder yet again. Still nothing happening at the other end of that aisle. It was only ten minutes after the hour, his watch told him. He was glad for the watch since he didn't have his phone handy. He glanced at the minister, who was sitting in a chair on the altar reading something, presumably his wedding sermon. The organist was still playing, although John noticed she'd transitioned into a different song. Well, if the wedding pros weren't going to worry, neither was he. Olivia was a complete knockout with baggy sweats and no makeup. With all this extra time and preparation, she'd look like a *Vogue* model. It really wasn't like her to be late. But hey, it was her wedding day. She could do whatever she wished, as far as he was concerned.

Hmmm…what was I thinking about? Oh yeah—Val.

They got married the summer before his senior year in college, and it had been perfect. As long as they were in college, that is. Because that's what their entire relationship had been based on—having fun together while going to school. As soon as they both graduated and had to tackle the real world—along with its jobs, rent, utilities, school loans, and car payments—things stopped being fun in a hurry.

Suddenly John noticed some movement. Olivia's dad was standing in the doorway at the base of the aisle.

Something was finally happening.

Chapter 6

Final Decision

"HONEY DID YOU hear me?" her dad, Charlie, asked, opening the door slowly and peeking into the room. "It's time to go get you marr—hey, what's wrong? You're white as a sheet."

"I'm the bride. I'm supposed to be white," Olivia replied, attempting a weak joke even though she didn't feel like laughing.

"Very funny, Miss Comedy," her dad said. "But I'm not talking about your dress; it's your complexion. You look like a ghost. Nervous?"

"Yeah, you could say that."

"About what, honey? Got last-minute cold feet?" Her dad fully entered the room then, closing the door softly behind him.

"I guess that's what it is. But it feels more like a full-blown panic attack." Her grip on the arms of the rocking chair was vice-like in its intensity.

"Is it the thought of walking out in front of the crowd? I know it's nerve-wracking to be the center of so much attention, but I'll be right there with you. I won't let you trip over your dress."

"Hadn't thought about that possibility. Thanks for planting that particular fear in my head." The laugh from her this time was strained and almost hysterical. Her dad had always been her closest confidante and best friend. *Maybe I should get his opinion on what I should do,* she thought as she looked into his concerned face.

"What's really the problem then?" he asked, a quizzical look making the lines between his eyes stand out on his wrinkled face. "You're starting to scare your old dad!"

"Sorry," she said, unclenching her hands from the rocking chair and standing up to enter his warm, comforting arms for a big hug. "I don't mean to scare you."

"Just tell me what's going on...." He patted her on the back like he was soothing a newborn.

"We don't really have time," Olivia said, nervously looking over his shoulder at the clock on the wall.

"Oh, you know that man would wait all day for you, so just spill it."

"Yes, yes he would," Olivia said, soothed by the love emanating from her father as she pulled back and looked into his face again. "He's a good man. I know he is."

"But...?" Charlie prodded.

"But...I don't know." Olivia decided at that moment to tell him everything. "I just can't help wondering if I didn't fall in love with the *idea* of finally getting married instead of with the groom."

"What? You don't love John?" Shock and concern marked her dad's face.

"Oh, yes, I love him. I'm just not sure I'm *in* love with him," Olivia confessed, hating that she'd waited so long to find this clarity. Why couldn't they have had this conversation a month ago? Or a week ago? Yesterday, even?

"You've been watching too many movies," her father said, his brow wrinkling in disapproval. "Love is about the long haul, not the chemistry."

"No, really Dad, I'm serious. I know what love is

supposed to be, but how do you know you've found the right person? How did you know Mom was the right person for you? How did you know she was the one you were meant to spend the rest of your life with?"

"Well, first of all, I made sure I asked myself those questions *before* the actual hour of my wedding ceremony," he said, his voice belying a hint of genuine disapproval.

"Yes, Dad, I know. I'm an idiot for waiting this long. But better late than never, right?" she asked with another attempt at a laugh. It came out more like a muffled choke.

"All right, Olivia. Just sit down first. You look like you're going to topple over." He gestured toward the rocking chair, and Olivia obediently sat as her father leaned against the wooden table, his gaze on her steady and unbroken as he struggled for the right advice to give his only child.

"The thing is, honey, you just *know*. I adored your mother and couldn't imagine a life without her. Now, unfortunately, it just so happened that I was forced to find out exactly what life without her would be like, but I wouldn't exchange a moment of the time we had together, even if it would have meant avoiding the grief and loneliness I've gone through since her death."

"I'm sorry Dad," Olivia said, still working desperately to hold back the tears that were threatening. "I didn't mean to make you sad."

"No, Olivia, *I'm* sorry. I was so happy that you'd found John. I thought for sure you'd create with him the same kind of love and life that I had with your mom. But if you have this many doubts about it, then it's not right. Or you're not ready for it. Either way, you need to go let that young man know there's not going to be a wedding today."

"I can't do that, Dad," Olivia replied, shaking her head and reaching for another tissue. "I just…can't."

"You *have* to, honey. You owe him that. You can't just walk out of here without saying a word to him. He deserves better than that, and I believe I raised you better than that, too."

"No, I'm not going to jilt him. I'm going through with it," Olivia decided, feeling her resolve build. There was absolutely no way she could run off and leave John alone at the altar to deal with the repercussions. No way. He didn't deserve *that*.

"What? You're going to marry him? Why?" her father asked, the questions firing at her like bullets from a gun as his tone rose in anger. "You'll be miserable for the rest of your life if you're not in love with him!"

"Dad, relax," Olivia said, praying no one could hear him. "Not for the rest of my life. Just for a month or so. It's just too mean to stand him up today. I'll let him down gently later."

"Olivia Marie Conte, you are not sitting there telling me that you're going to go through with this like it's some sort of game. I won't allow it!"

"Dad, I'm forty years old. I need your advice right now, not your permission," she snapped. "And keep your voice down!"

"Seems to me that you've made up your mind," Charlie snapped back in his sternest father-pouring-on-the-guilt voice. "I don't know why you bothered asking me about it if you already knew what you were going to do."

"I *hadn't* made up my mind," Olivia responded, "but after talking about it with you, well, I just know that I can't bear to make any other decision. And it *is* my decision, Dad. I'm a big girl now, you know."

"Well, too bad, because you'll always be my little girl," Charlie said, his tone turning loving again, at a mismatch with the disappointment still evident on his face.

"I know, Dad. I know. But just hear me out, okay?" She glanced at the clock. They'd been keeping everyone waiting for more than five minutes already.

"Go ahead," he said, sounding weary. "I'm listening."

"Jilting him right now is just too cruel. As you pointed out, he deserves much better. I think a quiet divorce or annulment later is just kinder. That's all I'm saying."

"So you're going to pretend this is the happiest day of your life? And I'm supposed to stand there and pretend too?" Charlie's voice was getting loud again. "There's a reason I didn't become a stage actor, Olivia Marie!"

"Please, Dad, *relax*. I wasn't sure before that this is the right way to go, but I am now. I can't humiliate him. I can't, and I won't. So don't do this for *me*, Dad. Do it for John."

"This can't be the only solution," he pleaded. "Olivia, come on, just be brave and strong like I know you are. Go tell him now!"

"Dad, please," Olivia responded, starting to feel very sorry she'd confided in him. "It's too awful. Everyone will know I'm the one doing the dumping. And right in front of his friends and his family. Please!"

Her father narrowed his eyes at her, his extreme displeasure rolling off him in waves. Finally, he sighed.

"Fine. I won't say anything. But I'm not happy about it, and I'm not really happy with *you*, either."

"We're even then," Olivia replied, "because this is far from one of my proudest moments."

"Let's get moving then," he said with a sigh. "You've got a couple lives to go ruin."

Olivia closed her eyes, took a deep breath, then exhaled slowly as she looked into her dad's disappointed face again.

"Let's go."

Chapter 7

The Ceremony

THERE HE WAS. Standing right where she'd been picturing him, looking eagerly down the aisle in her direction. He didn't even seem annoyed about the wait. Of course, he probably just thought she'd been powdering her nose this whole time or something. Honestly. In what scenario *would* this man get mad? He probably would have even forgiven her for walking out on him today. *He really is such a nice guy.*

Olivia sighed again.

"You still sure you're going to do this?" her dad whispered—actually, it was more of a hiss than a whisper—in her ear.

"Yes," she said through a forced smile as the music switched over to the wedding march. "I'm sure."

This day just keeps getting better and better, she thought ruefully as they made their way up the aisle. Familiar, happy faces swirled past her in a way she wasn't up to processing. She couldn't concentrate on what they were all thinking and how glad they were for the two of them. If they only knew. If *he* only knew....

John's face was the one detail she couldn't disregard. He looked so joyous and peaceful, so ready to make this huge commitment. And he looked so completely in love. *Ugh.* If he only knew.

Then they were there with John at the altar. Her dad turned, leaned down for the father–daughter kiss, and whispered in her ear, "There's still time."

She subtly shook her head no, then kissed his cheek.

"I love you," she whispered back.

"You too," he said, a bit of his usual tenderness showing through his mask of disapproval before he turned around to walk over and take his lonely place in the first pew on the bride's side. In that moment, Olivia felt sorrier than ever that she'd confided in him.

But there was no time to dwell on that now. She tucked her hand into the crook of John's waiting arm and flashed him a big smile as they turned toward the minister.

"You look gorgeous, Livvie," John said. "I love you so much."

She smiled at him again but was unable to say the words back. *Such a great guy. Why couldn't he have been the right guy for me?* How perfect that would have been. They really could have had a magical life together.

Olivia told herself to stop focusing on what could have been. She didn't need any further guilt about the "laws of God and man" heaped on her today. She felt terrible enough already.

"We are gathered here together," the minister began, "today in God's house to join together this man and this woman in the bonds of holy matrimony....."

She let these words wash over her while she tried to rationalize her decision for the millionth time. *I'm doing this for John. It's the kindhearted thing to do. Any other option is unthinkably mean and cruel.* She'd tell him after they got home. After Paris.

Paris.

And just how uncomfortable was this trip going to be? How could she possibly maintain this act with a man so in love with her? He was going to know something was wrong if she pleaded a headache for two weeks. Or would he be his usual laidback self and not even be bothered by the fact they weren't consummating the marriage? She couldn't sleep with him one minute and divorce him the next! Okay, maybe she *hadn't* thought this through enough. Now was probably a really bad time to run away, though.

"I do."

The two words snapped her attention back to the ceremony. That was John speaking. *Oh no! It's time for the vows!*

"And do you, Olivia Marie Conte, take this man, John Edward Daux, to be your lawfully wedded husband?…"

Did she? Would she?

She could feel the panic coming to a boil inside. She felt faint and nauseous. Had she eaten anything this morning? This was ridiculous. She was a forty-year-old professional woman acting like a child.

The minister stopped speaking, and suddenly the eyes of everyone in the church were riveted on her expectantly.

It felt like time had stopped. John's eyes were locked on her face, the love almost tangibly emanating from him. She could practically feel Charlie holding his breath, wondering if she'd finally come to her senses.

She had, in fact, done just that, she realized.

Just not in time to change anything….

"I do," she replied.

Chapter 8

The Receiving Line

THE RECEIVING LINE of well-wishers inched slowly out of the church as each person stopped to congratulate them, hug Olivia, and slap John on the back. It was an utterly overwhelming experience, with Olivia feeling a little shell-shocked. Or maybe a *lot* shell-shocked.

"You okay, Livvie?" John whispered in her ear.

"Sure," she said as her Aunt Lydia squealed over what beautiful babies they could have before swooping in for a rib-cracking hug. "Just a little, uh, overwhelmed, I guess."

"Yeah, that's what I figured," he said with a reassuring smile on his face. "This can all be a bit much."

"Thanks," she said with a quick smile back. *Such a nice guy*, she thought grumpily to herself. *Why did this have to be so complicated?* If he were a huge jerk, a quick dash out of here wouldn't have been so hard. Of course, if John *were* a jerk, she probably never would have been confused about her feelings for him in the first place. Despite her misgivings about him being *too* nice, she'd never been the type of woman who looked for the bad boy types who she could "fix." Life was complicated enough.

"Hey, Jed!"

"Val! Hey honey, you made it," John said, leaning over to embrace a radiantly beautiful, petite brunette who suddenly appeared in the line.

"And this is Olivia, of course," the woman said as she offered Olivia her hand.

"Oh, hello," Olivia replied in confusion as she met the woman's hand with a small shake. Val? A cousin? A coworker? She didn't remember hearing the name before.

"I'm John's..."

"...high school sweetheart," John filled in quickly for the green-eyed beauty. "She and I go way back."

"Oh, well I'm glad to meet you," Olivia said graciously, eyeing the woman with interest now. *He invited an ex-girlfriend?*

"Congratulations," Val said to her, a wistful smile on her face as she looked back at John again. "I'm so glad Jed has you in his life. He deserves nothing but happiness."

"You too, Val. It's great to have you here," John said, a funny look on his face that Olivia couldn't quite identify. Interesting, she thought as she studied the two of them. *Maybe John will have someone around to console him after the divorce after all.*

"Jed?" she asked, as Val walked away, and the line continued to move forward again.

"Yeah, it's an old nickname from high school," John explained. "You know, it's my initials: John Edward Daux. No one ever calls me that anymore."

"Jed!" someone else called out just then.

He and Olivia both laughed. Despite her overall misery, she couldn't help it—the timing was too perfect.

"Well, *hardly* ever," John said, turning to greet the man who'd said it—an old college buddy, apparently.

Jed....

Olivia rolled the nickname around in her mind. She liked it. She wondered idly if he'd mind if she started calling him that....

Then her musings trailed off abruptly as soon as they'd begun. She wasn't going to be around long enough to start giving him pet names anyway, she reminded herself. She couldn't get too wrapped up in this role she was acting out—she didn't want to do anything that would make their split even more painful for him. She turned to greet the college buddy, his wife, and then the others in the line.

They were all so nice. So warm and loving. Each of them clearly adored John—and would hate her with a passion in a matter of weeks. The thought was a tough one to carry around, especially where John's family was concerned. They'd been so welcoming and kind to her, and she was going to repay them by devastating their son. The façade got harder and harder to maintain the more she thought through the consequences.

Why couldn't I have realized my true feelings earlier? Even twenty-four hours earlier would have been soon enough to avoid this charade. She smiled at the woman John was introducing her to, not really concentrating on what he was saying. They were both looking at her expectantly.

Oops...

"I apologize," Olivia said, feeling foolish. "My mind wandered there for a minute, and I didn't catch your name."

"I'm Jackie, Jed's ex."

"Oh, another ex-girlfriend, huh?" she said with a forced smile as she extended her hand. These ex-girlfriends were getting more delicate and gorgeous by the minute.

Jackie laughed and turned a confused look toward John.

"I see you haven't even mentioned me, Jed. That hurts. No, I'm the other kind of ex. His ex-wife."

Olivia blanched, completely startled by the news, but tried her best to recover.

"Oh. I'm honored to be meeting the first wife," she said, trying to hide the embarrassing fact that she had no idea there even *was* a first wife.

"Nope, I don't have that honor," Jackie said, reaching up to kiss John on the cheek before moving along. "I'm Jed's *second* wife, darling."

This time Olivia couldn't even attempt to hide her shock. Her mouth fell open as she watched the beautiful blonde sashay away from them.

Second wife?

She turned to John with accusations all over her face. *Jed* had some explaining to do, she thought furiously.

Chapter 9

The Explanation

"WELL, THAT WAS awkward," John said, reaching for the next hand in the line.

"Hey guys, congratulations! I'm so happy for you both!" This was Donna, Olivia's friend since college. Donna was stunning—her deep mahogany skin was flawless and radiant, and her body was tall and willowy like a model's. Olivia was thin, but Donna made her feel like a linebacker by comparison. Donna probably knew her better than anyone aside from her father.

She gave John a big hug, then swooped over to Olivia to do the same, but stopped short as soon as she saw Olivia's face.

"What's wrong?" she asked.

"I am just *completely* overwhelmed by this day," Olivia said with a fake laugh as she tried to hide the anger and annoyance that threatened to contort her supposed-to-be-happy bridal face.

"Yeah, yeah, okay. I'll bet you are," Donna said. Then, giving her a second hug, she whispered, "Find me at the reception if you need to talk."

They pulled apart, and Olivia gave her another weak smile and a nod of her head. "I will."

"She'll be okay, Donna," John assured, looking down with a mixture of apology and love at Olivia. "I guarantee it."

Donna smiled quizzically at them both, then nodded before moving on with the line of people.

"I'm sorry that was a shock for you, honey," John said, concern lining his normally cheerful face.

"So, when exactly did you plan to tell me you'd been married twice before? Or, wait—are there more?" she asked, sarcastically looking through the assembled crowd for an even shorter and more beautiful wife number three.

"Very funny," he said. "No, just twice before. And, I don't know, it just never came up. You never seemed to care about anything to do with my past, and when I'm with you, I guess I just don't think about it, either."

"Classic," she snapped, startling the little old woman currently shaking her hand. "The universal 'you didn't ask' defense. Just classic."

"Can we please talk about this later?" he asked quietly as his sister and her family approached.

"Count on it," she said, inwardly bracing herself. Greeting his family was about to be miserably hard. But then being mad at John was a welcome relief compared to the guilt she'd been swimming through all day. Mr. Divorce would obviously be able to withstand her cutting out on their marriage. He was probably looking forward to adding her to his ex-wives' club. *I wonder if there are membership dues....*

Speaking of which, was Val the first wife, then? Maybe she really was his unrequited love, the one who would step in and pick up the pieces after Olivia left. *Why should I even care?* she thought indignantly as she allowed herself to be hugged by Kate and Steve. She forced a smile on her face as she accepted their words of congratulations.

I don't, she told herself. *I don't care at all.*
Still....

Her dad's stern, unhappy face was the next one in

line. Today was getting harder by the minute.

"Charlie! Thanks so much for everything," John said as they shook hands and exchanged a hug.

"Of course, son," Charlie said, drawing back from John to look in his face. "You're a good man."

John smiled at Olivia over Charlie's shoulder as she turned to hug her dad next.

"Thanks, Dad," she whispered in his ear.

Charlie pulled back from her hug stiffly and studied her face, then just sort of shook his head in quiet disapproval and walked away. Olivia felt as though she'd been kicked in the stomach. He didn't even want to talk to her or hug her, he was so mad. She rolled her eyes in frustration. Why was *he* so angry? She explained the situation to him—she went through with this for John's sake! Couldn't he see that?

Olivia glanced up at John, who was studying her quietly.

"What's wrong with Charlie?" he asked.

"He's, well, upset with me," she admitted.

"I can see that. What about?"

"Not now—here come your parents," Olivia said, grateful for the delay. Hopefully John would forget to loop back to this conversation.

"Okay, I'll drop it for now," he conceded. "But you'll tell me eventually?"

"Yeah, sure," she said, hoping again it never came back up. Well, at least until it came time to end it with him. She would definitely tell him everything that was going on and exactly what she was thinking...eventually.

He could count on it.

Chapter 10

Making It Official

THE LINE OF PEOPLE finally, blessedly, came to an end. Next were the formal pictures in the church, which required a level of acting that Olivia just did not possess. Her doubts, confusion, guilt, and now anger, were swarming through her with each pose and click of the camera. What were supposed to be smiles surely were more like grimaces. Pure misery *had* to be the only thing the camera was capturing; Olivia was convinced of it.

"Ready to go to the reception?" John asked, nodding his head toward the awaiting limo, its driver standing by the door. The pictures had finally, blissfully, ended.

"Like you wouldn't believe," Olivia replied, not even bothering to dial back her feelings of irritation as she turned to walk out of the church.

"Don't you have any belongings you need to grab?" John asked. "A purse or anything?"

"Oh, yes," Olivia said, remembering that her purse, phone, and makeup were all still in the church. "I'll be right back. Try not to marry anyone else while I'm gone."

Blocking his chance to reply, she brushed past him, grateful for a reprieve from his company for a few minutes. Because the moment they were alone together in the back of the limo, there would be a lot of explaining to do. *On both sides*, she reminded herself.

John needed to explain why he hadn't thought it necessary to share with her a little detail like the fact that he'd done all of this matrimony stuff before.

Twice.

And he'd probably remember to ask why Charlie was so mad at her, especially since John knew as well as she did that Charlie *never* got mad at her. John certainly must be aware now that something huge was going on.

Lies. Lies. Lies. Oh yes—and more lies.

Could this day get any worse? As she turned the corner toward the bridal room, she ran right into the minister.

"Excuse me, Pastor. I'm sorry," she said, startled out of her angry thoughts.

"Oh, Olivia, there you are. I'm glad I ran into you, although we didn't have to make it literal," Reverend Dickson said with a hearty laugh.

"Did we forget something?" she asked.

"Yes, the most important thing of all," he replied. "The marriage license. Your fathers already signed as witnesses, but we need you and John to sign it, too. Then I can mail it in and make this thing official. Where is he, by the way?"

"He's out front with the limo driver. I, uh, I'm just going to gather my things, then I'll join you."

"No problem. Be sure to grab John's things, too. I think I saw his phone in there." The reverend then turned to walk toward the front doors...and John.

Olivia took a deep breath and continued to the tiny room. She opened the door and gazed inside, still lost in thought and regret. She stopped to look at the rocking chair, where she had sat before the ceremony and pondered running away. *I should have gone with my first instinct and left*, she thought. What was truly kind or noble about any of this? Now she was going to have to go out there and sign her name to a legally binding document, making it all very official.

Olivia sighed, shaking herself out of those useless thoughts. It was done. Done and over. She'd already gone through with the hell of the ceremony and the second hell of that receiving line. Surely she could jot down her name on a piece of paper.

She grabbed her things and surveyed the room once more. Overwhelmed with an urge to lock the door and hide, she instead sighed, turned off the light, and went back out. Then she walked the church hallways once more, this time with a slow, "condemned prisoner on the way to the gallows" gait as she searched for the room with John's phone in it.

Life was so incredibly strange and complicated. What series of miscues and bad decisions and terrible timing had led her to this depressing moment in time? Where had she gone wrong? Should she never have accepted a first date with John? Or gone to the party at all that night? Is that how far back in time she'd have to go if she were to undo this mess? Perhaps even further? Had she *not* gone to a completely different party, say, five or ten years ago, and missed her chance to meet her real Mr. Right? Or was it that she just wasn't cut out to be married, and her mistake was believing she was?

She found John's phone and wallet. Picking them up, she sighed for what seemed like the millionth time that day before continuing her slow walk out of the building. Regardless of what, when, where, or why, she was here now, in this place and this marriage. She needed to snap out of her self-pitying wallow and *own* her choices. She'd done this thing, now she needed to see it through.

Following that last thought, she came to the open front door. John was standing out there chatting and laughing with the minister. She took a deep breath, then walked down the stairs to meet them.

"Ready to make this official?" she asked lightly.

Both men turned to her with smiles. Reverend Dickson pulled out the paper and a pen and handed it to John with a Bible underneath. Great. She was going to be signing this in the presence of God and this minister on a Bible! *Didn't Dante mention something about this scenario in* Inferno?

John quickly and neatly signed his name, then handed the pen to her. He held the license and Bible forward, then she leaned over to sign.

It was done.

Reverend Dickson gathered the items back from them, offered his congratulations again, and headed back into the church.

"Well, Mrs. Daux, are you ready?" John asked, a gorgeous smile on his face.

"For anything," she said, accepting his hand as they walked to the limo.

"OKAY, SO who goes first?" John asked as the limo pulled away from the curb.

"I think that the person in this vehicle who has been married the most times has to go first," she snapped. She was surprised by the intensity of her anger. *Why do I even care?*

John sighed and ran his fingers through his hair.

"Liv, I don't know what to say. I never purposely set out to deceive you, I promise you that, honey."

"Then why wouldn't you tell me this?" she asked, avoiding his gaze. "You don't...you don't have any children, do you?"

"No! No, of course not. I would have brought that up, you know. Children would directly affect our life together, but my ex-wives just don't. Besides, do you think I'm really the kind of guy who wouldn't be at all involved in my kids' lives?" He seemed genuinely hurt and confused by this idea.

"If the exes are so uninvolved in your life, then why were they at the wedding?" Olivia asked, ignoring the last question. "I assume Val is the other one?"

"We stayed friends. You know, for the kids' sake," John shot back.

"Very funny," she spit out.

"Yes, Val was my first wife," John went on, the sarcasm gone now. "We were high-school sweethearts who got married in college. We were too young, and it just wasn't right, and we quickly fell apart. I met Jackie at my first job—she's a CPA, too. I found out too late that she was looking for a society match and a tennis partner, not a husband. And I don't hate either of them because there just wasn't enough emotion involved to create that strong a reaction. We're friends because, I don't know, it just doesn't matter one way or the other. So why not have an amicable breakup?"

"Yeah, you're right. It doesn't matter," Olivia said, again wondering to herself why she even cared. "But why didn't you tell me?"

"With you, Livvie, the slate just felt washed clean. You never seemed like a woman on the prowl for a provider, or a trophy husband, or a sperm donor. You never quizzed me about my background or beliefs or political stances." John paused here to take her hand gently in his own. "You just loved *me*. Period. I felt like nothing in the past could touch us or affect us because you didn't care about that stuff. You loved me for who I am, and I just can't tell you how much that meant to me."

"That still doesn't explain why you didn't tell me," Olivia said softly, feeling her anger seep away to some degree, replaced by guilt and regret again. "You made me look like a fool in front of Jackie."

"I honestly didn't think about it," he went on. "I didn't even think about you three coming face-to-face in an awkward scene at the wedding when I added them to the guest list. My whole universe has been wrapped up in you." He looked directly into her eyes, the truth of his words ringing in his earnest tone. "I swear there was never a time when I thought, 'Oh, maybe I should drop the bomb on her now,' or 'I'll have to be sure and hide the truth about the first two marriages,' because when I'm with you, I never, ever think about things like the past or regrets and mistakes. Only about how wonderful you are and how great our life together is going to be."

Guilt slammed into Olivia full force.

"Why did you have to be so sweet?" she asked, looking back at him for the first time since they got into the limo.

John studied her quizzically for a moment. "So, you forgive me?" he asked.

"Of course," she said as they pulled to a stop in front of her father's old colonial. "I could never stay mad at you."

He opened the door and stepped out with surprising grace, considering his height and muscular build. Then he leaned over and offered his hand to help her. From there they walked together to the house in silence.

She was glad John hadn't had time to question her about why Charlie was mad at her. She hoped the reception would keep him busy and make him forget about it altogether.

After all, she still had a honeymoon to get through with this poor, sweet, and entirely unsuspecting man.

Chapter 12

The First Dance

THEIR THOUGHTFUL silence continued as they walked hand-in-hand through the house, where she dropped off their belongings before they went out the back door.

"And here's the happy couple now!" chirped the DJ from his table under one of the backyard tents erected to ward off rain or sun; luckily, sun had won out that day. "I'd like to introduce Mr. and Mrs. John and Olivia Daux! Let's get started with the couple's first dance!"

The DJ started the song they'd picked out, the gentle notes filling the air around them.

"May I have this dance?" John asked, turning to face her for the first time since they left the limo.

"Yes, of course," she said, allowing him to lead her forward. They went to the area set aside as a dance floor, ignoring the happy faces and clapping hands of their family and friends, who were looking on from their tables under the main tent.

He wrapped his arms around her tightly. She leaned her head against his cheek as they began to move and sway.

"I'm sorry, Livvie honey," he whispered.

"Please don't apologize," Olivia said, overwhelmed with guilt and thoughts that she was the one who should be apologizing. "It's okay."

"But it's not. I put a black mark on the memory of

this day for you, and it's just unforgivable." He dropped a kiss on top of her head. "I'm so sorry, honey."

"But I told you I forgive you, and it's the truth. Don't worry for another second about how I'll remember this day." Olivia raised her face so she could look directly into his kind, loving gaze. "Please?"

John studied her back, seemingly searching for answers, but he didn't appear to be sure what the questions were.

"Liv, is something else wrong?" he asked finally.

"What do you mean?" she asked, inwardly cringing. Wow, her acting skills were poor. Keep this ruse up for weeks or even months? *Hah, I can't fool him for an hour.*

"You just don't seem...I don't know, you don't seem yourself today."

"It's my wedding day," Olivia said lightly, hoping to divert his focus. "Of course I'm not my regular old self."

"No...," John nudged back gently, clearly not accepting the attempted redirect. "It's not that. I think I can distinguish what a carefree, radiant bride should look like."

"You certainly have had lots of practice," Olivia snapped, surprising herself the moment the words left her mouth. What was she doing bringing his former wives up again? That certainly wasn't the way to convince him that everything between them was okay.

"Ah-ha. You *aren't* as fine with this as you're trying to say you are," John told her, looking both guilty and upset. "I'm so sorry, Liv. But in so many ways, this *is* my first wedding day. I love you to depths of my soul they never touched, and I'm going to spend the rest of my life proving that to you. You're it for me, baby."

"Stop, John, please just stop," Olivia cried out, anguish evident in her voice as it sliced through her heart. She leaned her head down so that it rested on his shoulder, her face buried in his neck. "Just stop."

"Livvie, is this about Charlie? Did you two have a fight?"

"Yes," she said, her voice muffled. She distantly noticed that the DJ had shifted to another song.

"Does he not approve of me? Have I done something to make him think I'm not worthy of you, or that I won't make you happy?"

Olivia raised her head to look at him once more.

"No!" Olivia said emphatically. "Charlie *adores* you. He's your biggest fan."

"Then what is it?"

"I…I don't know. We just…," she stammered. She couldn't get into this with him now!

"And now it's time for the bride's dance with her father," the cheery DJ went on, saving her from having to answer.

He'll certainly be getting a nice tip, Olivia thought about the DJ as John gave up on getting an answer from her, squeezed her hand, and stepped aside while Charlie approached. Of course, she now had to deal with her angry father. *Great.* She could tell from Charlie's stone-faced demeanor as he approached that he hadn't gotten past his anger yet.

"Dad, you don't have to do this if you don't want to," she began as Charlie took her hand and put his other arm gently at her waist.

"I will if it means John won't be made to look like a fool today," he said, his voice low and still dripping with venom.

The words of the song Olivia had chosen—

"Unforgettable," the duet Natalie Cole recorded with her own father—washed over her. This was supposed to be one of the most joyful, unforgettable moments in her life. Dancing with her father at her wedding should have been fabulously heart-warming. Instead, it was an icy, awkward experience that couldn't end soon enough. She didn't have time or energy to get into it again with Charlie. Besides, what was really the point? Once he made up his mind about something, he could be the most stubborn man alive. It was too late anyway. And she didn't need to give John any further reasons to question her, which he certainly would if she and Charlie started arguing now.

She sighed as Charlie continued to circle her around the dance area. This day was less of a blessed event and more of an endurance test. *When will I have to scale a wall with ropes or run ten miles in full combat gear?* she asked herself, the stress of the day starting to break down her defenses. If the song went on much longer, she might just dissolve into tears.

Finally, blissfully, it ended, saving her from a tearful breakdown on the dance floor. John and his mom headed out to dance. *Yet another reprieve from having to talk to him,* she thought. *Thank God...and the DJ.*

Charlie stalked away without a word. Trying not to be devastated by this, Olivia headed toward the head table, where she and John were supposed to sit. One of the waiters hired by the caterer offered her a drink.

"Rum and Coke. On second thought, no Coke."

The young man smiled at her, and she smiled back. She wasn't joking, of course, but there was no need to frighten the waitstaff. She really wanted to minimize how many people she made miserable today. So far it was just Charlie and herself.

She silently prayed, as she gratefully accepted the drink from the young waiter, that John wouldn't be added to that list. He couldn't find out tonight how she really felt about him...well, make that how she *didn't* feel about him. If he did, then this whole act would have been for nothing. Her actions would only have moved the fireworks from the church to the reception.

She took a gulp and then another, hoping she could steady her nerves. She was desperately going to need them.

Chapter 13

The Toasts

"I'LL HAVE one more," Olivia told the waiter.

"Make that two—I'll have one of whatever she's having," John said, sliding into his chair next to her.

"How's your mom?" Olivia asked.

"Ecstatic. Like me, my parents think this time it's going to work out, and they couldn't be happier." Then John added, "Like your dad. No...wait a minute...."

"Very funny," Olivia said, anxious for the waiter to return. *Why can't John drop this?*

"No, it's not funny," John said. "Charlie's clearly beside himself with anger, and it seems to be directed at you. A little strange coming from the man who thinks you walk on water *and* control the interplanetary flow."

"What's the interplanetary flow?" Olivia asked, smiling despite herself.

"I don't know. But it sounded impressive," John replied, winking as he turned to accept their drinks.

"Thanks, Galileo," she said, taking her glass from his hand and immediately tossing back another gulp.

"See? Now it's this kind of banter that made me fall in love with you the first time we met," John said, looking into her eyes. His own feelings of love were clearly on display across his face.

He loved her *so* much, she could see. And he deserved so much better than this, she thought guiltily as she broke their eye contact in favor of another long sip.

"When are you going to tell me what this fight is about and what's really bothering you?" John asked.

Olivia swallowed, then took a deep breath. "Not tonight, okay? This just isn't the right time or place to get into it."

"You can tell me anything at any time, Liv," John replied, leaning closer. "What is it, baby?"

"John, please! *Please,* I don't want to talk about it! I don't want to start crying in front of our family and friends, which is definitely what will happen, okay?" Her eyes as well as her words were pleading with him.

"Yeah, of course, honey," he said finally, pulling back. "I don't want to ruin this day for you anymore than I already have. But you know I'm here for you when you're ready to talk, right?"

"Oh yes, I know."

"Good," John said as he leaned in again and gave her a long, soft kiss. Olivia kissed him back, if only out of tenderness for this sweet, understanding man. The loud cheering and catcalling of their guests brought them back to reality.

"I think it's time for speeches!" declared the DJ. "I believe the father of the bride wanted to say something first?"

Olivia audibly sucked in her breath as she turned to locate her father, who was seated with John's family at the next table.

No...!

Surely he wasn't going to give away her secret...was he? She held her breath as he stood, his glass extended in his right hand.

"Yes, yes, I did want to say something," he began after he cleared his throat.

Her dad had never been much of a spotlight seeker

or public speaker, so she knew this wasn't easy for him under any circumstances.

"My only child Olivia came to me several months ago and told me she was getting married. I had my doubts because I didn't think she'd known her young man long enough to make a wise decision." He paused here and surveyed the crowd before continuing.

"But then I got to know John, and I really *have* gotten to know him over these last several months. He's a good man, and I can now say from the bottom of my heart that there should be no reservations or hesitation about it."

Then Charlie was staring directly at Olivia, his eyes boring into her soul. "John is most definitely the right man for my daughter. She made the right choice, without a doubt."

A round of happy agreement rose from the tables around them as glasses clinked together to end the toast.

John tossed a quizzical look in her direction—was this man suddenly a mind reader?—as he took his own glass and stood up.

"I'd like to add a little something," John said, waiting a beat while the happy chatter stilled once more. "First off, I'd like to thank you all for coming today and sharing this wonderful celebration with me and my gorgeous bride. We're so honored and blessed to have each and every one of you here."

With that, he turned his gaze away from their guests and looked down into Olivia's eyes.

"But having you all here with us isn't the only way in which I've been honored and blessed. I can't believe I'm lucky enough to have this beautiful, smart, funny woman willing to spend the rest of her life with me.

Olivia, sweetheart, I love you from the depths of my heart and soul, and I'm going to spend the rest of my time on Earth proving that to you."

He leaned down to kiss her while clinking glasses and applause rose all around them to complete the toast.

"I don't...I, uh, I don't know what to say, John. That was beautiful," Olivia replied, not wanting to look at him any longer. His pure love and joy were just too painful to acknowledge. Not when she didn't have a big enough supply to give him in return.

"So, you had some second thoughts, huh?" John said, ignoring her comment as he turned to touch her glass with his own, before settling back in his chair to study her face. "Is that what this fight is about?"

"Wha…what gives you that idea?" Olivia stammered before taking another gulp of her drink. How had he switched gears so easily? And how had he figured that out?

"Charlie would never make a good spy or a master poker player, Liv," he said with a shrug. "He's as transparent as all these glasses."

"Yes, he is. And if I'm being truthful here, so am I," she agreed, setting hers back down on the table. "Okay, fine, you've worn me down. I had some cold feet, and I had the bad judgment of confiding those fears in Charlie."

"Completely freaked him out? That's why he's mad?"

"Yes, that about covers it."

"But it didn't completely freak *you* out, obviously, since you're still here. You're too strong-willed to go through with this if you didn't mean it. That much I know. So, really, what is there to worry about?"

Right, Olivia thought as she continued downing her drink.

What indeed?

Chapter 14

It's Going to Be Okay

THE HAPPY SOUNDS of eating, drinking, and laughter filled the spring air as the salad plates were removed and the first course—manicotti—was served. John sat back in his chair, studying Olivia as she moved from table to table, visiting with her coworkers, friends, and family.

She looked calmer than she had all day. Had she really let a little thing like a case of the jitters get her *that* worked up? he wondered. And why had Charlie come down so heavily on her about it? Everyone had fears and doubts when it came to getting married, didn't they?

John took a slow sip of his water as he pondered his own fears and doubts. The funny thing was, he really *hadn't* had any second thoughts when it came to Olivia. She was right for him, and that was all he needed to know. Things hadn't been so easy with the others. When he'd married Val, his fears were real and palpable. Were they too young? Could they support themselves while they finished school? And was he really ready for a wife and possibly children? He certainly loved Val, but he also wanted to experience more of life, travel and meet new people and build some memories outside the safe cocoon of college. But Val had persisted, arguing that they were ready and could do all those things together.

So he ignored his fears, and they got married. But,

of course, they'd had no money to spare, so they never had time for things like travel or entertainment. He'd done precisely what he didn't want to do—jump right into the "real world," with all its responsibilities and hassles and pressures. He worked a couple jobs while still going to school so he could finish his bachelor's and master's degrees. It was a very stressful time and a very rocky start for them.

And, of course, it was all those things that eventually brought the marriage to its predictable end. He had seen it coming and should've asked her to wait—if it had been right, she would have been able to do that. He should have graduated and immediately set off for parts unknown. He could have backpacked across Europe. Or climbed Mount Kilimanjaro. Or gone on a million other adventures. But he'd ignored that voice of doubt, and he'd paid the price with a broken marriage. He'd learned his lesson with Val and vowed to embrace life and always listen to his gut.

Once their marriage was over, and once he'd finished his studies and passed the test to become a CPA, he raised some money, put everything he owned in storage, and spent the next several years traveling the world, first with Habitat for Humanity and then the Peace Corps. He'd gone everywhere—Asia, the Middle East, Africa, Russia and Eastern Europe, all over South America and the Caribbean....

John smiled at the memories as he recalled them now. Those days seemed a million years ago in some respects. But in others they were with him all the time. They had changed him, touched him, forced him to grow up and look at the rest of the world beyond his tiny, sheltered life. He'd been working to help others, but they were helping him in return. His experiences had played a large part in creating the man he was today; developing, for example, his inability to stay mad at people. Life, as he'd seen firsthand all around the globe, was too short, fragile, and precious to spend being angry. He'd grown more accepting of people in general, of their beliefs and differences.

Of course, despite all his life lessons and experiences abroad, nothing had prepared him for Jackie. John shook out of his reverie and thanked the waiter for clearing away his half-eaten manicotti and Olivia's abandoned plate.

She glanced over at him from her current seat next to her friend Donna and offered a tentative smile. He raised his eyebrows and mimicked spooning something to his mouth, but she just shook her head no and mouthed *No thank you.*

Just as he suspected. And he was sure Donna was getting an earful about his twice-married, lying self. He sighed, then took another drink of his water; no more alcohol for him now. He wanted to remember this day, not drink it into oblivion.

He was glad Olivia had forgiven him, and he honestly didn't care if she had to get it out of her system with Donna. Whatever. As long as they were okay, he was okay. He truly hadn't meant to keep things from her. She was just so accepting of him. He had never given his past a single thought.

It was pretty stupid of him in retrospect.

Oh well, it was all over now.

The waiters came around with the main courses; he'd ordered the filet mignon. He had to convince Olivia to eat. There would be time to mingle with their guests afterward. He stood up and strolled to where she sat, still thick in her conversation with Donna.

"Hey Liv, honey, you're sure you're not going to eat?"

The two ladies looked up at him and smiled. *Well, at least Donna doesn't seem to hate me*, he noted. In fact, she sort of looked sorry for him. He studied her a bit more closely, but she neatly wiped the expression from her face.

"You guys picked a beautiful day for an outdoor reception," she said, her voice and facial expressions giving away nothing more.

"Yes, thanks, we were really lucky."

"Well, I guess I'll let you eat," Olivia told her, standing up and passing a final look that John couldn't see or interpret.

What was going on here? Had Donna's reaction to his first two marriages stirred up Olivia's anger again? If that was the case, wouldn't Donna be looking at him with accusations rather than pity?

Pity?

Unless Olivia had confided her last-minute jitters to Donna as part of her explanation of Charlie's angry behavior today. *Yeah, that was probably it*, he assured himself. Well, there was no reason for her to feel sorry for him. Olivia married him! Cold feet or not, she was his wife, and their life together was going to be great. Charlie and Donna would just have to move past this. Olivia certainly had.

He and Olivia sat back down at their table.

"You told Donna about my previous marriages and the last-minute jitters, too, right?" he asked as he settled his napkin in his lap and reached for the silverware.

"Yes. Yes, I did," Olivia replied. "I'm sorry."

"For what? Being human? I've had my share of

second thoughts and fears before, too. Just not with *this* marriage."

"Really?" Olivia asked, looking surprised. "You had second thoughts before?"

"Of course. With Val I worried we were too young and hadn't experienced enough of life, and I was right." He paused to take a drink of water. "And with Jackie, I worried I was rushing things and falling for a pretty face and not a true life partner. Once again, I was right."

"But you didn't have a single doubt about us?" Olivia pressed. "Not one?"

"Not one, not ever," John said, looking Olivia in the eyes and hoping she was really hearing what he was telling her. "I knew the first time I saw you that you were the one for me. I never doubted it. But it's okay if you did. You haven't been through this before. It's only natural, honey." He took her hand from her lap and surrounded it with both of his, trying to infuse her with the feeling of being thoroughly loved no matter what.

"It's going to be okay," he said. "I promise."

Chapter 15

Confiding the Truth

OLIVIA HAD, IN FACT, been spilling the whole story to Donna. From her initial panic attack to her confession to Charlie, right on through to the revelation about John's multiple ex-wives. Donna's reaction had been much more sympathetic and, frankly, satisfying than Charlie's had been.

"Oh, you poor thing!" Donna had whispered. "What are you gonna do now?" Luckily, the others at Donna's table were mostly John's friends and didn't seem too concerned about Olivia and Donna's private huddle.

"Keep up the act until after the honeymoon," Olivia admitted, sneaking a peek at John, who seemed lost in his own thoughts at their table. "Or try to, anyway. So far, he's managed to get a lot of it out of me. The man should interrogate suspects for the FBI."

"What? He knows you want to end it?"

"Shh!" Olivia warned. "No, no, of course not. But he knows Charlie's mad at me because I got cold feet before the wedding. And he's pretty sure something else is bothering me."

"Well, you can't say the man doesn't know you."

"At least one of our lives is an open book," Olivia replied tersely. "And it's definitely not his."

"Interesting," Donna said, sitting back in her chair with a smile.

"What? What's so interesting?"

"It's really bugging you, isn't it?"

"What is?" Olivia asked. "I don't know what you're getting at here."

"That John was married before. Oh, yeah, I can see that you're trying really hard to convince yourself it doesn't matter. But it sure seems to bug you. Quite a lot, I'd guess."

"No, it doesn't," Olivia denied with a shrug. "Honestly, why should it?"

"Point out the exes to me," Donna demanded, surveying the crowd.

"Um, okay.... The first wife, the high-school sweetheart, Val, is over there sitting with his sister Kate and her family." Olivia nodded subtly toward their table. "Her hair is brown and short, and she's really perky and pretty."

"Oh, okay. I see her," Donna said. "Ouch, she's sitting with *his* family. That's not at all uncomfortable. And the other one?"

"She's the blonde ice princess at the next table to the right," Olivia replied, trying not to be obvious. "Super petite and gorgeous."

"*Very* interesting," Donna observed.

"What? What's *very* interesting?"

"You met her for all of…what, one minute? And she's already an ice princess?"

"Leave it alone, Don," Olivia said, feeling frustration bubbling up inside her. Why couldn't anyone just take her words at face value?

"I'm just saying these aren't the words or actions of a supremely indifferent woman. My advice for you is to think long and hard about all of this while you're in Paris. Because you won't be able to undo the hurt once you inflict it." Donna paused to take a drink. "You better make sure this is really what you want. You married him. It's not too late to embrace this marriage with both arms and never look back."

"You think I should stay in this marriage, even though I'm not in love with him?" Olivia asked. "Honestly?"

"Olivia, I'm not telling you to do anything you don't want to do. I'm just asking you to make *absolutely sure* you know what's in your heart. Me personally, knowing you the way I do, well...."

"Say it," Olivia insisted as she chanced another look over at John. *He wants me to eat something?! Well, forget it. I'll never keep anything down with these nerves.*

"I think you're crazy about the man and that you'd be even crazier to let him go, hon," Donna said. "He's a keeper, girlfriend."

"I *know* he's a great guy," Olivia agreed. "Of course I do. But I can't stay with him and settle out of some sort of fear that I won't find the right guy before my ovaries shrivel up."

"You're truly a poet."

"You know what I'm saying. All the advice and folk wisdom out there says you have a better chance of getting, I don't know, hit by a meteor or something than getting married at my age. But I don't want to *settle* regardless." Olivia watched in mild horror as John stood up and started walking their way. "Don't give anything more away to him," she ordered. "Hopefully you're a better actor than Charlie is."

As John arrived and asked Olivia to eat again, Donna flashed a look of complete pity at him. Olivia wanted to kill her. Could no one she talked to keep up pretenses for even five minutes?

She stood to leave with him and mouthed a silent

Shh! to Donna for good measure. Clearly, she couldn't confide her secret to anyone else. She was already having trouble keeping John in the dark, and they'd barely been married a couple hours.

Chapter 16

The Ex-Wives

ONCE THE MEAL was over, John and Olivia went back to rounding the tables together and chatting with their guests. The DJ, meanwhile, was busy trying to entice people onto the dance floor.

Eventually, John sat with his sister and her husband while their kids were off running around, happy to get a break from the adults.

"The ceremony was really beautiful," Kate said, smiling.

"Well, you'd think I'd have the hang of planning these things by now," John joked, winking at Val, who was sitting nearby.

"Very funny," Val and Kate both said, unanimous in their mock indignation.

"Speaking of which, can I have a dance with the groom for old times' sake?" Val asked.

"Of course," John said, rising and taking her hand. He led her out, then wrapped his arms loosely around her and settled into a slow rhythm to match the love song currently playing.

"How have you been Jed? I've missed you," Val asked, looking into his face.

"I'm great," John answered truthfully. "The happiest I've been in years."

"So, you finally found the right woman, huh?"

"Well, I can't say I didn't have fun looking for her," he said teasingly. "But, yeah, she's The One."

"And she definitely feels the same way?"

"Been talking to my sister, by any chance?" John asked, now feeling annoyed. Kate should have kept her mouth shut.

"She's just worried about you," Val said, adding softly, "and so am I."

"There's no reason to be. Sure, Olivia might have had a case of pre-wedding jitters, but she got over them. She's here now, and she's in my life to stay."

"Pre-wedding jitters? Yeah, maybe that's all Katie was sensing," Val admitted. "Her female intuition might not be finely calibrated today or something."

"Trust me, everything's fine," John insisted. "You two can stop worrying."

"I'll always worry about you Jed. Because I still love you, you know."

"Of course, there will always be a bond between us," he replied. "You never fully get over your first love. But I'm a completely different man than I was back then."

Val nodded. "I've noticed."

"And you can't go back and recapture the past," John added, hoping she was really hearing him.

"I know, I know. But always remember that I'm here for you if you ever need me. No matter what."

"Thanks, Val," John said. "Really, thank you. But I'm fine. I won't need to take you up on that offer."

"That's good. I hope you don't. All I want is for you to be happy."

"Hey, is this a party anyone can attend?" Kate asked as she and Steve joined them on the dance floor. "Can I cut in and dance with my brother?"

"Of course," Val said, offering John one last smile before turning to Steve.

*   *   *

John scowled at Kate as soon as they started dancing.

"Hey! What did I do?" she asked, looking surprised and innocent.

"Oh, I don't know. How about the fact that you blabbed your theories about my new wife to my first wife?" he said, annoyed. "I told you everything is fine with Olivia and me."

"I see," Kate said, taking a deep breath. "She shouldn't have said anything. But we both care about you, and we're worried about you."

"In that case, I hope Jackie gets the press release, too. That way we can really make this as uncomfortable as possible."

"You know I don't talk to that woman!" Kate insisted.

"Yes, that's right. You don't like Jackie. Let me see...who else don't you like? Oh yes, that's right—Olivia. Apparently no one after Valerie has been good enough for me in your eyes."

"Well, Jackie sure wasn't," Kate said with a pout.

"I appreciate the fact you two have my best interests at heart. But if we're going to continue to be close and spend a lot of time together, you'd better exert a huge effort at making Olivia feel welcome in our family, because she's here to stay."

"Of course, John."

"And I expect more of an effort than you put into welcoming Jackie," he added. His family had never taken to her, and the lack of support hadn't exactly helped them when times got rough.

"Oh, come on, John, you know full well that Jackie is a total bi—"

"Did I hear my name?" Jackie asked sweetly, a knowing smirk telling them she'd heard precisely what Kate was about to say.

"I was just telling my brother here that he should dance with you," Kate said, her face flushed as she stepped aside while the DJ started a new song.

"Well, isn't that a fabulous coincidence?" Jackie asked, tossing a withering look at Kate as she moved into John's arms. "Because I was just on my way over here to ask for that very thing."

John quickly scanned the crowd, looking for his bride. He spotted his father asking her to dance. *Good, that's more like it*, he thought as he turned his attention back to the tiny blonde in his arms.

"Hey Jack, how's life been treating you?" he asked. He couldn't remember the last time they'd talked.

"Pretty well, actually. I'm getting married again, too," Jackie replied, the smile on her face tinged with a rare hint of shyness.

"Really? That's great, honey." John gave her a hug. "Who's the lucky guy and when's the big day?"

"Actually, he's my boss. Harrison Pennington the Third."

John laughed. "Mr. the Third wouldn't happen to be filthy rich, would he?"

"But of course," Jackie said, laughing back. "Put it this way: I probably won't have to work too much longer if I don't want to."

"Your hours at the yacht club are just too demanding?" John teased, although he was genuinely pleased for her. She'd obviously found precisely what she'd been looking for all these years.

"Something like that. Anyway, I think we're going to get married in France. Harrison has a home and a small vineyard, so we'll honeymoon there."

"That's where we're going, too. Well, not to Harry's vineyard. We're going to Paris for a couple weeks."

"Have a wonderful time, Jed," Jackie said, her smile now full of sincerity. "I wish you all the happiness in the world."

"You too, Jack," he replied, and meant it with his whole heart. Just because theirs wasn't a forever kind of love didn't mean he wished anything but happiness for her. For Val, too, for that matter.

With that, the romantic music came to an end, and the DJ switched to an up-tempo rock song.

"Well, that's it for me," John said, releasing Jackie's hand and looking for Olivia. "I've got a bride to find."

"Right behind you," Olivia said.

John turned around.

"Should I request the DJ play 'To All the Girls I've Loved Before'?" Olivia asked, her tone unreadable.

"Hilarious," John said, sweeping her gently into his arms. "Is that a tone of jealousy I detect?"

"No!" she said, a little too sharply.

"You're mad," he teased. "Admit it."

Olivia leaned up against his shoulder, hiding her face from him.

"No, I'm really not," she said, ending the conversation.

Chapter 17

The Talk with Charlie

"HEY, CHARLIE," John said to his new father-in-law as he waved to some guests who were heading out. "I guess this party is winding down, huh?"

"Yes, it looks that way," Charlie agreed.

"I just wanted to thank you for everything—the use of your yard and, of course, for your help during all of this." John was genuinely grateful for the support of this wonderful man, who had shown him nothing but kindness.

"You're welcome, son," Charlie said. "It was my pleasure."

"Well, I know you've done more than your share in backing me up with Olivia," John went on, curious how Charlie would respond if he referenced the fight between Olivia and her dad.

"What do you mean?"

"I know Olivia had a case of pre-wedding jitters," John said, "and I do believe you gave her hell for it."

Charlie turned to meet his gaze. "She told you?"

"It doesn't take much of a student of human behavior to see you're mad at her. You're *never* mad at her, so I asked her why, and she told me about the argument."

Now Charlie looked anguished. "I'm so sorry, son. I didn't think she was going to unload this on you so quickly."

"Well, believe me, I had to do some prodding. But

I could tell something was on her mind all day."

"You're sure taking it calmly," Charlie said, studying John with a curious look on his face.

"It's just a case of cold feet," John replied, studying Charlie back now while trying to understand why this bothered him so much. "Nothing to get upset about."

"You think so? Really? You think she'll change her mind and give this a try?"

"She married me. She's already gotten over—wait...what exactly did she tell you?"

"What did she tell *you?*" Charlie asked, confusion written all over his face now.

"That she admitted to having second thoughts about getting married, and that you got upset with her when she confided this to you. That's it, right?"

"Oh, yes. Yes, that's what happened," Charlie agreed—but perhaps a little too quickly.

"It was more than that, wasn't it?" John asked, his eyes narrowing with suspicion. Charlie was *such* a bad liar.

"No, not at all," Charlie answered, his discomfort clear. "Just go on this honeymoon and have the time of your lives. Everything will work out as it should."

"Yeah, okay. Thanks," John answered although he remained unconvinced. But he decided to drop the line of questioning for now. It was Olivia who owed him the whole story, not her poor father. "Well, as long as we're having true confessions, I need to tell you something that I neglected to tell Olivia until today."

"What's that, son?" Charlie asked.

"I've been married before," John said, wincing. "Twice."

"You're a widower?" Charlie asked, looking shocked.

"No, no. Just the victim of youthful mistakes. Not this time though. Third time's a charm and all that."

"So, wait...you've been divorced twice?" Charlie asked. "What did Olivia have to say about that?"

"She was taken off guard and angry—and rightfully so. But I just never think about the past when I'm with her. I didn't set out to deceive her. She never seemed to care anything about my past, so I guess I didn't either."

"Did she forgive you?"

"Yes, she did," John said, a small smile on his face. "She's an amazing woman, your daughter."

"Oh, yes," Charlie said, his tone still off. "She's something all right."

John continued studying him. Something weird was definitely going on. This man absolutely idolized his only daughter, yet today he seemed angry and judgmental about her. Simply over a case of pre-wedding jitters? No way. John decided then that Charlie and Olivia were both definitely hiding something from him—something big.

"Hey, you two," Olivia said, walking over to join them. "What are you talking about?"

"Your pre-wedding argument with your dad," John said, hoping to get a reaction out of her.

Olivia stopped and visibly paled. *Interesting*, John thought. *Yep, she's definitely hiding something.*

"Really? What did you say?" she asked, shooting daggers at Charlie.

"Oh, nothing much," John replied quickly, putting his arm around her waist and bringing her to his side. "Nothing to worry about, anyway. But let's get going. We have a hotel to check into tonight, and a flight to catch tomorrow."

"Yes, okay, let me just go change and get my

things," Olivia said, chancing one more questioning look at both of them before pulling from John's embrace and heading toward the house.

John smiled at her retreating figure. He had two weeks alone in Paris ahead of him with his new and very secretive bride. He was confident that he'd get the whole story out of her soon enough. And how bad could it really be? She loved him. She'd married him. Those were the only two things he needed to know.

The rest would work itself out, right?

Chapter 18

The Hotel Room

"I'M ABSOLUTELY exhausted," Olivia said, flinging down her suitcase and collapsing backward onto the bed. The emotional toll of the day had left her completely limp and weary.

"Me too," John concurred as he tossed his suitcase on the desk and headed into the bathroom.

Happy for the moment alone, Olivia closed her eyes and tried to empty her mind of all thoughts. But there was no escaping the memories of the past day. Her inner turmoil, her deception, her fight with her father, John's revelations about his previous marriages, the hurt she was going to eventually inflict on him....

She shook her head and pressed her eyelids together more tightly, but once again the swirl of the day's negativity attacked her without mercy. How was she ever going to get any sleep if her mind was conducting a full assault on itself? And worse than that, how was she going to survive these next two weeks? Or the weeks after *that*, when she would have to end things with John and start her life all over again?!

Thank God they hadn't moved in together. She at least had her own apartment, so there would be no ugly moving-out scene. She'd break the news to him gently, they'd talk it over like the mature adults they were, and then she'd go home and forever close this chapter of her life.

Well, okay, so the wedding presents would have to

be returned. That and the wedding and honeymoon debt they'd have to pay off would make any simple scenario a little more complicated. But basically she would be free to start over.

And start over how, exactly? she wondered. *By entering the dating scene again? Ugh!* Just thinking about having to go out on first dates made her head pound. Perhaps her new life should include a serious look at moving to a convent.

The door to the bathroom opened and John walked out, clad only in low-slung sweats. His hair was wet, so he'd obviously showered. Olivia had been so lost in her thoughts she hadn't even heard the water running.

"Your turn," he said, sleepily shuffling over to his suitcase and opening it.

"I'll be in there a bit longer than you were," Olivia told him, pulling herself back off the bed and picking up her own suitcase in its entirety. "It'll take at least an hour just to pry out all these bobby pins and another hour to wash out the hairspray."

"Mmm, good luck with that," John said, still rifling through his clothes. "I'm afraid I might fall asleep the second my head hits the pillow. Unless you need help with any of that?"

"No," Olivia said, hoping relief wasn't evident on her face. "No problem. Go to sleep. We have two weeks ahead of us you know."

"That we do," he said, returning her smile.

He looked so sweet and sexy with his wet hair sticking up and his sleepy eyes struggling to stay open that she couldn't resist walking over and giving him a quick kiss. John caught her around the waist and drew her into a tighter embrace, lengthening the kiss. Olivia was sorry she'd initiated anything. He'd just looked so irresistibly cute. But he was obviously waking up now, and she wasn't prepared to carry this lie any further. Not tonight, anyway. She put her hands up to his chest and pushed him away gently.

"Go to bed, sleepyhead. We have lots of time, remember?"

"But I'm suddenly not so tired," he said, sitting on the edge of the bed and holding his arms out to her. "Come here, sweetheart."

"Nope," she said, taking another step back, but feeling like a complete jerk. "I've got so much metal on my head I'm probably pulling satellites out of orbit. Let me just de-pin and hit the shower before I collapse, too."

"Okay, honey," John said, dropping his arms. "You're right. We've got lots of time."

She held his gaze a minute longer, then headed into the bathroom and closed the door. As she drew it shut, she could see John still on the edge of the bed, watching her.

Is he studying me again?

She leaned against the door and shut her eyes. He seemed to know something was going on. He obviously hadn't bought the story about Charlie getting mad over a small case of pre-wedding jitters. Did he know the whole truth? Had Charlie revealed everything? Had John been testing her just then?

"You're getting paranoid," she muttered to herself as she pushed away from the door and walked over to the mirror.

She looked completely exhausted; although, to her hairdresser's credit, not one strand was out of place. With the amount of hairspray that was used, her hair wouldn't dare move for fear of breaking off. She smiled at the mental picture of her scared hair, then started tugging the pins out one by one. She tried not to think about John and what he knew or suspected or wondered about. Panicking on the very first night of her honeymoon wasn't a great way to launch her plan to gently and maturely break things off with him.

"Remember, we have two more weeks," she whispered to her reflection.

When she finally finished pulling all the metal off her head, she got undressed and wearily climbed into the shower. The hot water felt wonderful as it coursed over her skin. She wished it would be this easy to wash away the guilt. Guilt and regret and sadness had assaulted her all day. And she saw no immediate end to it, either.

Why? Why did this have to happen? Why couldn't John have been the right man? Why couldn't this day have been truly and fully joyful for her?

She finally gave into the despair and allowed her tears to join the water and makeup in a cascade that ran down her face, then the rest of her body, and finally—symbolically—down the drain.

Chapter 19

Heading to Paris

"WE MADE IT," John said, pausing to stow their bags in an overhead bin as Olivia ducked into their seats to claim the one by the window.

"Finally," she said as she dug around for the bands of her seatbelt.

They'd gotten up early and headed to New York's JFK Airport. They spent hours either slogging through the winding security lines or waiting for coffee in painfully long queues in the terminal and laughing about their mega-fun honeymoon. It felt good to be laughing and relaxing with her, although he could tell something still wasn't quite right. It was all there in the looks of sadness that she kept trying to hide, he could tell. The small sighs or moments where she appeared lost in thought. And was that remorse on her face? Why would there be signs of sadness when they should be in the middle of the happiest time of their lives? They were finally on their flight to Paris, and John couldn't have been happier about it. But he desperately needed to figure out why Olivia clearly wasn't on the same page.

"The ceremony and the reception were great, but I'm glad they're over," he said as he got in his seat and felt around for the belt.

"I couldn't agree more," Olivia replied, her eyes closing as she eased herself into the amazingly comfortable first-class seat. "This feels heavenly."

"Tell me that again in seven or eight hours," John suggested, smiling at his new wife but still wondering what was going on in her head.

Wife....

It was certainly a word he was familiar with. But it meant so much more to him than it ever had before with Olivia. This was so right—whatever was holding her back, whatever was bothering her, well...it would wash away. They'd spend two beautiful weeks together, and they'd talk, and eventually she'd unload whatever was burdening her. And he'd be right there to comfort her, to reassure her, to...whatever she needed, he'd provide it.

He reluctantly turned his gaze from her beautiful face and sat back. "Mmm...I see what you mean."

They remained in a state of companionable silence as the other passengers continued to file in. Eventually they both fell asleep, missing takeoff and the first hour of the flight.

"Sir, would you like something to drink?" The flight attendant whispered. Though the question was aimed at the businessman across the aisle, it awoke John with a start.

"Oh, I'm sorry to wake you," the attendant said. "Would the two of you care for something to drink?"

"Umm, yeah," he said, shaking off his sleepiness as he glanced over at Olivia, who was starting to stir as well. "Liv, wine?"

"Mmm, no," she said. "Ginger ale."

"Okay, I guess we'll take two ginger ales," John said, watching the attendant as she placed ice in two plastic cups and poured the soda over it. He took them from her with a smile, then waited while Olivia pulled out their tray tables before setting down the cups. "Why ginger ale? Aren't you feeling well?"

"Yeah, my stomach is kind of a mess," she said before taking a small sip.

"You're probably starving. You ate very little between the reception and the hotel." John looked genuinely worried now. "Are you coming down with something?"

"Oh, no. Really, it's nothing." She offered him a half-smile. "Probably still decompressing from the wedding nerves."

"You mean from your pre-wedding jitters and the reason Charlie's so mad at you?" John asked, hoping this might finally be his chance to get her to open up to him.

"Yes...well, no...." Olivia stammered before adding, "Seriously it was nothing, and my uneasy stomach is nothing, too. Please John."

He studied her profile as she took another sip of the ginger ale, then placed it back on the tray table. After that, a small sigh escaped her lips.

"Okay, that's it," John said, turning toward her. He had to get to the bottom of this, because whatever was wrong was clearly eating her up inside. "Spill it."

"My drink?" Olivia asked in a lame attempt at humor.

"What's on your mind? And don't tell me it's nothing, because I know that's a lie." He was beyond frustrated now. "This has something to do with Charlie and why he's so mad at you. Why can't you just tell me? You're so upset that you can't eat. Just get it off your chest so you can enjoy our trip."

"Now's not the time, John," Olivia said with another sigh.

"Oh yes it is. Actually, it's the *perfect* time. We've

got hours in front of us, and I can't stand another minute of your silent misery. We're married now, remember? I'm your husband, and you can tell me anything." As if to emphasize this point, he reached over and took her hand in his own.

"I know, John, really I do. And I do confess there's something on my mind. But I refuse to ruin our honeymoon discussing it. And you have to trust me when I say it would definitely ruin the honeymoon. So please, *please* just drop it, okay?"

But he couldn't. The love of his life was miserable, and he couldn't just sit there and let her stew without attempting to lift the load off her shoulders.

"Olivia, baby, you're obviously in a lot of pain about something. Knowing that you're hurting is going to ruin the honeymoon for me anyway. So you may as well tell me."

"John!" she said sharply. Then, much more quietly, "John...no. I can't tell you. Eventually I will. I promise. But not now. Not here and not today."

"It's got something to do with your argument with Charlie," he insisted, stubbornly *not* dropping the subject. He was so frustrated with her now. *Why is she being this obstinate?* "Something about your pre-wedding jitters. You made Charlie worry that we shouldn't be getting married, right?"

Olivia turned toward the window, her body language screaming that she was trying to shut out those last words and put an end to the conversation.

"But what did it really matter?" John said. "You still married me. You *love* me. What could be so horrible? Why is Charlie mad, Liv?"

Olivia's head whipped around toward him. Now she was getting angry; it was written all over her face.

"Drop it," she demanded. "*Now*."

"I can't. You're unhappy, so I'm unhappy. Liv, what's going on? You were upset all day yesterday, and I just can't sit back and watch you slog miserably through our honeymoon."

"Fine!" Olivia snapped. "Yes, I said something to Charlie that made him believe we shouldn't get married, but I married you anyway. So now he's mad. Period."

"What did you say?"

"Stop pressing me on this, John," she insisted. "I'm not kidding. Stop it before you get hurt."

"So, you said something about me specifically," he pressed on. "What was it?"

"Nothing."

"It's *not* nothing," John said. "Tell me!"

"Drop it!" she repeated.

"I *won't* drop it," John replied. "Come on already. We've come this far. Let's just bury this topic for good."

"Stop it, John! Just stop it!" Olivia insisted, anger woven around every syllable.

"No, Liv. What did you say to him?"

"Fine! Oh my gosh you're so stubborn," she snapped. "I told him I didn't want to marry you!"

"What?" John asked, shocked. "That's crazy. I know I said this before, but you *did* marry me. You're in love with me. So what's the problem?"

"That *is* the problem, John! I'm *not* in love with you!"

Olivia looked straight into his eyes now.

"And I don't think I ever was!"

Chapter 20

The Explanation

PAIN SLICED through John, but denial stepped in quickly to stop the bleeding.

"That's not funny, Liv," he said, releasing her hand.

"No, it's not," she said, sorrow etching her features. "Trust me, I know that nothing about this is funny. But it's the truth."

"Would you like another?" the flight attendant asked, suddenly reappearing to collect their glasses.

"No!" they both barked a little too harshly and without turning to acknowledge her.

"Ooookay," she said, rolling her eyes and moving on.

"What are you *talking* about?" John asked. "We just got married! This wasn't some arranged thing. I didn't knock you up in Victorian times. You weren't in some kind of a trap. You don't marry someone you don't love these days."

"*I* did," Olivia said gently.

"Olivia, this is crazy," John said, praying she'd take the words back. *Or maybe I misunderstood...or misheard her.* "We've been together for a year. At any point you could have just walked away."

"I didn't know. I...I...." She closed her eyes and took a deep breath. "I didn't realize it until yesterday morning. I don't think I slowed down long enough in the last year to really think about it before yesterday."

John remained silent, afraid if he tried to speak again the pain would overwhelm him. This wasn't a misunderstanding. He'd heard her very clearly. She wasn't taking any of it back. Not now, not ever.

"So, yesterday," Olivia continued, "I got dressed and put on my makeup and had my hair done, and I went through the other motions of being a happy bride. But I wasn't. So I sat down and really thought about it, and I realized it was because I was making a mistake in marrying you."

John had rarely cried a day in his life—he couldn't even remember any examples since he was maybe ten when his family dog died—so he didn't know how to release the flood of grief that was bubbling inside of him. He also wasn't accustomed to rage and anger, either. He'd never been that kind of man, even in the middle of his divorces. And he wasn't a violent man either. But the urge to hit something was suddenly overwhelming.

Hit...yell...kick...demolish...destroy....

Any of those choices sounded good to him at that moment. Anything to release the pain and make the bleeding stop. And yet he sat mutely next to Olivia, powerless to do anything other than let her continue annihilating him. Never in his life had he felt this raw and exposed.

"But I didn't want to embarrass you by jilting you," Olivia went on, clearly determined to spill everything now that he'd broken through her defenses. He guessed he deserved that—she *had* warned him after all. "It just seemed too cruel. You deserve so much better than that. So I went through with it, thinking that I would just tell you after we got back from Paris and quietly end it then. It just felt like a much kinder plan, even though it meant having to lie to you and keep up an act in front of everyone we know."

John continued to stare as her words rang in the air between them. He felt unable to say anything at all for fear of what might come out of his mouth. She looked so beautiful and loving, and he'd believed in her so deeply and completely. How could he have missed this? How could he not have known?

"Good plan," he finally choked out.

"John, I know you're upset and hurting," Olivia said, "but I just want to say that I am *so* sorry about this. I wish more than anything in the world that it could have been right between us, because I know what an amazing person you are, and I just wish you had been The One."

He still didn't know what to say or do; the shock and grief were just too much. He had to leave. Get away from her before he exploded.

"John, are you okay?" she asked, reaching out to touch his face.

"Don't. Touch. Me." The words were quiet, but the devastation and anger in each one was crystal clear. Palpable, even.

Olivia awkwardly pulled her hand back.

"I'm so sorry," she said, as the tears welled up again in her eyes. "So, so very sorry."

"Save it," he told her, unhooking his seatbelt and standing up. Her tears seemed to be the key to unlocking his paralysis. As he stood, the businessman across the aisle shot him a look of pure pity. So everyone on the flight knew what a sap he was.

Great...and where else have I seen that look of pity? he wondered as he stalked down the aisle toward the bathrooms at the back. It was as far away from Olivia as he could possibly get right now without flinging himself off the plane, which actually was a tantalizing option right now.

Donna....

Of course. Donna had given him that same look of pure pity when he'd interrupted her conversation with Olivia at the reception yesterday. Now it was all starting to make sense. Olivia had told Charlie she didn't love John, and the kind old man had been furious with her. When she then told Donna about it, her best friend had felt sorry for him.

John entered the tiny bathroom, locked the door, sat on the toilet lid, and leaned forward, holding his head between his hands.

The shock started to lift and, in its place, came rolling waves of agony.

He couldn't hold it back any longer.

For the first time in longer than he could remember, tears filled his eyes and began dropping silently to the bathroom floor.

Chapter 21

Leaving First Class

HE KNEW HE couldn't spend the rest of his life sitting in the airplane bathroom, regardless of how tempting that seemed. So he first dragged himself off the toilet lid and stood to look in the mirror. Olivia's confession had already taken a visible toll on him. His eyes were red and swollen, and he looked about ten years older. The lines and shadows on his face seemed deeply etched, as though in stone.

"Great," he said as he leaned forward to splash cool water on his face. No small task since he had to use one hand to keep the water running in the tiny sink. He did what he could, then grabbed a thin, rough towel and used it to dry off. He looked in the mirror again. No improvement. He still looked like he'd been run over by a dump truck. And he sort of wished he *had* been. Those wounds would either heal eventually or they'd kill him. But the wounds Olivia had inflicted would never go away.

His love, his trusting nature, his ability to let go of anger, his easygoing demeanor. Those things were gone, all of them. He could feel their absence because they'd always been such a huge part of him. Now he felt like someone he didn't recognize. Hard. Bitter. Angry. Sad. Embarrassed. Foolish....

He reached for the door, then noticed the wedding ring shining on his left hand. It seemed to be taunting him with everything they *could* have had together but now never would. Before he knew what he was doing, he'd yanked it off and thrust it into his pocket.

With a sigh, he finally unlocked the bathroom door and walked out, trying to ignore the impatient line of passengers who were looking at him with annoyance. How long had he been in there? *A long time, I hope*, he thought. The sooner this flight was over, the better.

"Are there any empty seats?" he asked the nearest flight attendant.

"We're pretty crowded. We'd prefer it if you returned to your assigned seat," she replied kindly.

"I'm on my honeymoon, and my new wife just told me she never loved me."

"I'll find something for you," she answered quickly, her eyes filling with pity. He supposed he was going to have to get used to that, since everyone who found out would now be flashing it at him for a long time to come.

"Is the seat next to you empty?" she asked a passenger who appeared to be sitting by herself.

"Yes," the pretty passenger answered, flashing a friendly and slightly flirty smile at John.

He attempted a smile of thanks at the flight attendant, but it came out as more of a grimace.

"Can I get you your meal?" she asked him then. "Did you miss the food?"

"I did, but I doubt I could eat right now," he told her, collapsing into the new seat. "Could you get me a drink instead?"

"Should I make it a double?"

"Definitely," he said, a smile coming more naturally this time.

All right, so maybe he could still be nice and easygoing. With well-meaning strangers anyway. But could he ever truly trust anyone again? And at his age, why did he even care? He was obviously destined to be alone. A bachelor with three failed marriages and no kids. Now *that* was depressing.

As soon as the flight attendant returned with his drink, he tossed it down his throat, unconscious of what she'd even served him. The fiery trail that it left behind felt soothing somehow. He closed his eyes and leaned back, letting the depression wrap itself tightly around him like a fist.

No wife. No kids. Three divorces. These ugly facts were beating a drumbeat in his mind, a relentless rhythm of failure. Tears were trying to return to his eyes, but he fought them back. He wouldn't let her destroy him. He absolutely would not give her that satisfaction.

"Where did you come from?" the passenger next to him asked. "I didn't see you before."

John opened his eyes and looked over at her for the first time. She was stunningly beautiful. Long, light brown hair and gorgeous brown eyes—just like Olivia's—that were looking at him with interest, patiently waiting for a response.

"I was in first class," he said finally.

"Slumming now?" she asked with a light laugh.

"It's the first day of my honeymoon, and my new wife just told me she never loved me, and that she wants to divorce me as soon as we get home," John replied. *I'm going to have to get used to saying all that at some point anyway,* he thought as he tossed back another gulp of the drink. "I literally ripped off my wedding band in the bathroom about a minute ago."

The woman's beautiful brown eyes were now wide with sympathy.

"You're not lying, are you?" she asked after studying him another moment.

"Trust me, I couldn't make this stuff up," he said as the flight attendant brought another drink.

"It's on me," she said with a wink before heading back up the aisle.

"Thanks...."

"But wait," the woman next to him went on, "I'm confused. Why did she marry you?"

"Because it was kinder than jilting me at the altar," he answered. "Or at least that's what she said. If this was the kind approach, I'm pretty damn sure the harsh one would have killed me."

"You poor man," she said. "What are you going to do?"

"I don't know," John admitted. "This literally just happened. I can't even wrap my mind around it yet, let alone think about the future."

"I take it your honeymoon was supposed to be time together in Paris," she guessed. "Do you think you'll stay there?"

"Yeah. Probably. I guess so." John tossed back the new drink in one gulp. "You can see I haven't given this a lot of thought."

"Have you ever been to Paris before?" she asked, obviously trying to change the subject.

In spite of all the other emotions swirling through him, he found himself appreciative of the effort. "Yes. I've pretty much been around the world. I spent several years in the Peace Corps."

"Really? That's wonderful. *Parlez vous Francais?*" she asked.

"*Oui,*" John replied, switching their conversation to French. "What are you going to be doing in Paris?"

"I'm here on business," she said. "I'm a fashion journalist, so I'm scoping out the new trends, designers, fabrics, and shows. I'll have some time to myself, though, if you wanted to get together and do some sightseeing or have dinner or whatever." Then she added, "I'm single, by the way. Just so we're clear on that."

John smiled at her offer. "Thanks. You're just what my battered ego needed."

"So, say you'll meet me," she pressed.

"I'm not exactly great company right now," John said. "Besides, I don't even know your name."

"Samantha. Samantha Anderson," she said, extending her right hand.

"John Daux," he said, shaking the hand while bracing for the laughter at the sound of his surname. But none came. "D-a-u-x," he added, not wanting her to think he was lying. "But my friends call me Jed."

"Nice to meet you Jed," Samantha told him as she retrieved paper and pen from her bag. Then she wrote down her name and number, along with the name and address of her hotel. She handed it to John, who glanced at it briefly before putting it in the pocket of his shirt.

"So there you are," Olivia said, suddenly standing next to him in the aisle with a murderous look on her face.

JOHN SEEMED startled by the sound of her voice.

"Aah, here's the little woman now," he said to his new friend before adding something else to her in French.

"She's beautiful," Samantha said, reaching up to shake Olivia's hand.

"Sam, this is my third ex-wife Olivia. Olivia, this is Sam."

"Samantha Anderson," Samantha said.

"Olivia Conte," she replied, taking the outstretched hand in confusion. She'd been worrying herself sick about John, and he was back here *dating?* And speaking French? *He speaks French?!* She had no idea. "And we're still married," she added, surprising herself. She almost sounded like she cared.

"Barely," John said, looking beyond annoyed.

"Jed was just telling me about his time in the Peace Corps," Samantha chirped sunnily.

Olivia battled to keep the shock off her face. *He'd been in the Peace Corps, too? When was this?!*

"Why don't you come back to our seats?" she said finally, trying to ignore Samantha's beautiful face or the stab of jealousy that it was causing. "We've got a lot to talk about."

"No, I really don't think we have a thing to say to each other," John replied before saying something else to Samantha in French, a language she couldn't understand.

"Please John," she said, not wanting to beg but also not wanting to draw out the domestic drama for Samantha any further.

"Go ahead Jed," Samantha said with a smile. "You know where to find me."

"Yeah, okay," John said with a sigh. He gave Samantha's hand a small squeeze before he stood up. "Thanks for everything."

"Anytime. Take care, Jed."

"You too." Then he turned back to Olivia and said, "Lead the way, Ms. Conte."

She turned sharply and practically ran back to their seats. She couldn't believe this was happening. They were still married after all, and he was making it quite obvious that she could be replaced in a matter of minutes. Maybe it was a blessing for both of them that she'd ended things the way she did. Now he could get back on his rigorous dating schedule.

"Was that wife number four?" Olivia asked as she crawled back into her seat.

"Hey, maybe," John said, sitting down and closing his eyes. "Who knows?"

"Well, you certainly don't waste any time, do you *Jed?*"

"Save the jealousy act, *Olivia*," he said, matching her tone. "We both know you wouldn't care if I dropped dead right now."

"That's not true!"

"I obviously don't know a single thing when it comes to you," he replied, his eyes still closed.

"Well, that makes two of us. First, I find out on our wedding day that you were married twice before.

Now, on the first day of our honeymoon, I discover that you were in the Peace Corps? And you speak French? What else have you been hiding from me?"

"Only that I'm really a secret agent playboy who's been assigned to tally up as many ex-wives as possible," he snapped back. "Your country thanks you for your assistance in this vital work."

"That's not funny," Olivia replied, still shocked at herself. Why was she so mad at him? Why did the fact that Samantha had called him "Jed" and seemed to know more about him than she did hurt so much? Why in the world did it feel like jealousy? What did she even care at this point? Nothing was making sense.

"Ah yes, but the rest of this comedy-filled day sure has been," John replied, startling her out of her inner turmoil.

"You certainly seem to have gotten over it rather quickly," Olivia told him, again surprising herself. She should be thrilled that John was not only able but clearly willing to move on. Instead, she was picking away at him. What was her problem?

"Don't you *dare* tell me how I'm feeling," he said, turning an icy glare on her now. "You've *destroyed* me. Is that what you want to hear? It's not enough to rip my heart out and throw it on the floor? Now you want to see it bleed?"

"No, John, I—" Olivia started before being cut off.

"Just stop," he said. "That woman was being nice to me, and in my current state, it felt pretty damn good. Considering that the love of my life had just told me she *never* was in love with me—not that she'd fallen *out* of love with me, but that she *never once* was in love with me in the first place—I think you're just going to have to accept that I chose to let someone else help me feel better, if only for a few minutes."

"I'm so sorry—" she tried again.

"Please stop talking to me," he replied acidly, turning away and closing his eyes again. "Just stop apologizing and stop haranguing me about Samantha. Just stop all of it."

"Okay," she said, before facing toward the window. "I'm sorry."

What was wrong with her? Was he right? Did she just want to see him suffer some more? Why? This man had done nothing wrong except choose the wrong woman to love. Why was she beating him up about any attempts he made to move past it? When had she become such an unfeeling monster?

The silence between them, once comfortable, now hung over their heads like a black cloud. Olivia finally couldn't take it anymore.

"When were you in the Peace Corps?" she asked.

"It seems the information you don't know about me is infinite," he replied.

"Whose fault is that?" Olivia asked.

"Well now, that's a good question. I've spent the last year living under the misguided delusion that you loved me exactly as I was, and that's why you didn't seem to have questions about anything in my past— that all you cared about was being with me and building our lives together. Now I realize, of course, that it was because you didn't care about anything to do with me at all—past, present, or future. So I don't know, you tell me: Is that my fault for being the world's most deluded and romantic sap? Or is it your fault for being the world's least self-aware human being?"

"My fault," she said quickly, wishing she could

undo some of the damage she'd inflicted on this kind man. "You've done nothing wrong here. It's all me."

"So, wow, that's great. I guess this all boils down to the classic 'it's not you, it's me' breakup line," John said. "Well, you're nothing if not magnanimous."

She deserved a lot worse than some angry sarcasm, so she let his comment go by without a response. She couldn't stop watching him though, wondering what he was thinking and wishing she could take his pain away.

"Are you staying in Paris?" she finally asked.

"Yeah, I guess so," he said with a shrug. "Racing home to return wedding presents and hire a divorce attorney doesn't sound so appealing right now."

"Maybe he'll give you a volume discount." The line slipped from her mouth before she could even think about it, and she was horrified with herself as soon as she said it. What was *wrong* with her? She may not be in love with John, but she did care about him. She couldn't believe she kept actively trying to hurt this wonderful man.

"If I had another drink in me, I'd probably laugh at that," he said with a weak smile.

"I'm so sorry, John," Olivia said, shaking her head now. "I don't know what's wrong with me, I really don't. I can't believe I just said that—it was *such* a cruel joke."

"But an accurate one," he pointed out. "I *am*, officially, a three-time loser now."

"Stop it, John. This one doesn't even count. We never even consummated it last night—I don't think you could even call it a marriage, let alone a divorce."

"Gosh, yeah, that helps. I feel so much better."

Olivia winced. "I'm sorry," she added yet again.

"Stop. Apologizing."

"I'm sorry," she said before she could stop the words, then she offered a tentative smile.

He stared at her for a moment, the expression on his face not giving her any clues to what he was thinking just then, before he silently turned away from her one more time.

She watched him in return as he worked to ignore and avoid her. Then she leaned her head back, closed her eyes, and fought off another round of tears. It was going to be a really long flight.

And a *really* long honeymoon.

Chapter 23

The Aftermath

"WHY DID YOU introduce yourself as Jed to her?" Olivia asked later, clearly unable to tolerate the silence.

"Because it's my name," John said with a sigh. Was she ever going to shut up? Was this flight ever going to end? "My nickname, anyway."

"Okay, but why didn't you introduce yourself to *me* as Jed?" Olivia pressed.

"I don't know," he answered honestly. "I guess because you were having too much fun teasing me about my last name for me to get a word in edgewise."

"Oh...ugh...I'm sorry."

John shot a glaring look at her, which she answered with a shrug. "Habit, I guess. Sorr...uh, it won't happen again."

John thought about her question more seriously. Honestly, why *hadn't* he told her his old nickname? He hadn't been lying to Samantha before when he told her that his friends typically called him Jed.

"I wanted everything with you to be different and new," he said after a few moments. "I fell for you almost immediately and, well...I guess I never bothered giving you the nickname because it was so nice having you call me John, which was unlike what anyone called me in previous relationships. It was just one more thing about us that was fresh for me. You were so unique, and I wanted what we had together to be unique, too."

"Oh...."

He felt even more exposed and raw than ever. He couldn't believe he'd just opened up to her that way. He squeezed his eyes shut, praying for relief from the heartache that was still curling around him, squeezing tightly, and leaving him feeling like he needed to gasp for air.

"Tell me about the Peace Corps, if you wouldn't mind."

"Tell me why you care first," he snapped back, trying desperately to use anger to hold himself together.

"I'm curious about you."

"Really? You're curious? So curious that it took you a year to string together three questions about me?"

Olivia drew in a deep breath, looking like she was trying to find the right words to say in reply. But, really, what could possibly be the right thing to say now? Even if she suddenly declared she had been kidding and that she desperately loved him and wanted their marriage to work, it was too late. The damage had been done, and the pieces of their relationship lay scattered all around them. No one and nothing could put them back together again.

"I....," she started, then stopped. The words just didn't seem to be there.

"Don't," John demanded. "Nothing you say will make this better. Nothing's going to fix it. Gamely playing a few rounds of 'get to know me better' isn't going to put a bandage on the wounds you carved into me today. So just...don't."

"I know, John. Really, I do," Olivia replied softly. "I know you're hurting, because I'm hurting, too. I can't make sense of how we got here. I was so sure yesterday that I was doing the wrong thing by marrying you, but...."

"But?" John asked, intensely angry now. What kind of game was she playing here? "What could possibly be the end of that sentence that isn't going to gut me more?"

"I don't *want* to hurt you more!" Olivia said, shaking her head and fidgeting with the strap on her seatbelt. "Of course, I don't! But I keep asking myself *why?* Like, why did I get so upset when I learned about Val and Jackie? Why did it hurt when I saw you back there chatting up Samantha? Why am I dying to learn more about your time in the Peace Corps? It's not idle chatter, John! It isn't! I...I don't know what it is, if I'm being honest here. I thought I knew what I wanted, really I did. But now? Well...now I'm wondering if maybe it really *was* just cold feet. But...I...I don't know! Maybe it wasn't! I clearly don't have the answers to anything anymore!"

John listened, astonished that he could actually feel a flicker of hope trying to ignite in his shattered heart. Was she saying she'd gotten it wrong? That she really did love hi—wait, no! No *way*. He was *not* going to let this woman have any more power over him. He could not allow her to fan those flames and somehow turn them into an actual fire raging inside him. Never again. He had to shut her down before it got worse.

"Olivia, stop yourself," he said forcefully. "That confusion you think you feel? It's just regret that you hurt me. You feel bad. That's it. It's really quite simple if you think about it. So there you go: You have proof you're not a complete monster, because hey, look at that! You feel bad for hurting me. But stop with whatever else you're considering or implying there. I heard you the first time—I get it. We're over. Don't start in with some sort of 'hey maybe I was wrong' do-over scenario. I'm telling you right now that it will never happen."

"No, really this isn't just me waffling or feeling sorry now that you know and are hurting," she argued. "Donna warned me about this very same thing at the reception."

"Huh? What are you talking about?"

"When I told her about my freak out before the wedding and my decision to end things with you quietly later, she said she didn't think I really was indifferent or not in love with you. She said that my angry reaction to finding out about Val and Jackie was proof that maybe I wasn't as in touch with my true feelings as I thought. I didn't really consider her words then, but now...I just don't know what to think anymore."

"Holy hell you've got to stop this," John said as fresh agony coursed through him, clouding his thoughts and baffling him even further. "If you were so conflicted, the words 'I don't think I ever loved you' would not have come out of your mouth! What was it? Only an *hour* ago? Stop torturing me! You've done enough!"

"But this is precisely *why* I told you I wasn't ready to talk about this!" Olivia shot back. "I begged you to leave it alone, but you kept pushing me and pushing me. I needed more time to think about this. Maybe if you'd let it go, then I would have had time to realize I needed to learn more about you...that maybe I can't truly know...."

"Stop!" John cried, unable to hear anymore. "Stop, Olivia, for the love of God, stop! I don't want to hear it, I don't want to consider it, I don't want to even think about it. It's *over*. It doesn't matter one bit what you think you maybe kinda perhaps, under the right set of circumstances and given the perfect lighting and atmosphere, could possibly feel for me. *It. Doesn't. Matter.*"

"Of course, it matters, John!" Olivia shot back, a stubborn look on her face. "It's *everything.* I just need time!"

"Well, fine then," John said. "Have it your way. You can spend the next two weeks in Paris doing all the soul searching you need to do. But I'm telling you right now, you have to leave me out of it. This is it; we're done. No matter what huge revelations you uncover, there's no going back. Do you hear me? Regardless of how much you're trying to talk yourself into it, there's nothing left to save."

"I'm not trying to talk myself into anything," she said. "I need to get to the truth, and I think you need me to as well."

"Good luck with that," John said, closing his eyes once again and hoping she'd finally get the hint. As far as he was concerned, this conversation was over and so was this ridiculous relationship. She'd figure out eventually how right he was.

Somehow he mercifully nodded off, the anguish too much to bear any longer. It wasn't long enough, though, and soon he was opening his eyes, gasping as the mere memories of Olivia's words carved up his heart once again.

I'm not in love with you. I don't think I ever was.

None of the shock and pain had diminished in the short time since she'd said them. How long would he need before this stopped hurting? A few months? A few years? A lifetime?

"Hey there, how're you doing, honey?"

The flight attendant who had been so kind to John

earlier was back to check on him, thankfully distracting him.

John flashed her a tired smile as he tried to stretch some of the cramped muscles in his neck and shoulders.

"About as well as you might expect, I guess," he said, glancing over at Olivia. She was either asleep or faking it. Then again, it didn't matter whether she heard or not. The flight attendant—Marie, according to her nametag—had addressed him in French.

"Is that her?" Marie asked, shooting a look of pure hatred in Olivia's direction.

"Yep, that's the little missus," he said, hoping a touch of humor would help. His nap hadn't helped him feel any better; if anything, waking up and remembering what had happened had just made him feel worse—if such a thing was even possible.

"What are you going to do?" Marie asked, her genuine concern evident on her pretty face.

"I really haven't thought about it too much, but I guess I'm going to use the time in Paris to lick my wounds and figure out what I'm going to do with my life."

"I'm based out of Paris," Marie told him. "Would you like to get together and just talk?"

"Oh...uh, maybe," John replied. Not that it was necessarily helping anything, but he suddenly realized that *Hi, my wife never loved me* was apparently a great pickup line. Too bad he couldn't fathom ever trusting any woman again, let alone loving her.

"Here's my number," Marie said as she handed him a card. He glanced at it, gave her a smile of appreciation, and put it in his pocket with Samantha's.

"If meeting up later doesn't end up working out, I

just want to thank you for your kindness," he told her. "You've been great."

Marie leaned down to give him a kiss on the cheek. "She's a fool," she whispered. Then she stood up again, shot one last malevolent look at Olivia, and headed back into the coach section of the plane.

Moments later, Olivia said, "Well, you're certainly getting a lot of action on this flight," as she rolled her neck around, presumably to work out any kinks.

John glanced at her. So, she had been only pretending to be asleep. How much of that exchange had she witnes—

Oh come on, who cares? he thought. Like it would really matter if she got jealous. That would just prove she was petty in addition to being completely heartless.

"So, is this the silent treatment?" she asked.

"You've said more to me on this flight than you said in the last year cumulatively. Give it up, okay? I still can't tell if you're trying to make yourself feel better, or if this is some misguided attempt to soothe *me*. But you're turning this flight into the seventh circle of hell. So just shut your pie hole."

Olivia barked out a short laugh. John cast a sideways look at her, fought back a smile, and turned back to face forward.

"I always loved your laugh," he said, begrudgingly.

"Thanks," she said softly.

John shut his eyes again, attempting to block her out, but there was no removing her from his thoughts.

How long? he wondered again. *How long is this going to hurt?*

Chapter 24

Arriving in Paris

SHE TURNED AWAY from him again. She hadn't gotten a bit of sleep. She'd been too busy tormenting herself about what she'd done, so she witnessed his exchange with the stewardess. Although she didn't know exactly what they were saying, she knew the basics. How many women had he told his tale of woe to? How many phone numbers had he collected already? Is that how the next two weeks were going to be—watching him date the entire passenger roster and crew from this flight? Perhaps there were also some baggage handlers he could chat up after they landed?

She sighed and looked out the window. They were over land now, so they would be reaching Paris soon. *Thank God....*

She tried to relax, but all thoughts kept leading back to the man who was—at least for the moment—her husband. *Pie hole*, he'd said. The goofy words floated through her mind again, causing her to smile and glance over at him. Despite everything that had happened since this plane left New York, he still had his sense of humor. Maybe a guy who some people might label as being "too nice" was exactly what she needed. Regardless of how deeply she'd wounded him, he was still sitting next to her and trying to make her laugh, no matter how hard he fought it. What a great person. Traits that had seemed smothering and dull yesterday were suddenly appealing to her.

But then the same question kept echoing in her mind—*What is wrong with me?* She had to get off this plane and away from him. She obviously needed time alone to think before she went crazy second-guessing herself. She'd made her decision, so it was over, right...? That's what he just said very clearly to her. She needed to get on with the rest of her life.

The rest of my life....

What was that phrase reminding her of? She suddenly recalled John's toast at the reception—

I can't believe I'm lucky enough to have this beautiful, smart, funny woman next to me, ready to spend the rest of her life with me. Olivia, sweetheart, I love you from the depths of my heart and soul, and I'm going to spend the rest of my life proving that to you.

Bitter tears gathered in her eyes. She kept her gaze turned toward the window and away from him as she allowed them to fall. She hadn't been lying to him before: She really *was* conflicted. What had seemed very clear to her moments before the wedding now seemed murky and confusing. She knew she loved him. But as she had walked down the aisle to marry him, she had been convinced she wasn't *in* love with him. *Convinced!*

So why was she feeling so hurt that she didn't know his nickname? Why was she angry to learn that he'd been married before, to two stunning women who apparently were both still in his life? Why did the attention Samantha and that flight attendant were giving him make envy course through her veins? If he was so darn boring, why was he such a chick magnet? No one who spent time in the Peace Corps and who spoke fluent French could be *that* boring! And who knew what else he hadn't told her?!

She didn't know what to do. Charlie and Donna

had both warned her to think this through, yet she'd somehow managed to do just the opposite and blurt out everything. How had she reached the age of forty and still managed to be this spectacularly unable to understand her own feelings? And while she was trying to sort them out, how dare she annihilate the loving heart of this wonderful man?

Regret assaulted her as she squeezed her eyes shut. What was she going to do? Her breathing became more rapid and shallow, so she worked actively to try to calm herself down. A full-blown panic attack wasn't the solution, that much she knew. *Come on now...happy thoughts, relaxing thoughts, calming thoughts.* She worked to clear her mind and block the panic. They just had to get to Paris, and then they could figure out a plan, right? She still had two weeks with him—hopefully in that time she could figure out her true feelings and what to do about them.

Eventually she was able to drift off—but just moments later, it seemed, one of the flight attendants was welcoming everyone to France. *Probably one of John's new girlfriends,* Olivia thought crabbily.

"I swear to God I thought we'd never get here," John grumbled once the plane pulled to a stop, unbuckling his seatbelt and standing to gather their bags from the overhead compartment. He thrust her small bag at her, offering no further conversation.

She unfastened her seatbelt and slid over to John's newly vacant seat. She was dying to know what was going to happen now, but she was afraid to set off another sparring match by asking more questions. Still...they had so much to figure out. Would they share a cab to the hotel? And would they get separate rooms after they arrived, or was John planning to go his own way entirely? Would this be the last time she would ever see him? Their quickie, no-contest divorce would scarcely require them to face each other in court. They maintained separate apartments, so they didn't have a common home waiting back in the States. And they wouldn't necessarily stick with their original return flight. In fact, she was sure John would do anything—pay any penalty fee or whatever—to avoid being stuck in confined quarters for such a prolonged amount of time with her again.

This could really be it.

She quickly looked up at him, still in the aisle and waiting for the doors to open. The thought of never seeing him after this moment sparked an emotion she couldn't quite identify. *Must be indifference, right? Or relief? Or maybe the sensation of freedom mixing gleefully with joy?* Couldn't be remorse or panic or doubts. That would be ridiculous. Really, she was still being so utterly ridiculous.

Still....

She studied his handsome profile again. What if she'd been wrong? What if this was the biggest mistake of her life? What if this man really was perfect for her, and she was too stupid to realize it?

No! This is so ridiculous, she thought. These panicky feelings were the ones that got her into this mess to begin with. Certainly she must have stayed in this relationship from some misguided fear about still being single at this age. *Then again, I never actually felt symptoms of anxiety until the wedding day....*

"Let's go," John said, never looking toward her as he waited to let her walk out first.

She grabbed her purse and bag and mindlessly did as he suggested, leading their way off the plane even as the questions continued to pound through her head relentlessly.

They went through the airport gate and started following signs for the baggage claim and customs areas. *This is what I wanted, right? My freedom and two weeks to explore Paris. This is what I wanted...really, this is what I wanted...it is.... John is too comfortable, too boring, too nice. There were no sparks. Yes—this really is what I wanted.*

By the time they reached the carousel, she had successfully regulated her breathing and reduced her panic. It didn't matter what happened now—she was a strong, successful, attractive woman. There was no reason to think that her life wouldn't be wonderful, fulfilling, and exciting. She just needed to say goodbye to this temporary husband of hers, and whether she did it now or in two weeks, it didn't matter. Like he himself had said, this marriage had ended. John was not the right man for her. It was over.

This is what I wanted.... This is what I wanted....

She closed her eyes and took a deep breath, then released it slowly. *Okay, better....*

"There you are!" Samantha said brightly as she approached John. "How was the rest of your flight?"

"Well, unless my doctor had called me to say I had three hours to live, it probably couldn't have gone much worse," he replied, flashing a smile at her.

"Well, I, for one, am very glad that call didn't come," Samantha told him, now in full flirt mode.

Olivia rolled her eyes. Honestly, had he always been such a player? How had she never noticed the effect he seemed to have on women or the charm that he had exhibited over the last two days toward Val, Jackie, Samantha, and the French-speaking stewardess? Or were these pathetic women only attracted to him because *he* was married? *If that's true, then he'd better enjoy his two weeks in Paris. Because he won't be wearing that wedding ring for long.*

On that thought, she glanced down at John's left hand, visible to her because his arms were crossed as he stood talking with Samantha. The ring was already gone. He'd already taken it off!

She looked down at her own left hand, still shining with the diamond solitaire. He certainly didn't waste any time. Maybe this wasn't as big of a heartbreak for him as he was letting on. In the handful of hours that had passed since her agonizing declaration, he'd already ditched his ring and picked up at least two women on the plane!

What a jerk! No wonder he's been married three times. He can't work his way through us fast enough.

Thank God she'd come to her senses and ended this relationship before *she* was the one to get hurt. *No*—*before* anyone *got hurt*, she quickly amended.

Because it was quite obvious that John was going to be just fine.

Chapter 25

The Cab

JOHN WASN'T SURE he was going to survive. How could any man live with this much pain—and with the source of that pain sitting next to him in the back of a cab? Just feeling the warmth from her body was enough to drive him insane.

Samantha—who was obviously a saint in the making—was crammed into the taxi on his other side. She had agreed to share a ride with them, then proceeded to fill the awkward silences by cheerfully commenting on the various buildings and historic sites they drove past. He had managed a few polite replies along the way, but Olivia's stony silence was practically a tourist destination all its own.

What was her problem anyway? She was getting everything she wanted, right? She should be giggling with delight, not acting pouty and sullen. She wasn't the wronged party here; so why did he get the distinct impression that on top of everything else, she was mad at *him*?

Well, she had been acting weirdly jealous about Samantha and Madeline, right?

No, Madeline wasn't her name, he realized. Monica? Marie? Well, regardless, Olivia had been clearly jealous about her, too. Completely indifferent women didn't get jealous, did they?

At that moment, he felt a leap of hope bound through his damaged heart. Olivia really *was* in love with him! She just didn't know it! She....

Wait, no—no, no, no....

John cut off these ridiculous thoughts, furious with himself for even allowing them to flicker through his mind. The only way he could possibly become more hurt was if he allowed himself to *hope*. And there was no way he could live through this pain if it got any worse. He'd never felt this way before. Never. Which was pretty amazing, considering he was a man with two divorces under his belt already.

But those marriages had lasted awhile; there had been actual love and good times and laughter before things died out. And in both of those marriages, he'd known the end was coming long before they'd actually reached it. Neither divorce had really been much of a surprise.

When it came to Olivia, however, he hadn't seen it coming at all. She had succeeded in completely blindsiding him. So, for his own sanity, he could *never* allow himself to entertain any serious hope where Ms. Conte was concerned. If he was going to pick up the shattered pieces of his life, he had to go about the business of putting her and this joke of a marriage completely out of mind. It was over. Finished. Done.

He just had to make himself find a way to believe that.

The car finally stopped at Samantha's hotel. She opened the door and got out, and John impulsively decided to follow her. *Why not try to get a room here?* After all, the faster he got away from Olivia, the better.

They pulled their bags out of the trunk, then he leaned down to look inside. He was unable to prevent himself from catching one last glimpse of Olivia. Despite their long plane ride, she was as gorgeous and unruffled as ever. It hurt him deeply just to look at her.

"Well, see ya," he managed to choke out, overwhelmed by the thought of never seeing her again. *Why in the world did this hurt so much?*

"John, you can't just abandon me and go shack up with your new girlfriend," Olivia snapped, surprising him once again with her venomously jealous tone.

"Can and will," he said, not bothering to correct her assumption that he'd be staying with Samantha. She was unreal! Like he really was looking for someone new within hours of pledging to love and cherish her for the rest of their lives.

"The reservations are in your name," Olivia went on. "Those same reservations were made with your credit card. The tickets, museum passes, tours, and everything else we prearranged are also in your name and on your credit card." Angry impatience was dripping from her tone. "Will you please just take an hour or two from your hectic social life to come to the hotel with me, get us checked in, and talk about how we're going to handle the next two weeks, like mature adults?"

"Mature adults? Like the kind who don't know they're not in love until they're already married?" he flung back, not caring that Samantha and the cab driver and countless other passersby were overhearing their fight.

"Yes! That's right! The same kind of mature adult who can't seem to go one whole day without picking out new wife applicants. Speaking of which, do I have any duties in that regard? Do the guidelines call for me to teach them the secret handshake and passwords, or do I let them read the handbook?"

"You are *such* a piece of work!" John snapped.

"How can you sit there and talk to me this way after what you've done to me? After the way you *decimated* me on that plane?"

"Riiight," Olivia fired back. "*Decimated.* Sure. Is that from the Latin root 'deci' meaning 'decided to take off the wedding ring already' and 'mated' meaning 'with anyone, anytime, anywhere'?"

Soft laughter floated behind them. John stood up and whipped around to see Samantha struggling to smother another outburst.

"Glad this is so entertaining for you," Olivia snapped, still buried in the depths of the cab.

"Sorry—that just struck me as really funny," Samantha said, looking a little embarrassed. "Well, I guess now that I've got your attention, I'd just like to point out that you're paying for this fight at whatever price he comes up with." She nodded her head toward the unperturbed cab driver, who was leaning against the front of the car and nonchalantly cleaning under his fingernails with a pocketknife.

John sighed. She was right—if they were going to fight, they should do it in the privacy of the hotel room that had already been figured into the budget.

"Right, well, I think Olivia's got a point. The hotel is on my card, so I guess I'll go see how we can settle this," John said to Samantha as he ran his fingers through his hair in annoyance.

"Listen, it's been great getting to meet you, and I appreciate the shared cab ride. Do whatever you need to do, Jed, but just take care of yourself, okay?" Samantha leaned over to give him a short kiss on the cheek and handed him several bills for the fare.

"Thanks. You too," he said, watching as she picked up her bags and headed toward the lobby. He sighed again, then turned back to the driver, gave him the name of their hotel, and climbed back into the cab.

For the rest of the trip, the two of them sat as far apart as they could manage while remaining in the backseat.

Chapter 26

The Honeymoon Suite

"AHH, THE HONEYMOON suite!" the hotel clerk said with a knowing smile on his face. "You two young lovers are anxious to get checked in?"

"Do you have any other rooms available?" John asked as Olivia looked around the lobby.

"You do not want the honeymoon suite?"

"No, we need two *separate* rooms."

Man, this is embarrassing, John thought as he tossed an idle look over his shoulder at his current bride, who appeared to be pretending she was with someone else and was obviously embarrassed, too.

The clerk's smirk changed to a look of confusion. "You are not on your honeymoon?"

"No, we're not," John said, unable to censor the spitefulness from his tone. "Must be some mix-up with the reservation. I barely know this woman."

"I am so sorry, sir, but we have no other rooms! It's the high season for tourists—you won't find another room in the city."

"Of course not," John said, rubbing his temple with the heel of his hand in frustration. They couldn't have planned this trip for February or some other equally bad season for travel?

"There is a sofa in the honeymoon suite," the clerk offered.

"Okay, thank you," John said. This certainly wasn't the clerk's fault. "That'll be just fine."

He finished with the paperwork, got their keys, grabbed his bags, and walked toward the elevator without sparing a word or a glance toward Olivia.

* * *

This was all her fault, he reminded himself yet again. This whole miserable scenario was *her fault*. But why? Why did she do this to him? To *them?* If she was going to dump him, why wait until now? What had he done to deserve this hellish nightmare of a "honeymoon"?

He stopped in front of the elevator, pushed the button with the upward arrow, and struggled to quiet the self-pity coursing through him. Feeling sorry for himself certainly wasn't going to numb the hurt or change the miserable outcome of his third marriage.

The elevator doors creaked open.

"I think we're seeing our first genuine French artifact," Olivia said, looking dubiously at the rickety contraption.

"Feel free to take the stairs," John said, walking into the elevator and turning to push the button for the top floor.

Olivia wordlessly slid inside just before the doors closed again. There was barely enough room for the two of them—had either of them not packed lightly, they never would have gotten into the confined area with their baggage.

There was also no room for Olivia to turn around; she was facing him, practically pressed against his chest. As the elevator slowly rose, John closed his eyes and tried to block out her scent. It felt so comfortable and so right to have her near him like this, and every fiber of his body was straining toward her. He would have given anything at that moment just to put his arms around her again. But the weight of his bags—not to mention his dignity—kept his arms firmly in place. *Thank God*, he thought. The last thing he needed was *her* pity. His own self-pity was bad enough. The anger and the weirdly misplaced jealousy that he'd been getting from her since the plane landed were much more preferable, no doubt about it.

The elevator jerked to a halt, and Olivia, unable to hold her balance, fell against him. Instinctively, he dropped his bags and reached out to steady her.

"Thanks," she said with a nervous laugh. "Of course, I think this elevator's too small for me to actually fall down."

John suddenly realized he was still holding her; he dropped his hands from her sides as though he'd been burned.

"The door's open now," he said with a nod of his head.

"Oh, yes, of course," she said, looking as flustered as he felt as she backed out of the elevator.

John picked his bags up and followed her, grateful for the space between them now. He obviously couldn't trust his body not to react to her as it always had; holding her in the elevator just then felt right. Very comfortable and—unfortunately—wonderful. Living with her in this hotel for two weeks without touching her or holding her would be sheer torture. The self-pity threatened to overwhelm him again as he searched for the key and gave her the room number. They followed the signs on the walls in silence until they found the right door.

"Here it is," she said.

John numbly handed her the key, and she unlocked the door. Then, after a brief survey of the tiny room, she said, "I think the word *suite* was a bit generous."

"So was the word *sofa*," John replied, looking at the small, high-backed, museum piece of a love seat that was regally perched under the window.

Both their gazes landed on the full-size bed at the same time.

"I really am in hell, right? John said, looking over at Olivia, who looked equally uncomfortable. "The plane actually crashed after take-off, and I just went straight to hell. Okay, so now what?"

"Well, at least you've got company in hell," she said, clearly trying to lighten the mood.

"Yeah, and you're exactly who I'd choose to bring along," John fired back, effectively ending Olivia's attempts at humor.

"Okay, fine," she said as she dropped her bags in the entryway and closed the door. "So what *are* we going to do?"

John flung his bags on the bed and pulled out his phone.

"I'm going to find another room," he said. "I can't imagine there really isn't a single room available in the entire city."

"Okay, but before you start calling every hotel in town, can we discuss what we're going to do about our time here? We've got joint passes to everything. Do you want to forfeit them, or can we be mature adults and just enjoy the city the way we planned?"

"There's that phrase again. 'Mature adults.' Do you really want to have another face-off about who's been more mature during the last twenty-four hours?" John snapped, wondering again how she could be so cool about all of this.

Because her heart wasn't the one shattered in a million

pieces, he realized then, with another jolt of pain. *It wouldn't affect her one bit if I stayed here, slept in that tiny bed with her for two weeks, and tromped with her through every museum, church, catacomb, historical landmark, and tourist trap within a fifty-mile radius.*

She had the complete advantage in this situation because it didn't matter to her one way or the other. And if he continued to throw a fit about it, it would just give her more power and provide more proof of exactly how deeply he loved her, making him look like an even bigger fool than he already did. So maybe he *should* stay, just to show her he could.

But he first needed to get away from her in order to help himself try to heal. That much was stunningly obvious. Every time he caught a glimpse of her, and every time he heard her voice or saw her smile or smelled her perfume, it was going to be pure torture. Knowing how much she meant to him, and also knowing how little he meant to her, was going to be unthinkably painful. He needed time to adjust, to go over the past year, and to figure out where he'd gone wrong. He also wanted to wallow in his self-pity and think about how bleak the years to come were starting to look. And finally, he wanted to make some kind of a plan for the future.

But Olivia didn't need to know any of that.

"Fine, yeah, you're right," he finally said with a sigh. "We'll stick to the original plan."

"The original plan to stay here together?" she asked.

"No, sorry, no way. We'll take tours and enter museums together, but once we've gotten into places, we'll go our separate ways," he clarified. "As far as a place for me to stay, I'll figure something else out."

"Or some*one*," Olivia said, still sounding jealous for reasons he couldn't comprehend.

"Yes, that's right. I'm going to sleep my way through the city, one hot French babe at a time," John said icily. "Let's hurry up and figure out where we're meeting tomorrow, because I need to get started."

"Fine," Olivia said. She pulled up an email on her phone to show him. "We have a pass that's good for ten days and gets us into all these museums." Then, pointing, "I guess we should pick one of these for tomorrow?"

"The *Louvre* will be fine," John said, gathering his bags. "I'll meet you out front at the glass pyramid at opening time tomorrow."

"Don't you want to sit and make those calls before you leave? You don't know where you're going yet."

"I'll figure something out," he repeated.

"But what if the guy downstairs was right? What if there really aren't any rooms available? What will you do?"

"Your concern for me would be touching if it was at all sincere."

"John, come on, enough of this," Olivia said. "You know that I care what happens to you. Caring about you wasn't the issue."

"Yeah, that feels better every time you say it. Thanks."

"I'm sorry. I just really don't want you to race out of here and not have a plan," Olivia pleaded. "I'll sleep better tonight if I know you're safe. Please, John."

"Your sleep or the lack thereof isn't my problem," John said, becoming truly angry now. "I'm a big boy, and I've survived much worse than you."

With that he opened the door, sailed through it,

and slammed it behind him.

*   *   *

He felt like an idiot because she was right; he really needed a plan. But he couldn't stand there and look at her beautiful face or listen to her fake jealousy or hear her say again that she didn't love him. Listening to her talk about how much she cared for him, but not how much she loved him, had sliced through him just now as though he was hearing it for the first time. It had been all he could do to get out of there without begging her to take him back.

He entered the small elevator and pushed the button for the lobby.

So, seriously, what am I going to do?

And he didn't just mean for that night. What was he going to do with the rest of his *life?* How was he going to live without her? He couldn't even imagine an answer to those questions. This was supposed to be his honeymoon, and this hotel was supposed to be where they celebrated the beginning of their new life together as a married couple. He had to fight to hold back the tears again as he left the lobby and walked out onto the street.

Alone.

Chapter 27

Needing to Know

OLIVIA WAS completely exhausted now, worn down by guilt, tears, and doubt, not to mention the fighting....

But the exhaustion wasn't just mental—she hadn't slept more than an hour or two of their flight. Those same feelings of guilt and doubt and pain had kept her awake during most of the trip.

After John slammed out of their honeymoon suite, she tried to focus on small tasks. Unpacking. Organizing. Planning. But the weariness soon overwhelmed her. She took a quick shower just to relax, then climbed into the soft, warm bed. There she found herself staring at the ceiling and trying desperately to block out the onslaught of memories that were barraging her weary mind.

Some had to do with Charlie and how right he'd been—marrying John had obviously been anything but kind. How was she going to patch up her damaged relationship with her father?

Then there was the future. She would be forty with no husband, no children, and a serious doubt that she'd ever end up with either. How could she trust her instincts again, let alone start a relationship with someone new?

But mostly her thoughts were about John. Where was he right now? Had he run directly into Samantha's arms? Were they together right at that very moment having the wedding night she forfeited? Was he really over her so quickly?

She had to admit, though, the one overriding question that was assaulting her senses was why did thoughts of John being with another woman hurt so much? It just didn't make any sense. She'd done nothing but attack him since she found him sitting next to Samantha on the plane. But why? Why hadn't she just left him there, happy in the knowledge that he'd be okay? She hadn't done that at all. She'd become unreasonably furious, stalked down the aisle, and proceeded to start an hours-long verbal war with him.

She didn't want to think of herself as petty and shrewish, but that certainly was the way she'd been acting. No wonder John had stormed out of their hotel room with no place to go. Had she ever been a particularly jealous person in other relationships? Was this her standard operating procedure? She let her mind wander back to her previous boyfriends.

Justin from high school had barely been more than a buddy, so he didn't really count. Terrance and Gage, both exes from her college and law-school days, had been serious boyfriends. Terrance had been a frat boy—the life of every party—and women had loved him for it. Had she been jealous of the sorority sisters clamoring around him? *Not particularly.* He just loved to have fun, and he was only a professional flirt. She'd never worried for a moment about his feelings for her. It was his partying ways that had eventually worn against her much more serious and studious nature and finally caused the relationship to end, mutually.

She'd met Gage in the law library. Driven and smart, he seemed to be a perfect match. They'd spent the rest of law school together, studying, debating, and sharing their love for the law—and each other. But everything changed after graduation. Gage had been heavily recruited by several large firms, then he'd sailed through the bar exam and headed off to California to start building his fortune. She didn't want to work for a high-powered firm a million hours a week or pull down an amazing six-figure salary. She wanted to have a much simpler life, and she didn't want to be that far from her father. So she let him go without a fight and wasn't too surprised to learn of his engagement months later to a fellow attorney at his company.

Even then she hadn't really been jealous; the news rolled right off her without leaving much heartache in its wake. They hadn't wanted the same things, and he'd found someone who did. She'd been hurt, of course. And a little lonely. But never jealous. Other dates and short-term relationships had followed, but nothing serious had come along in all those years. Until John, that is.

And with him, apparently, the first real taste of jealousy....

How odd, she thought as she lay there in the middle of what was supposed to be her honeymoon bed. Why now? And why him, when *she* had been the one to end things? She wasn't a woman scorned, despite her angry musings earlier that day. She knew without a single doubt that John had been faithful to her since she met him, and she also knew that he had loved her deeply. The conclusions she'd leapt to earlier had been ridiculous, and she knew it. So why had she been acting this way all day? She barely even knew the man!

So was that the *real* heart of the problem? The fact that she hadn't gotten to really know him in this last year—and now that she was beginning to, she was jealous of losing what she might have had? How pathetic. How childish! *And how true*, she thought as she turned on her side and pulled what would have been John's pillow into her arms. She didn't know whether she loved this man or not because she'd never given him a chance. She'd met him, liked him, learned his name, and then decided on the spot that he was just a boring old "John Doe."

And why was that, exactly?

If those were truly the conclusions she'd drawn, why had she gone out with him even once? And then for a year? And then married him! And all without knowing his nickname was Jed. Or that he'd been married twice before, spoke French, and spent time in the Peace Corps. What else didn't she know about him?

Quite a lot, apparently.

Okay, I'm being overdramatic, she reasoned with herself. Of course she knew *something* about him. You couldn't spend a whole year with someone and not notice a few preferences or pick up a handful of trivia.

She supposed that had she really been pressed with the question, she would have eventually remembered his drink preferences or what his favorite book was. She knew he was right-handed, for example. He loved going to the movies, but not streaming them. He had an innate appreciation of expensive things, but he never sought them out for himself. He revered Billy Joel like some sort of god. And she knew he loved animals and children and someday wanted a home with a family and pets.

She stopped trying to frantically create a laundry list. Okay, so she knew him to some degree. But she also acknowledged that she'd never really questioned him or pushed for more details or stories from his youth. Why? *Who knows*, she thought, squeezing the pillow even more tightly. *Maybe it's because he really is the dull creature I assumed him to be.*

Or maybe he wasn't.

She sat up suddenly, struck by a very intriguing thought. In order to move past this and let herself off the roller coaster of accusations and self-doubt, she had to *know* if she'd done the right thing. And the only way to do that would be to truly get to know John better.

Yes, that would do it. Definitely.

She settled back onto her pillow, a calm falling over her that she hadn't felt in days. She was going to spend the next two weeks learning all she could about him and spending as much time with him as he could tolerate. She wanted the answers to all those questions that were still lurking in her mind. That way she'd finally know whether she'd done the right thing.

If he turned out to not really intrigue her—as she'd suspected all along—and they didn't share the same dreams and goals and visions of their future, well then she'd have the proof she needed. She could forgive herself for this catastrophe, get that divorce, and really, honestly move on with her life. But if she found she'd been wrong, and if in getting to know her husband she realized she'd made a horrible mistake....

She found she couldn't finish that train of thought. Because she actually had no say in the matter. She'd devastated him. How could he forgive her or trust her again? He certainly wouldn't give her a second chance at falling in *love* with him. But maybe it would still be enough. She would have learned an incredibly valuable lesson, and she'd spend the rest of her days making sure she really got to know the people around her. She'd never make this mistake again.

With that thought, her tired eyes finally closed. She soon fell into a deep, dreamless sleep, the pillow still tightly clutched in her arms.

Chapter 28

Making a Plan

OKAY, SO THE hotel clerk had been right—there wasn't a single decent room available in town. Of course, he hadn't bothered calling any youth hostels or wherever it was that people stayed while backpacking through Europe or trying to see it on ten dollars a day. He needed time alone to think and to heal, not trade travel tips with kids half his age.

He'd spent the day getting recommendations for hotels all over the city. The end result was always the same—no rooms and no vacancies on the horizon for any time in the next two weeks. The city really was filled to capacity. There had to be some sort of festival going on, maybe a fashion convention, too.

Weary, he had stopped in a little café so he could consider his options. Going back to the honeymoon love nest was out of the question. He couldn't even imagine spending one more minute in Olivia's company, so there certainly was no way he was going to sleep in the same bed with her. Or even in the same room with her, except maybe on the floor. Just wasn't going to happen. Especially after the way he'd stormed out of there while she begged him to stop and make his plans first. No, his dignity was already in shreds; no need to set it on fire as well.

So what did that leave? He reached into his pocket and pulled out two slips of paper—the addresses and phone numbers he'd been given on the plane.

One was for...*Marie. That was her name.* The flight attendant who had been very, very nice to him. Still, he doubted that was really going to extend to, "Hi, can I come crash at your place?" For one thing, he didn't remember formally introducing himself to her, so she likely wouldn't even know who he was if he *did* call. And second—he thought as he took a bite of the sandwich he'd ordered—all she'd said was something like, "If you want to get together and talk, give me a call." Again, that didn't seem like an invitation to stay over for two weeks with no strings attached.

He sighed as he took a drink of the wine he'd foolishly ordered. He was way too tired for wine; he'd be asleep on his plate if he didn't watch out. His mind traveled grudgingly back to his dilemma. *What to do...where to go....* What he really wanted was to be alone. Completely alone for the entire two weeks. He didn't want to stay with anyone, or talk to anyone, or explain himself to anyone, or have to—God forbid—talk about his *feelings* with anyone. Nevertheless, it was looking more and more like he was going to have to impose himself on Samantha's hospitality. And if he did, he'd probably have to be around her and talk to her and be somewhat social and civilized.

But hey—at least *she* knew his name. She also knew a bit more about his situation than Marie. And he was pretty sure she understood that this wasn't a romantic come on; although he would have to make that abundantly clear, just in case. There was no way he could handle her pain while in the middle of his own.

He finished his meal, paid the waiter, and headed out to the sidewalk with his luggage still in tow. The weather was warm and inviting, so he started walking aimlessly. All around him swirled the crowds of tourists, the rich aromas drifting out of the bakeries and cafes, and the rushing sounds of the traffic. But he wasn't really absorbing or appreciating any of it, which only deepened the depression.

His thoughts had temporarily abandoned the dilemma of where to stay and instead focused on another completely maddening question, the one that had plagued him most since Olivia's declaration: How had he not seen any of this coming? Other than the fact that she hadn't made much of an effort to learn about his past—which he'd stupidly chalked up to loving acceptance—he'd had absolutely no warning.

He suddenly stopped walking, causing a pile-up of irritated pedestrians behind him. He apologized, then started forward again. But the memory that had resurfaced continued to assault him mercilessly. He *had* received a warning. He'd just chosen to ignore it. His sister Kate's words to him on the day of the wedding rapidly came flooding back into his mind—

John, I'm not trying to spoil this day for you, I'm really not. But for some reason I feel that something's just not right with the two of you, and I'm really worried that you're not thinking this through. It's only been a year—why jump into marriage so soon?

What else had she said? Oh yes—

Does she love you? I want you to really think about it. You're positive?

What was she, the Oracle of Delphi? She'd precisely summed up the problem on the first try. Things *weren't* right between them, and apparently he was the only person stupid enough not to have noticed that his blushing bride wasn't in love with him. He was going to have to enter the Witness Protection Program just to avoid facing his sister again. John knew Katie loved him too much to say I told you so, but he couldn't stand to see the pity and concern in her face, either. Or his parents' faces, for that matter. Even Val had expressed concern for him that day. But he didn't listen to any of them. He'd even given Kate a lecture on welcoming Olivia into the family. *Well, she'll certainly be saved from that fate.* In fact, Olivia might be the one forced into hiding once his family and friends learned what had happened.

John smiled at the thought, although he seriously doubted he'd ever give them the whole story. It was just too painful and raw and embarrassing to chat about over Sunday dinner. He'd probably condense the story down to something like "we just decided it wasn't working" and let them wonder about the rest. He'd be in too much shock and pain for anyone to grill him about it anyway. He did know that it wasn't healthy to bottle it up. He'd have to tell someone at some point. Maybe that was the role Samantha was meant to play in all this—a stranger with a sympathetic ear who could listen while he poured out all the heartbreak.

No...too soon. He couldn't imagine doing that already. If he didn't talk about it, it might seem less real. And he knew the reality of the situation was more torturous than he could face at the present.

Maybe this time away *was* the answer. Maybe after two weeks, he'd feel a little less devastated and a little more ready to handle the rest of his life alone. But Paris was supposed to be a vacation they experienced together. Everywhere he turned, every sight he saw, and every experience he had in the next two weeks were just going to remind him that he was supposed to be doing those things and seeing those sights with his loving wife.

Okay, so he needed to get away from it all—this

life, that wife, *and* the current vacation. Where should he go? Jamaica? Hawaii? Japan? The moon?

How about everywhere? a small voice in the back of his mind suggested. Of course! He could travel with the Peace Corps or Habitat for Humanity again. It had helped him heal from one divorce, why not two? He was sure he could take a leave of absence from work without too much trouble. And he was certain either program would welcome him back with open arms.

A feeling of calm came over him now. He had a plan! And it was a way to make himself feel whole again while focusing on helping others. Better that than swimming around in his own misery for months.

What a great idea!

Buoyed by the thought, he unfolded the scrap of paper from his pocket again that had Samantha's handwriting on it and pulled out his phone.

Chapter 29

Finally a Bed

"I'M SO GLAD you called," Samantha said with a wide smile, opening the door of her hotel room to let him in. "You absolutely did the right thing."

"I appreciate this more than you'll ever know," John told her. "But I was worried about it, too—I just didn't want to mislead you or make you think I'm—"

"Say no more," Samantha cut in. "I completely understand that you're strictly here as a friend in need of a place to crash."

"Thank you for understanding," John replied with a flood of relief. "I know this is completely crazy, but...."

Samantha closed the door behind him. "Hey, it's okay. I saw quite clearly today what you're going through. There's no way I'd want to try to complicate your life further. And you're in luck. They gave me two twin beds, so you don't even have to sleep on the floor."

John's tired eyes eagerly sought out the bed she'd mentioned. It looked wonderful. *How rude would it be to just collapse on it now without another word?* he wondered.

"I can't believe I couldn't find a single room after looking all day."

"I'm not using the desk," Samantha said as though he hadn't spoken, clearing some space. "So feel free to put your things on it."

John gratefully complied, thrilled beyond words to

finally be free of the bags he'd been lugging around.

Samantha continued to fuss over him, urging him to unpack, get organized, and take a shower to relax. She even ordered their dinners, insisting it was her treat. Though he really wasn't all that hungry, John didn't argue with her as she took complete control of the situation. Being worried over by a beautiful woman actually felt kind of nice. *Too bad my lovely wife isn't the one doing the worrying,* he reflected ruefully.

When he was out of the shower and comfortable in a pair of sweatpants and an old college t-shirt, the food arrived. They sat on the edges of their beds, the tray resting on a chair from the desk in between them. It made for a passable, if makeshift, table.

"Aah, the elegance of fine French dining," Samantha said, breaking the silence.

"Nope, this is perfect. I never could have pulled off 'elegant' tonight."

"So what happened with Olivia, exactly?" Samantha asked. "If you don't mind me prying a little bit, that is."

"We got checked in to our honeymoon closet, but there weren't any other rooms, and there wasn't space enough for me to even consider staying," John told her. "I just can't see her right now, and I definitely can't share a bed with her."

"Completely understandable," Samantha said, taking a sip of water. "What about the other items she mentioned—the tours and passes and other things you've already purchased?"

"We didn't exactly sit down and work out a new itinerary. I just told her we'd meet at places, get in, then split up and go our separate ways. Tomorrow we'll be at the *Louvre.*"

"Good plan."

"So how long are *you* here?" John asked, hoping to permanently change the subject.

"This is my big business trip for the year. I typically stay about a month."

"Oh, nice. So you'll get to spend some time here not having to play nursemaid to me. We're only here for two weeks."

"Not that I mind one minute of this small favor. Really and truly, Jed, it's nice to have the company. Speaking of which," she said, turning around and reaching for her purse, "here's a spare key. I went and got another after you called."

"How do you know you can even trust me with this? What if I'm a high-class pickpocket who set this whole thing up to rob you blind? Maybe Olivia's in on it with me, and she's just back at our lair waiting for me as we speak."

"Lair?" Samantha said with a chuckle before seeming to realize John was serious. She struggled a moment to wipe the smile off her face before adding, "No, you're right. I *don't* know that for sure. And if this is just a setup, then I guess I'll be learning a valuable lesson."

"Seriously, though," John said, the look on his face surely making it clear that he was blown away by this stranger's kindness, "why are you doing this?"

"I'm just a hopelessly nice person, I guess. I trust my instincts when it comes to reading people, and I decided on the plane that I believe that you are indeed a good person who's suffered a terrible blow. It makes me feel good to know I'm helping you through this in some small way."

"You're a saint," John said after studying her face

for another moment and deciding to take her words at face value. She was doing the same with him, after all.

"I wouldn't go that far," Samantha said with a laugh.

"Well, considering that I'd be sleeping at the front gate of the American Embassy tonight if it weren't for you, I'd say the Papal decree is in the mail."

"Does the Pope mail his own decrees, do you think?" Samantha asked with a smirk.

"Nah, probably not," John said, returning her smile. Samantha's goofiness was a breath of fresh air in his currently too-heavy life, and he really appreciated it—and her. Maybe under another set of circumstances....

He quickly brushed aside that thought; he had enough problems on his hands without inventing more.

"Speaking of saintly behavior," he went on, changing the subject again, "I think I have a plan for getting through this divorce nightmare while actually thinking about something other than my own pathetic life."

Samantha raised her eyebrows and looked at him expectantly. "Spill it! What's this brilliant plan?"

"I think I'm going to take a leave of absence from work—or, frankly, I'll just quit if I have to—and do some more volunteering. I'm going to see if I can join up with Habitat for Humanity or the Peace Corps again."

"What a great idea! You'll be getting away for a while and focusing on *other* people's problems! Ingenious, really."

"Yeah, well, it was this kind of wacky forward thinking that helped me get through my first divorce without losing it," he said. "So I figured why not apply the same techniques to the third?"

"I'd love to do something like that," she said, a wistful look on her face.

"Well, you're certainly welcome to join me, although I have to warn you there's probably going to be a hefty out-of-pocket expense, depending on what we do and where we go, unless you can whip up some fundraising activities for us." Then John added, "Although you know what? It's been so long since I did a trip like this, I honestly have no idea how it works. I'm starting from scratch here."

"If it were necessary, I've got money stashed away," she told him.

"Okay, well, when I figure out more, I'll let you know."

"Please do. How long do you think you'll take off from your real life?"

"Oh, I don't know. Maybe six months or so? But you certainly wouldn't have to dive into such a huge commitment. A couple of weeks is probably more typical." John gave a tired smile as he put down his fork and stretched his arms above his head. "I'm absolutely exhausted. I know it's only like eight or something, but would you mind if I went to sleep now? I'm so beat that you could watch TV at full volume or tap dance all night and I wouldn't hear a thing."

"Go ahead. I'm going to read a while. And then, you know, maybe I *will* do some tap dancing."

John smiled at her as they stood to clean up the dinner tray and set it out in the hall. He brushed his teeth, and Samantha set the alarm on her phone before taking her turn in the bathroom.

John crawled into his bed and pulled the covers over himself with a blissful sigh. *Sleep*.... That was definitely what his weary body and soul needed. Sweet, wonderful sleep.

He never even heard Samantha leave the bathroom only moments later. He was out for the rest of the night.

Chapter 30

The Louvre

OLIVIA FELT LIKE she was going on a first date. She was nervous and flustered, and she took an inordinate amount of time fixing her hair and makeup and deciding what to wear. She knew it was an odd reaction to her current and very bizarre set of circumstances. John wasn't a first date; he was the husband she'd scorned only...what? Was it really just one day ago? She needed to get herself under control if she was going to survive two weeks of weaving in and out of his company.

She was standing by the *Louvre*'s glass pyramid, as they'd agreed. It was a large modern architectural monument surrounded by fountains in the plaza in front of the museum. As time crawled by, she became more and more worried. What if something had happened to him? Should she call? Text? She was likely the last person he wanted to hear from, and his pride would've led him to sleep on a park bench before he came back to her. She would never forgive herself if he'd been mugged, or hurt, or worse.

She'd been standing there for about thirty minutes, tapping her foot anxiously, worrying, and debating endlessly about whether she should reach out to him. Then she caught a glimpse of him walking toward her through a crowd of tourists. *Thank God*, she thought, feeling a little breathless as he got closer. He looked incredibly handsome. He was wearing a pair of faded jeans and a navy blue t-shirt, a color she'd always loved on him. His worn pair of brown walking shoes completed this casual wardrobe. All in all, he looked great. Certainly better rested than the last time she'd seen him. And the air of anger around him seemed to have dissipated a little, too. *Good*, she thought, *maybe he'll be more open to talking with me.*

An odd look that she couldn't quite read was on his face as he approached.

"Sorry I'm late," he said tersely, stopping before he got all the way to her. "Let's get in line."

"Is everything okay?" she asked as she practically had to chase after his rapidly retreating form. *So much for him being less furious with me.*

"Just as terrific as it's ever been," he answered somewhat sharply.

Okay, so maybe he wouldn't just be opening up to her and sharing his most intimate thoughts, memories, and feelings. *I'll be lucky if he says anything more to me at all*, she told herself. He'd stopped at the end of the line for admission, which had tripled in length since she arrived. He stood stiffly, scanning the crowd, and not even acknowledging her presence.

"Did you find yourself a hotel room yesterday?" she pressed on, uncomfortable and desperate to start a friendly conversation with him.

"Nope," he said, still looking away.

"So where did you go?" she asked, adding before she thought it through, "With Samantha?"

"Yeah. And she says hi," John answered.

Olivia felt like she'd been kicked in the stomach. So, he *had* run into Samantha's sympathetic arms! His confirmation of her suspicions was so unreasonably painful—and it absolutely should *not* be hurting so much. She knew it shouldn't, and she knew she had forfeited all claims to this man and his time and affections already. But for some reason, at that precise moment, she would have done anything just to see him smile at her.

"I'm glad you weren't shot while sleeping under a bridge," she blurted out, sounding falsely chipper and maybe a little deranged.

"What?" he said, looking in her direction for the first time.

"When you didn't show up on time, I started to get worried that you'd, I don't know, gotten hurt or something." This conversation wasn't going at all like she'd planned.

"Yes, I'm sure you were terrified."

"Stop it. You know I care about you. I just—"

"You say it again, and I'm walking away and never coming back, museum passes be damned."

"I wasn't going t—"

Olivia stopped herself and took a deep breath.

Then, "I had really hoped we could be civil with each other these next two weeks. I would love nothing more than to take this time to see Paris with you as a friend, and talk with you and, I don't know, get to know you better, maybe."

He turned to look at her again, his face awash in astonishment. And was that...*horror* in his eyes, too?

"You want to be my *friend?* You want to get to know me *better?!*"

"Yes, I really do," Olivia said, nervous now at his cold reaction.

"*WHY?!*" he yelled, causing nearby tourists and a few museum guards to turn and stare at them uneasily.

"John—"

"Why," he started again, much more quietly but with equal fury. "Why would you want to do that? And why, in the name of all that's holy, would I *let* you?"

"Because I was an idiot this whole year. I know silly trivial stuff about you, but I obviously don't know the real you or any significant details about you. I want...no, I *need* to get to know you better."

"That makes no sense," John snapped. "After these two weeks are over, you'll never see me again, God willing. What does it matter if you know that I can play the guitar or that I've traveled the world or that I can list all the American Presidents?"

"You play the guitar?" she asked, intrigued.

John rolled his eyes at her and stepped forward with the slow-moving line.

"Acoustic or electric?"

"Just leave me alone," he told her. "I think you've done enough damage to me for one lifetime. You really don't need to try to top yourself."

She sighed. He was right. *What am I doing?* She couldn't just force the man to play an enormous, two-weeks-long game of twenty questions with her. She was an idiot to even try. She'd had her chance to get to know him, and she'd chosen not to take advantage of it. Now it was too late.

"I'm sorry," she said quietly. "That was a dumb, pitiful effort at soothing my guilty conscience and my...." She faltered here, knowing it would be unthinkably cruel to let him know she was having doubts about what she'd done. "I didn't mean to hurt you again," she finished lamely.

"You didn't," he said, his voice sounding cooler and more detached. "I'm sorry I made you stand here and wait so long. I was doing some research and sending some emails. The time got away from me."

"Honeymoon update to your family and friends?"

"Hardly. I'll never admit any of this to anyone," he said. "As far as I'm concerned, everyone can think we're still happily married fifty years from now."

Olivia laughed despite herself. "Yeah, my social media posts won't be very detailed, either."

John considered her face for a moment before answering. "Why? You're not the loser who got dumped on his honeymoon."

"You are *not* a loser, John! *I* am, because I'm the idiot who didn't stop to think about what she was doing or attempt to get to truly know her husband-to-be *for an entire year*. The local Mensa chapter won't be sending me an application form anytime soon, that's for sure."

"Neither one of us knew enough about each other. That much is painfully obvious," he continued as they reached the head of the line. They showed their passes, got their tickets and maps, and walked inside.

"Why didn't I realize that sooner?" Olivia asked, truly perplexed by her own ignorance.

"Why didn't *I?*" John countered. "Well, actually, I think I did know there were large gaps in what we knew about each other. But I just kept ignoring that fact and assuming we had the rest of our lives to figure those things out. Good plan, huh?"

They were inside now and faced with the decision of which collections to view first.

"Can we continue this conversation? See the museum together? I would like nothing more," Olivia said, a hint of pleading in her voice.

John ran his fingers through his hair and looked down at her as he thought about it. She met his gaze and could have sworn she saw a flicker of tenderness and love there. But he drew it back inside so quickly that she couldn't be sure what it had really been.

She held her breath, waiting for his reply and feeling thrilled he was even considering it.

"Sorry, no," he finally said. "I just can't." Then he turned and disappeared into the crowd.

She stood anchored to the floor like one of the museum's statues, shocked numb by how much his rejection hurt. Of course, she had to keep reminding herself, it was justified. What she was feeling was only a fraction of the pain she'd caused him, and she knew that.

Justified...everything he's feeling now is fully and completely justified....

She started to walk in the opposite direction, tears blurring her vision.

Chapter 31

Mona Lisa

I WAS KIDDING myself if I thought I was going to survive this divorce, John told himself as he collapsed on a museum bench just around the corner from where he'd abandoned Olivia.

Any progress he thought he'd made toward survival had been completely undone when he had spotted her earlier, waiting for him in the plaza in her yellow sundress and light cotton sweater as the sun shone off her beautiful black hair. She'd left it loose in a riot of long curls, making her look even more sexy than usual. Just seeing her—his wife, and yet not even his friend—had hurt as much as hearing her initial confession on the plane. Which was why he'd been so childishly snappy with her. It hurt too much, seeing her and wanting her and loving her...and wishing he could hate her but failing miserably.

He sighed and leaned his head back, trying to work the kinks out of his neck. He'd slept straight through the night—almost twelve hours! Now he felt fuzzy and a little worn. *A head cold would make this trip even more magical,* he thought as he looked at the crowd milling past him, all the tourists intent on locating the museum's many treasures.

Which is what I should be doing, he thought as he tried to summon the resolve it would take to harvest any enjoyment from the day. He opened the map and surveyed his choices. He'd been to Paris before, but he had never spent much time at the *Louvre*. Crowds and lines had always interfered with seeing the museum's most famous pieces, like the *Mona Lisa, Winged Victory,* or the *Venus D'Milo*. Now, with a whole day to fill, he decided to hit the highlights. What would it matter if he had to stand in a few slow lines? He had to find some way to distract himself and get through the next two weeks. Standing around a museum was as good a way to start as any.

And after these two weeks were over, he was going to take a semi-permanent break from reality, he'd decided. He would immediately leave his job, put his things in storage, say goodbye to his family and friends, and take off. When he'd gone online that morning, he'd found several upcoming trips listed with Habitat, and he was leaning toward taking one of them. If Samantha was serious about coming along, it'd be easier for her to join that than formally applying for a typically lengthier Peace Corps assignment.

He had gone ahead and filled out the online application form and forwarded the link to her, although he was actually indifferent to whether or not she accompanied him. She was a nice person, and he certainly owed her one. But he didn't want to lead her on in any way. And he really didn't want to talk with her about Olivia and what had happened any more than he already had. Hopefully she would get the hint. It was nothing against her personally—he didn't want to rehash it with anyone.

He knew, rationally, that what he really needed was time. Even heartache this debilitating would diminish given the right number of days and space and distance. But exactly how *much* time would be needed was what worried him most. A year? Two? Twenty?

Twenty sounds about right, he thought as he reached into his pocket and pulled out his wedding ring. Although he'd yanked it off his finger almost immediately after Olivia dumped him, he couldn't seem to leave it behind in the hotel room either. Wearing it hurt as much as not wearing it did.

He stared at it as he rolled it through his fingers, the shiny platinum band still warm from his body heat. *What a disaster....* Such a waste of time and money. Such a lot of loneliness and pain and self-recrimination. He squeezed his eyes shut and tried to shake off the grief and self-pity that continued clawing at him. When was life going to be bearable again? Seeing Olivia this morning had been way too hard—like ripping the scab off a still-fresh wound. And to think he still had two weeks with her to go.

Had she really thought he would be able to spend today recounting his life story to her? Why in the world had she even said that? What were her exact words? Something about easing her guilt? That just didn't sound plausible—wouldn't she just want to stay as far away from him as possible if her real objective was to escape her guilt?

Unless she's having doubts and second thoughts about what she said, and she really wants to spend time with me to get me back! Yes! That's it! She—

No..stop! Stop this right now!

John's brain was struggling to drown out the chorus of hope working its way into his heart. He *had* to stop letting himself cling to this relationship. His emotions and self-esteem were already in shreds, and he knew that holding onto imaginary evidence of a second chance was only going to hurt him more and make him look like an even bigger fool.

He was strong, he reminded himself. He'd gotten over broken relationships before. He'd gotten over broken *marriages* before. Marriages that had lasted a whole lot longer than this one. *I can do it again,* he thought. *I don't need her, and I'll be fine.* What should it matter if he saw her every day and talked to her for the next two weeks?

It doesn't, he thought stubbornly, feeling slightly better after the mental pep talk. Regardless of what Olivia did or said while they were together—and regardless of how amazing she looked—he was going to be indifferent to it. To *her.* If he let her bother him whenever they saw each other, then he would be giving her more power. And that would keep ripping open his wounds.

He slid the ring back in his pocket, determined to shake off his earlier grief and sadness. *The time for mourning is over.*

He picked up the museum map and found where the *Mona Lisa* was displayed. He then walked in that direction with a renewed sense of purpose, trying not to be too hard on himself when he realized every woman with black hair made him turn his head. Why was he hoping to get another glimpse of Olivia? He was supremely indifferent to her, right?

Well, okay, maybe not supremely *indifferent* he thought with a small, sad smile as he realized he really was searching for her in the crowd. It was going to take time—a *lot* of time—to truly reach a state of indifference. But he made a promise to himself that he would be all right eventually. He just had to be strong. Mind over matter.

*   *   *

He spent about an hour in line before reaching

170

what was very likely the most famous portrait in the world. But he didn't mind. The brushstrokes and colors were amazing—seeing the original felt worth the wait, even if it was safely encased in bulletproof glass and smaller than he had imagined. But the model's gentle, secretive smile, coupled with her long, dark hair, yanked his thoughts immediately back to Olivia.

She'd certainly had her secrets, too. He still couldn't believe she'd gone through the entire wedding ceremony and reception out of pity for him. He'd known something was up that day, but she'd maintained the act. Out of *kindness* for him? "Kindness" seemed like such a ridiculous word when he also thought about the pain of hearing her confess that she didn't love him. A pain that was still ricocheting through his body.

But would he *really* have preferred it if she had just jilted him? Honestly?

No.

He couldn't truthfully say that he would have wanted to face a church filled with their family and friends and admit his bride had abandoned him. And he wouldn't have known why, either, which would have made it even harder. Instead, she'd stuck around, saved him from embarrassment, and given him a private, face-to-face explanation.

He took a deep breath and closed his eyes, turning away from the portrait and walking blindly out of the room. The pain was numbing. He didn't *want* to admire Olivia for what she'd done. He didn't want to be grateful to her for how she'd dumped him or label her honorable for going through with the ceremony. The raw truth was that she'd chosen the toughest path possible, given the list of choices she'd had that day at the church. She even incurred her aging—and otherwise doting—father's wrath rather than risk completely humiliating him.

The pain and the embarrassment were still there, and he knew they'd be his constant companions for a long, long time. But he could feel a little of his anger toward her melting away. No matter how awful it had all turned out, she really had tried to be kind.

He reached a large hallway and studied his map silently. Maybe the next piece of art would help take his mind off her. Da Vinci's masterpiece certainly hadn't.

Chapter 32

Venus D'Milo

OLIVIA COULDN'T believe how devastated she felt as she mindlessly paced the halls of the *Louvre*, passing by the priceless works of art like they were nothing more than road signs. Why was John's rejection so painful? Or at all surprising, for that matter? She'd had a whole year to get to know him! Why was it suddenly so important to do so now?

She thought about the things she'd learned about him in the past few days. He'd been married twice…okay, make that three times. What had her reaction been when she'd stumbled across that bit of information? Fury. And an unreasonable amount of jealousy, given the circumstances. But why? Why did she even care? She'd also learned that he had been with the Peace Corps. Is that how he'd traveled so much? Is that why he knew how to speak French? And how had she never realized that he had such a profound drive to help others? That he was so giving of himself?

What else…oh, that he played the guitar! How could she forget that one? She'd always had a secret attraction to men who played the guitar. She found herself wishing she could hear him play someday, but then she tried to shake off that thought. It was never going to happen anyway.

And the other thing she'd learned about him—the thing that probably surprised her the most—was that women seemed to throw themselves at him. He'd gotten the numbers of at least two different gorgeous women during the flight alone! And she'd seen a few heads turn when he was outside the museum that morning. Why had she never noticed the effect he had on other women before? And why was the thought suddenly making her feel so jealous and territorial?

So what was the summary then...?

He was a world traveler who obviously cared passionately about helping other people. He was smart enough to pick up another language and speak it fluently. Musical and talented enough to play the guitar. Handsome and sexy enough that women flocked to him.

She spotted an empty bench and collapsed onto it in defeat. She almost felt dizzy as the remorse and self-doubt assailed her. How could she have been so blind to all these wonderful qualities he embodied? What had she been thinking before the wedding? That he was dull? That he was some kind of simpleton she'd latched onto during a midlife spinster crisis? Where had she come up with an assessment that was so far off the mark? She felt like a complete fool. She sighed, then took a deep breath to calm herself down.

If she had the whole thing to do over again, she would have kept her mouth shut on the plane and used the honeymoon as an opportunity to get to know and hopefully fall in love with him. If only she could turn back time and take away those horrible things she'd said! But she couldn't. It was over. And it really came down to a lack of faith, both in him and in her own ability to choose a good person to spend her life with. She hadn't been willing to put much effort into this relationship. She had childishly determined that if she wasn't struck by lightning and instantly in love, then it wasn't going to happen.

And they'd had such a great foundation to build their futures on! They had been compatible and comfortable with each other. He had slid into her world with absolutely no problems. How wonderful would it be to have a husband—best friend, confidante, lover—with whom she was so at ease? She could tell him anything, and he'd understand. She knew that. He was easygoing, accepting, funny, kind, strong...all the things anyone could possibly want in a husband.

And she'd thrown it all away. The remorse hit her again with a vengeance, taking her breath away. She'd made a huge mistake. She knew that now. The marriage would surely have worked if she'd given it a chance.

Okay, now I'm just getting hysterical, she thought angrily. There wasn't any *guarantee* she would fall in love with him, even given all the time in the world and all the second chances she could ever wish for. Despite the painful way it had all played out, she might have done the right thing after all, saving them both a lot of time and heartache.

The unfortunate part was that she'd never know which way it would've gone. She couldn't get that second chance now. What if she begged John for another shot at making things work, then found out she would never fall in love with him? She couldn't break his heart a second time—that would be so cruel!

She shook her head, trying to clear it out. She felt weary and beaten down by all the second-guessing and guilt. It was time to force her mind off her predicament and enjoy a bit of this trip.

She pulled out her museum map and studied it carefully. She'd never been to Paris before; it was inexcusable to throw away this opportunity to see some of history's most famous works of art just because she was having a nervous breakdown.

The Venus D'Milo *is here*, she realized. How could she have forgotten about that? She'd always thought it was breathtaking, and now she had a chance to examine it up close.

She stood and set off in search of it.

* * *

Her new sense of purpose propelled her down the ornate hallways and through the magnificent galleries of a museum that had once been a royal palace. She focused on trying to actually *see* its opulence and beauty. But she found herself surveying the crowds instead, hoping to run into John. Once again, she felt like she owed the man an apology. He must think her so unbelievably thoughtless and cruel for her bungled attempt at a conversation earlier.

She came across the *Venus*, which was standing in a small room, light shining from a window and casting shadows on the white marble features of its serene face. Olivia gasped, overwhelmed by the beautiful masterpiece and touched by the opportunity to stand so close to it. The crowd was inexplicably light at the moment, giving Olivia the opportunity to walk all the way around the statue and really absorb its presence.

After circling several times, she noticed the information cards in boxes posted on the wall, so she walked over and looked through them. They were in a variety of languages, a few she recognized and a few she didn't. But none were in English. *Where is my bilingual husband when I need him?* she thought, but the joke didn't get a laugh out of her. In fact, just the thought of him alone somewhere in the museum, experiencing it without her, made her want to cry.

She set the cards down, moved over to the corner

of the tiny room and slid listlessly down the wall until she was sitting on the floor. She made sure her dress wasn't flipped up and giving museum visitors an extra exhibit, then leaned her head back against the wall and closed her eyes. *When is this pain and remorse going to go away?*

Then she sensed someone next to her.

Great, I'm probably going to get thrown out by a museum guard and really make this day memorable, she thought. She continued to sit there defiantly, not bothering to open her eyes.

"Are you okay, Liv?"

Her eyes flew open, and she found John standing there. He was looking down, concern etched on his face.

She didn't answer him, but continued to stare in surprise as joy flooded her body and assaulted her senses. He really *was* so handsome. And so smart...and kind and caring and funny....

And so not mine anymore.

She felt embarrassed as tears welled in her eyes. Noticing this, John knelt on the floor next to her.

"Livvie, what's wrong?" he asked as he gently reached over to wipe the tears away.

He hadn't spoken so kindly to her, or used that familiar nickname, or even touched her, since their breakup. It felt so good to hear the softness in his voice and to feel his concern, something she thought she'd never experience again.

"It's nothing," she finally said, struggling to get in control of her emotions. "It's just...really good to see you."

John gave her a small, sad smile, but said nothing. Then he sat against the wall next to her and guided her head gently to his shoulder.

They remained that way for a long time, watching the crowds swirl around the *Venus D'Milo*. And she felt so grateful simply to be near him again.

Chapter 33

A Small Truce

"ISN'T SHE BEAUTIFUL?" Olivia finally asked, breaking the comfortable silence that had surrounded them.

"Yeah, she is," John replied. "I'm glad I'm finally getting to see her."

"Oh, you've never been here before?" she asked. *Great, something else I don't know about this man.*

"To the *Louvre?* Yes, I have. But I've never made it in to see their most famous works. I never wanted to stand in the lines."

"It's my first time," she said.

"And what have you seen today?"

"Just this, actually," she answered sheepishly.

"You've been sitting here for hours?" John asked, looking shocked.

"Well, not exactly. I just wandered for a while until I made it to this room. I was really overwhelmed by her, and I wanted to read more, but I couldn't find the English information card." She gestured toward the box of cards on the wall. "It made me wish....," she began, then trailed off, not wanting to confess anything further.

"It made you wish you were bilingual?" he guessed.

"Well, yeah," Olivia said, still withholding what she *really* had wanted.

"It made you wish *I* was here?" he added cautiously, the question nothing more than a whisper.

"Yes," Olivia admitted finally, also in a whisper.

Silence hung between them again, but it was not as comfortable as before. Olivia didn't want to risk hurting him further, and she was still somewhat confused by how happy she felt having him there.

He pulled away, stood up, and walked over to the cards. The traffic in the room had started to increase, so it didn't look like there were many left to choose from. Nevertheless, he grabbed one, came back, and sat down again.

"The French one was there?" she asked.

"Nope. They had Spanish and German though," he replied, as though that explained anything.

"Oh, that's too bad. So, what do you have there?"

"I picked Spanish," he said with a shrug.

"Wait, what? Don't tell me you speak Spanish, too?" she all but shrieked, turning to look him in the eye.

"And German," he continued. "Although I'm stronger with Spanish than German, which is why I picked it."

"How many other languages do you speak?"

"Well once you know one Romance language, you basically know them all."

"What does that mean?" she snapped.

"Italian wasn't so hard to pick up," he told her, a confused look on his face. "You look mad. Did I say something wrong?"

"No...I'm sorry," she said, leaning against the wall again and closing her eyes. *Is that a headache starting to build up in my head...or just an enormous tidal wave of self-recrimination?* "I'm just so furious with myself. I literally cannot believe how much about you I don't know. It's absolutely making me crazy."

"I don't think there are any more big surprises," he replied with an apologetic smile.

"You speak like fifty different languages! The fact that I didn't know that alone is inexcusable, but it's barely a drop in the bucket compared to what I've learned in the last few days."

"It's over and done with now. Stop beating yourself up about it."

"I don't think I'll *ever* be able to forgive myself for everything that's happened," she said. "I really don't."

"Just let it go," he insisted, shocking her even more than his list of languages.

"Does that mean *you* have?" Olivia asked, looking at him again in astonishment. "You've forgiven me so easily? And so soon?"

John studied her face for a long moment before answering.

"I wish sometimes that I was the kind of guy who could really stay angry about something or really be able to nurse a grudge," he said. "But somehow I always find myself completely unable to hold onto the rage."

"But that's a wonderful quality!" she told him.

"I guess so. It doesn't make this hurt any less. And it doesn't change the fact that you should have figured all of this out a long time before our wedding day, and that I should have been more forthcoming in the past, too. But I can see now that...well, that you took the tough route that day, Liv. And I *am* grateful you didn't just leave me there to explain it to everyone. I wouldn't have had any idea what I was explaining or why."

"You don't have to do this, John," she said, shaking her head. "I don't deserve it."

"Yeah, well, I wanted to. I think I needed to say it."

"Then thank you for telling me," she said softly, wishing in that moment she could reach out and take his hand, but knowing that would break the small truce they'd reached. "Really, it means more to me than you'll ever know."

"You're welcome," John replied. And it seemed for just a moment that he might actually be leaning toward her, like maybe he was leaning in…for a kiss? Was he really going to kiss her? As astonishment raced through her body, so did longing, she quickly realized. There was absolutely nothing in the world she wanted more than for him to close the gap between them.

She caught her breath in anticipation. *Do it, do it, do it,* she chanted silently, even as she froze, afraid the slightest movement would make him change his mind.

Then, as quickly as it had begun, the moment was over. John pulled back and broke his gaze with her. She could feel the letdown coursing through her. Then she became quiet, uncertain what to say. John looked like he was upset. Would it be the right thing or the wrong thing to admit that she'd wanted him to kiss her? She didn't know. What should she do? This was sheer torture.

Maybe she just needed to let the moment pass. Simply change the subject and fill the awkward silence? Since she was no closer to knowing how she felt than before, she decided that was probably the right path.

"Will you read to me about the statue?" she finally asked.

"Sure."

He brought the card up close and read the information to her, telling of the statue's history and about several theories about how it had originally looked before it was damaged.

"Wow, I think she looks better *without* the arms," Olivia said with a laugh as she looked over John's shoulder at the sketches of how it might have looked when it was complete.

"You're just used to seeing her this way," he replied, looking back at her over his shoulder. "You'd never want the arms taken off if they'd been there all along."

"Yeah, you're right. I guess it *is* just that I'm used to seeing her this way," Olivia said softly, suddenly realizing that they were getting kind of close again.

"Listen, I'm really getting hungry," he announced, abruptly changing the subject as he stood up and stretched. "I think I'm going to go find some lunch. Are you coming?"

Olivia wanted to spend the rest of the day with him. She was dying to, actually. But she felt so guilty; she'd done nothing but lead him on. For his sake, she had to keep her distance while she pulled herself together and figured out how she felt. Tomorrow would be soon enough to see him again.

Olivia stood up so she could look him in the eye. "No, I'd better not," she said.

"Oh, okay," John said awkwardly, a look of vulnerability flickering over his face.

Olivia wavered. *Am I hurting him again?* She didn't want to be the cause of any more of his pain, especially after he'd gone out of his way to help relieve some of her guilt.

"Maybe we could meet for dinner?" she found herself asking before she thought it through.

"I'm meeting Samantha," he said tersely.

"Oh, of course," she replied quickly, feeling a stab of unreasonable jealousy slice through her yet again.

"Okay. Well, what are you doing tomorrow? Maybe we could meet again?"

"I don't know," John said with a sigh as he ran his fingers through his hair. "You should really see Notre Dame," he added.

"Will you see it with me?" she asked, holding her breath expectantly. Why did it mean so much to her? She really should be trying to keep her distance. The last hour had certainly proven that.

John stared at her silently for a moment. He was obviously trying to protect himself from her, but—just like her—seemed to be fighting to stay away.

"Yeah, okay," he said eventually.

"Great!" Olivia replied with a tentative smile.

"I'll meet you in front of the cathedral tomorrow," he offered. "How's nine?"

"Perfect. I'll see you at nine."

He nodded once and turned to leave.

"John?" she asked, catching him by the arm.

"Yes?" he said, turning back around as another couple wandered past them.

Olivia took a step closer.

"Thanks. For today, I mean. And for what you said."

He looked at her for a moment, gave her another one of his sad smiles, then walked away.

Chapter 34

Arc de Triomphe

WHAT IN THE WORLD just happened? he asked himself as he flew down the stairs and back outside. Why couldn't he control himself when Olivia was around? She didn't love him! What more did he need to know?

But she looked so vulnerable and lost and beautiful sitting there on the floor of the museum, with those silent tears running down her face.... What had been wrong? He'd never really figured that out—was it just frustration about not being able to read about the statue? Surely not. Had she actually been sitting there missing *him?* No!

Why would she miss a guy she *dumped?*

He seriously needed to put an end to this ridiculous war raging inside his head. Especially if he was going to be spending more time with her these next two weeks. He couldn't be trying to kiss her at every opportunity. With every move he made like that, he was also making himself look more foolish. And he obviously *was* a fool. In the last hour alone, he'd comforted her, forgiven her, tried to kiss her, and made plans to spend tomorrow with her.

Why don't I just propose marriage again and really *be a loser?* he pondered as he walked briskly under a nearby arch and onto the grassy area beyond it. Confusion plagued his every thought. Would she have let him kiss her? She'd seemed willing. But why? Why would she? Guilt over what she'd done? Gratitude that he was still talking to her? Loneliness because he was the only person she knew in Paris?

And why had he even tried to kiss her in the first place? He had just gotten done, barely a few hours before, giving himself a mental pep talk about how indifferent he was going to be to her and her charms. Why wasn't he able to pull it off and be indifferent— even for five minutes? Or to at least *pretend* that indifference? And, really, why wasn't he repulsed by someone who had hurt him this badly?

But if he was being totally honest with himself, he wasn't indifferent. And he certainly wasn't repulsed, either. Despite all his efforts to the contrary, he was still very much in love with her. How could he make his love for her die out and leave his heart intact? The questions were flying through his brain faster than he could process them. The mental inquisition was exhausting.

Time, he reminded himself. *I just need more time.* Only time could make all these questions and heartaches fade.

He'd already made plans to set that healing in motion by taking himself far, far away from her. His volunteer work was the best approach he could imagine toward healing.

But—again—it was looking like he couldn't stay away from her while they were both in Paris. His original plan to enter museums and attractions together and then avoid each other hadn't started off so great. Today he'd been pulled toward her like they were connected with an invisible rope.

So, really, what was the answer here? Was he going to have to spend the next two weeks walking around like a raw, exposed wound while mooning after her?

No, he couldn't do that, either. He couldn't leave himself that vulnerable again, regardless of whether the hurt was inflicted intentionally or not. He had to toughen up where she was concerned. No more trying to kiss her, no more thinking of them as married, and no more games. It was over, and he had to treat it that way. She was a friend, nothing more. An acquaintance. Whatever. She was just off-limits to him. He'd be friendly but restrained, nice but not flirtatious. It was a good plan, he decided. Any man who could be on good enough terms with his first two wives to invite them to his third wedding could manage anything, right?

He sighed, tired of all the mental pep talks, then abruptly stopped walking. He looked around, then strained to read the nearest street sign. *Where am I?* He'd been so lost in his thoughts that he hadn't paid any attention to where he was going. He continued to the corner, where he saw a queue of cabs by a hotel. He walked over and secured one, asking the driver to take him to *Champs-Élysées*. If he was going to wander aimlessly, he may as well do it among tourists on a trendy street.

The cab driver dropped him off near the *Arc de Triomphe*. Then he stood on the sidewalk, letting the crowds flow around him as he studied Napoleon's famous arch. *The Arch of Triumph—what a sick joke that is at the moment....* He had a lot of feelings coursing through his body, but "triumph" definitely wasn't one of them. In fact, he was feeling exactly the opposite: defeated. His shoulders sagged as he let the sorrow overwhelm him again, but he tried to stem the surge of grief this time.

This was no way to go about implementing his plan, he decided. No more sorrow and no more resignation. He was in control of his emotions and his destiny! He would be strong and detached. *And yes, even triumphant*, he thought with a laugh and a final look toward the arch, which towered majestically over the busy street, mindless of the traffic swirling around it.

His confidence renewed, he started walking in search of a place to eat. He eventually wandered into a café, lured by the smell of pastries and coffee. He ordered a sandwich, practiced his flirting with the waitress, and gave himself a mental pat on the back when two consecutive minutes passed by without entertaining any thoughts of Olivia.

Yeah, I can do this, he told himself. No problem.

Chapter 35

Window Shopping

OLIVIA MEANDERED out of the museum in a haze of confusion. She'd completely ruined her trip to the *Louvre*; she'd only really seen one statue! And she'd sent all sorts of crazy mixed signals to John—a man she was supposed to be surreptitiously getting to know, *not* continuing to emotionally cripple.

And yet...he'd almost leaned into kiss her. She'd wanted him to do that with every cell in her body. So what was *wrong* with her? She didn't even know whether she could actually love him...right? Only a few days ago, she'd seriously considered jilting him at the altar because a lifetime of marriage to him was so unthinkable. That's what happened, right?

So why did she feel his absence so acutely right now? Why did the short time they'd spent together in the *Venus d'Milo* room of the *Louvre* feel like the happiest she'd known in a long time? And why did the thought of him having a cozy, romantic dinner with Samantha tonight send shards of pain and panic slicing through her heart?

It just didn't make any sense. Nothing made sense anymore. And she was a logical person, so she had to find a way to locate the reason and order in all of this chaos.

She hailed a cab and impulsively decided to go shopping. Nothing like a little retail therapy to get her mind off John and cheer herself up. The midday traffic was light, and it wasn't long before she was climbing back out of the cab and paying the driver. He'd taken her to the very expensive *Champs-Élysées* area. She looked around at the beautiful storefronts and quaint cafés with a little guilt and hesitation. Maybe shopping wasn't such a great idea after all, especially considering how much money she'd just thrown away on the wedding.

Opting for window shopping instead, she randomly picked a direction and started wandering. The day was sunny and beautiful, and she tried to let that boost her spirits as she walked along. A wild pair of strappy pink sandals in a trendy boutique window caught her eye. She almost went inside, but she hesitated as the price tag of her wedding again floated through her mind. So she kept walking.

A café caught her eye, and she decided to go in. She wasn't necessarily up to eating anything big. Maybe a small pastry and some coffee or tea would be a nice treat, she thought as she drew closer. She glanced in the window as she was heading for the door, and what she saw brought her to a complete stop.

It was John, sitting at one of the tables. A waitress approached him, and they began to talk. He must have said something funny, because she started to laugh.

Flirting. He was *flirting* with her!

John suddenly had more babes flocking around him than a Hollywood star, she thought with considerable annoyance. In fact, she wanted to scream in frustration as she watched the little scene play out. Part of her wanted to barge inside, plop herself right down at his table, flash her wedding ring around, and let the waitress know she was out of luck. But the other part—the part that remembered how deeply she'd hurt him and how much she wanted the chance to get to know him these next two weeks—kept her there on the sidewalk, very much alone.

If she flew in there and started making a bunch of ridiculous, snarky comments about his fast-paced dating life, she'd only alienate him further. So she forced herself to stay where she was, a stranger looking in on her own life like it was a zoo exhibit. And that was exactly where she wanted to be anyway, right? On the *outside* of a life with John?

Right...?

Well, yes. But she also wanted a chance at some friendly conversation and time to get to know him better. She just wanted to find out if she could have fallen in love with him to either ease her guilt or learn a valuable lesson.

She took a deep breath, gave him one last lingering look, and walked away. Whatever small burst of enthusiasm she'd summoned for her window-shopping adventure had withered away. She wanted so badly to run back to that café and be with him! *Why?* her tormented mind screamed back at her.

Yes, why indeed? Why am I doing this to myself?

No more! She'd had enough of the anxiety and doubt and pain. It was time to remember her indifference to this man and to recall the feelings toward him that had surfaced on her wedding day. There was no reason to be in this kind of turmoil now. None at all.

With a new burst of resolve, she buried her raw emotions as she walked down the busy street, unmindful of the sights and smells that swirled around her.

Chapter 36

Sainte Chapelle

THE NEXT DAY they met as planned in the plaza in front of Notre Dame Cathedral, its square twin Gothic towers hulking above them in the early morning sunlight.

"Hi," Olivia said shyly as John approached. She felt unsure of what else to say and could only offer a hesitant smile.

John studied her for a moment, also seemingly at a loss for words. A soft look of emotion fluttered across his face, almost before she could spot it. She looked at him in wonder, again amazed that this kind, handsome, fascinating man was still speaking to her and meeting up with her after what she'd put him through. Her next smile had greater force of emotion behind it. She was feeling lighter now, just happy to have this opportunity to spend the day with him and see the magnificent city of Paris.

John looked up in the sky, as though he were trying to locate the sun's position—or maybe he was offering a silent prayer for continued calm in the stormy seas of their relationship and current situation.

"Before we walk around the cathedral, there's something else I think I want to show you," he said. "If we're going to do it, the lighting is just right and now's the perfect time."

"What's that?" she asked with a turn of the head, still unaccountably elated that he wanted to be with her at all, let alone show her something special.

"You'll see."

To her amazement, he reached out and grabbed her hand, gently tugging her off the spot where she had felt almost rooted moments earlier. Then they walked away from the cathedral, across the plaza, and down the block.

"I have to admit you've got me really intrigued," she told him, undeniably thrilled to have the close connection to him through their laced fingers. She'd thought he would *never* touch her again, and she marveled at the tingly feelings of electricity that were emanating from their joined hands, working their way through her body, and finally nestling somewhere near her heart. *My heart? Electricity?!* Weren't those the very things she thought their relationship didn't have?

"Trust me, you'll love it," he said. Then they stopped walking as if in silent agreement. Olivia felt transfixed by the moment and the feelings rushing through her.

"Love it," Olivia finally whispered. "Yes, I...I'm sure I will."

Her voice seemed to bring John back to reality; he dropped her hand as though he'd just been burned by her touch and looked away as he ran his hand through his hair.

"Let's get going. We don't want to lose the morning sun," he said with a sigh as he started walking again.

The magic of the moment was gone, and Olivia instantly felt its absence bitterly. She mentally kicked herself for being so disappointed as she started to trail after him—she was still getting precisely what she wanted after all, right? She was spending time with John and getting to know him. That was certainly all that she deserved from him. She sighed quietly too and tried to shake off the disappointment and squash the urge to grab his hand again.

He continued walking resolutely ahead as she followed, genuinely bewildered by where he might be taking her. She didn't remember seeing any other nearby sites when she'd researched for the trip. Her confusion doubled when John pulled to a stop in front of what appeared to be a police barracks of some sort, judging by the uniformed men standing around the gates of the entrance.

"Okay, really, where are we?" she asked with a slightly nervous laugh.

"This is the *Palais du Justice*," John said as though the words cleared up any possible question she might have.

"So...you're having me arrested?" she asked. "Do I get a trial first? Am I going to have to act as my own attorney?"

"Very funny." He pulled out his passport. "They'll probably want to check these before we can get through the gates."

"Oookay," she said, rifling through her purse.

They passed through the gates after a brief inspection of their passports and her bag. John chatted for a moment in French with one of the guards or policemen or whoever they were. Olivia couldn't make any sense at all of what was happening.

"Is this what you brought me to see?" she asked as he started walking again toward a chapel in the center of the courtyard.

"Almost there," he said, stubbornly maintaining the mystery of their destination.

They joined a line of tourists and stood waiting in sustained awkward silence. Olivia wanted to knock down the walls John had built between them, but she honestly didn't even know where to begin, so she let the silence build. When they finally made their way inside, he led them through the chapel doors, where tourists were wandering around a quaint, tiny, and extremely old church sanctuary.

"Oh, John, this is really beautiful," she said, taking in the surprisingly colorful paint on the walls and altar. *Fleur-de-lys* covered the walls, and stars were painted on the ceiling above the altar.

"Yes it is, but it's not the surprise," he said, tentatively taking her hand again. "Close your eyes."

"What? Why?" she asked, really surprised now.

"Just be patient and close your eyes," he urged, a soft expression in his own as he stood waiting for her to comply.

She had no idea where they were or what was happening between the two of them, but one thing she knew for certain: She trusted this man implicitly. She offered him a tentative smile and then did as he asked.

"Now you're going to have to just trust me to guide you," he told her, taking her arm gently. "I won't let anything happen to you."

"I trust you," she replied.

"Okay, we're going to be walking upstairs, so be careful." When he added, "And no peeking," she laughed with anticipation.

He led her up what felt like a very narrow and winding stairway. At the top, she heard the quiet whispers and footsteps of fellow tourists around her, and the sounds seemed to echo around the room.

"Keep your eyes closed, but turn your face up,"

John said. She felt his eyes on her as she did what he asked, angling her face up toward the ceiling.

"Okay, you can look," he said finally, and with emotions wrapped around each word that she couldn't identify.

She opened her eyes slowly and gasped in wonder. They were in a long, narrow room—a church sanctuary—brilliantly surrounded by stained-glass windows. The morning sun sparkled through the tall, narrow panels of color that stretched from the floor to the sky all around the room. It felt like she was standing inside a jeweled crown.

"Oh, John, what is this beautiful place?" she asked as she turned slowly. "There aren't any walls!"

He smiled at her, watching her with an expression she didn't recognize.

"I knew you'd like it. It's *Sainte Chapelle*. As Gothic chapels go, it's not as famous as Notre Dame, but it's one of my favorite places in all of Europe. Maybe in the world."

"I can see why," she said breathlessly, meeting his eyes. She felt overwhelmed by the beauty of it, and by the feelings that raced through her as she gazed at him.

Then John pulled away again. "Let's look around some more," he said.

They walked slowly along the edges of the sanctuary as he pointed out the different scenes from the Bible depicted in the glass.

"Supposedly there are more than 1,000 biblical scenes displayed here," he explained. "This was the king's private chapel—Louis IX had it built in the courtyard of what used to be a royal residence to house relics like the crown of thorns."

"And now it's a police station?" she asked.

"Well, no, the residence is courts and legal offices. But it's guarded by the Republican Guard and *gendarmes*, which is why it looks like a police station."

"Why didn't you tell me about it when we were planning our trip?" she asked. "I never would have wanted to miss this. It's so incredible."

"I knew you'd love it as much as I do," John said. "It was always my plan to surprise you with it. But after...well, after everything that's happened, I wasn't going to bring you here. It just seemed too..."

"Too special...too personal?" Olivia quietly guessed.

"Yeah, I guess so. It's very special to me, and I only wanted to share it with...the woman I loved," he admitted quietly. "But when I saw you standing out in the morning sun earlier, I just couldn't let the opportunity go and cause you to miss this amazing experience."

"Thank you, John," she said, looking up into his green eyes, her own filling with unshed tears. "I'll never forget this."

"Did you want to take some pictures?"

"Oh, yes!" she said, pulling out her phone. She walked away from him then to snap a few shots of the sun filtering through the room and casting its colors everywhere. It felt good to throw herself into tourist mode, thinking about how best to capture the lighting and the stunning beauty of the room instead of thinking about her problems.

After she'd made her way around the room again, John asked, "Ready to go?"

"Yes, I guess so," she said, looking around once more, attempting to take mental snapshots of this beautiful memory.

"Would you like me to take a picture of the two of you together?" asked an American woman standing near them.

"No," John replied just as Olivia said, "Yes!"

The woman laughed as Olivia handed her phone over. "Thank you so much," she told the woman gratefully. "I'd love to have a picture of the two of us here."

John sort of looked like he was being tortured, but Olivia couldn't let the opportunity pass. She wrapped her arm around his waist and held him tightly for the pose, even as she wondered why it felt so right to be touching him and why she could feel tingling electricity all around them. John, she couldn't help but notice, did not wrap his arm around her in reply, instead standing stiffly next to her.

"Smile!" the woman said as she held Olivia's phone up and snapped several shots, some vertically and some horizontally.

Olivia beamed, and then found herself unwilling to pull away from John when the woman handed the phone back. She thanked her and turned to smile up at John, but the scowl he was giving her melted the happy expression right off her face.

He pulled away from her embrace then, put his hand up to his neck like he was trying to work out the kinks, and closed his eyes. Olivia was frozen in worry— had she just done it again? Had she hurt him more? She'd thought they were making progress today. Things had felt so much better between them that she figured a little photograph couldn't hurt...but clearly she'd pushed him too hard and too fast.

Another awkwardly quiet moment ticked by, the silence between them heavy and uncomfortable, before

John finally spoke.

"Doubt I'll ever come back here again," he said, before turning and walking toward the exit.

Chapter 37

Notre Dame

THEY WALKED in silence, without any further hand-holding or touches, back to Notre Dame. Olivia took some pictures of the famous façade before they walked around the circumference of the building. John was still being very quiet, but she didn't want to push him any further. She knew he'd taken an emotional chance by sharing his stained-glass treasure with her, and it didn't take much imagination to figure out that the whole experience had probably left him feeling melancholy, raw, and exposed.

If only things were different. If only I'd realized how much I love him sooner, she thought, then hastily stopped herself in amazed confusion. *If only I realized how much I* didn't *love him sooner. That's what I meant, right?*

She shook her head as though she were trying to will the mental error from her memory. *I still don't know if I'm in love with him, because I never gave those emotions a chance to grow. I never tried to get to know him. That's what I'm doing now.* She repeated the plan to herself like a mantra as a cathedral tour guide whizzed past her with a small group in tow. *I could* love *him, but I don't know yet. I couldn't possibly know yet.*

She glanced nervously at him, hoping the man wasn't a mind reader. He appeared to be listening attentively to the history of the stained glass that the guide was giving the nearby group. *Good,* she thought. The last thing he needed to be subject to right now was any knowledge of her internal turmoil regarding her feelings for him. His poor bruised heart definitely couldn't take any more of this, she was certain. Of course, hers was feeling a little sore and beaten too. The only thing that could possibly hurt more right now would be if John totally pushed her away. She could only hope that their current plan to see the city together would hold out.

Please don't turn me away and shut me out, she silently pleaded as she watched him follow the group. *I really, really need this time together.*

As though he felt her watching him, John turned around and met her gaze. They stared at each other over the heads of the other tourists in quiet contemplation. Then John slowly walked away from the guide and retraced his steps back to where she was standing.

"What's wrong, Livvie?" he asked quietly.

A tiny gasp escaped her lips when she heard the familiar endearment.

"What?" he asked again, more quietly than before. "What is it?"

"John, will you...." Olivia started. Then she paused, chewing on her bottom lip in nervous contemplation before continuing. "Will you keep seeing the city with me this way?"

"Why though?" he asked, looking like he was stalling before giving a real answer.

"I know today's been hard on you emotionally," Olivia said. "It's been hard on me, too."

"I'm sure," he said, a hint of the old bitterness sneaking back into his tone.

"No, John, don't," she pleaded. "Please don't be mad. I just wanted to let you know how very much it means to me to be spending this time with you."

"Don't mention it," he bit off, still sounding angry and tense.

"And that I really hope we can do this again tomorrow," she continued as though he hadn't spoken.

John studied her face, his expression unreadable. She held her breath in anticipation. She knew she couldn't blame him if he turned and walked away from the cathedral and out of her life forever. But still she found herself feeling hopeful in that moment. The electric feelings that had come from the simple touch of his hand earlier flashed through her mind then. She gulped in a rush of air, her nerves making even her most basic functions—like breathing or blinking—difficult.

John closed his eyes and sighed.

Then, reopening them, he asked, "Where do you want to go tomorrow?"

"I've heard the catacombs are good, creepy fun," she said, trying to smile.

"Really?" John asked, looking dubious now.

"Really what?"

"I just didn't figure you for the type who would enjoy slogging through dark tunnels under the city filled with human remains."

"You mean it's not a must-see, top-ten honeymoon destination?" she asked, tentatively attempting to tease him again.

"Oh, it's more than appropriate for *this* honeymoon, no doubt. You just surprised me, that's all." His tone was suddenly a bit lighter. "I don't remember you bringing it up when we were researching this trip."

"It definitely piqued my curiosity when I heard

about it," Olivia replied, happy John seemed somewhat comfortable with their banter. Still, not wanting to push her luck, she tried to steer the conversation away from the subject of their hellish honeymoon. "The thought of it strikes me as so terribly, hauntingly sad. But also sort of fascinating, in a macabre way. You know I've always been a sucker for late-night horror movies."

"Well, stick with me then," John said, not falling for the redirect. "Given how this honeymoon is going, I'm pretty sure we're a few unsuspecting teenagers at a lake away from living *in* a horror film right now."

"Very funny. So, you're in?"

John looked at her again, a small, reluctant smile on his face.

"Okay, Liv, you've got a deal. Catacombs it is. How about if we meet in the lobby of your hotel tomorrow morning, say at ten?"

"Perfect!" she said, beaming. "Let's go find some lunch now. I'm starving."

A look of regret ran across John's face as he glanced at his watch.

"I'm meeting Samantha this afternoon," he said. "We're going on a river cruise."

Cold stabs of jealousy shot through Olivia's heart as she attempted to keep a smile pasted on her face. "Sure. Sounds romantic," she choked out.

"Could be, I guess," John said with a shrug.

"You two are really getting close, aren't you?" she asked, unable to stop herself. She knew it was completely wrong of her to be pushing him on this subject, but her heart was talking now, not her mind.

"Samantha's been a wonderful friend to me at a time in my life when I needed one the most," he answered.

"Oh," Olivia said softly, afraid to know more but unable to stop herself from adding, "Are you going to see her after we get back home?"

"You know that's none of your business," he replied, his voice also quiet as he appeared to be struggling with the decision about whether to say more.

Olivia held her breath, aching with every fiber of her body to hear him deny that his relationship with Samantha had grown that deep. Or *could* grow that deep.

"Okay, okay, yes," John finally said, shattering her hopes. "We might be doing some traveling together soon."

"*What?!*" Olivia cried out before she could stop herself.

"I'm taking some time off from life when we get back. Doing some volunteer work for a while—maybe six months or so," John said as though he hadn't noticed her emotional reaction. "And Sam might come with me."

Olivia couldn't breathe. The pain and the jealousy were coursing through her body, and she found herself struggling to remain calm—or *appear* calm, anyway.

"Oh, John," she said, tears pooling in her eyes despite her attempts to stop them. "That just seems so soon."

"Olivia, I've got to take the time away. I can't get over what happened between us and move on with my life without a break." He said this with more kindness than she probably deserved. "And helping people who have real life and death problems like not having a place to sleep is a perfect way to take my mind off my troubles."

"I understand that, of course I do," she said as she

blinked back the tears. "I just don't understand why you'd want to start a relationship with Samantha so quickly. I thought you loved me."

John stared at her, his mouth dropping open in amazement. She met his gaze, but she wasn't sure what she saw there. Anger? Laughter? Disdain? She had no idea what he was thinking. She nervously wished she'd kept her mouth shut.

"I can't believe you just said that to me," he said finally.

"I'm sorry John. I wasn't thinking. I—" she started.

"Don't *ever* speak to me about love again." Anger was cascading off him like a waterfall. "I don't think you know what the word means."

"John, I'm so sorry! The last thing I wanted to do was to spoil the truce between us or to hurt you again. I'm just so very sorry." She was dying to throw herself into his arms but knew that would be yet another terrible move. Tears coursed down her face now. She was so mad at herself for having hurt this wonderful man for the millionth time in a few short days.

He appeared to be waging an internal war with himself, perhaps torn between walking away or maybe stashing her body in the cathedral's crypt.

"See?" he said with a sigh. "My life *is* a horror film. You look like Carrie after the prom."

"Gee thanks," Olivia managed to say with a laugh as he reached over and gently wiped a few tears off her cheek with his thumb. The warmth of his touch ran through her body; she leaned into his hand and closed her eyes, reveling in the tenderness she felt in his fingertips.

Then he whispered, "Tomorrow at ten," before

turning and walking away.

Olivia watched him go. He'd forgiven her *again!* She couldn't believe it. The man was either a fool or a priceless treasure.

But, of course, she knew in her heart that he definitely wasn't a fool.

Chapter 38

A Night Out

JOHN FELT LIKE he'd spent the past few days doing nothing more than dashing out of Parisian landmarks to run away from Olivia. But he couldn't seem to help it. There was only so much together-time with her that he could take.

The most recent conversation with her was absolutely the icing on the cake of his misery and confusion. Why was she acting so emotional and jealous about Samantha? No matter how he thought about it or how he took it apart and analyzed it in his mind, it didn't add up. That is, unless he chose to believe one of two things about her as truth. Maybe she was a petty game player who was only interested in men she couldn't have but would then dump them once the thrill of the chase was over. Or perhaps she had, in fact, discovered too late that she really was in love with him.

He couldn't believe the first scenario. She'd risked a lot of personal pain and censorship from her family and friends by having the wedding ceremony merely to avoid embarrassing him. The sort of woman who would do that just wasn't into playing games. But, unfortunately, he couldn't fathom the second option, either. To do so would be to open himself up to more heartache, and he refused to do that. The walls were starting to build up around his broken heart. She didn't love him, and he felt he could at least accept that as the truth. It may still be the most painful thing he'd ever experienced, but he did believe it now. She didn't love him and never would. Period.

But by dismissing those two theories out of hand, he was still confused about her jealousy where Samantha was concerned, plus her welcoming and emotional responses when they were together the past couple of days.

After three marriages, he would have thought he'd understand women even a bit by now. But maybe that was the reason he couldn't make those unions last—he clearly didn't know anything. If he did, he would have seen Olivia's indifference to him a long time ago.

Tired of thinking and agonizing about all of it, he turned his thoughts to Samantha as he descended into a metro station. She really had been a life saver this week, and not just because she took him in when he had nowhere else to go. She'd been a great friend, never pushing him to talk about Olivia or questioning why he was continuing to spend time with her.

When Samantha suggested the afternoon river cruise, he happily accepted. Being around her was comfortable and fun. And, frankly, dedicating time to her was a great excuse to tear himself away from Olivia, who he seemed to keep returning to no matter how self-destructive it was, like a moth fluttering over a flame.

If he was a different kind of man, he was certain he'd be sleeping with Samantha by now. He sensed a willingness in her, but he'd been careful not to do anything to pursue the subject. Regardless of how pathetic his marriage was, he still considered himself a married man. Not that he'd bother reassuring Olivia of that again. As she had been pointing out for days now, she never really knew him. If she did, she wouldn't have to ask about his faithfulness and would never have reason to feel even a trace of jealousy.

He filed into the mostly empty subway car with a few other tourists and sat down, trying once again to block Olivia from his thoughts. He was frustrated with himself for letting his mind go back to her so often. He needed to be thinking about Samantha, right?

He tried to bring a vision of her into his mind, focusing on her silky, light brown hair and the way it hung down past her shoulders, framed her delicate face, and called attention to her brown eyes. Those eyes startled him every time he looked at her.

Of course, that's probably because they remind me so much of another pair of dark brown eyes....

He shook his head in frustration, trying to remove the image of Olivia that had suddenly formed there and eclipsed the one of Samantha that he'd been conjuring. Okay, so Samantha was no Olivia and never would be. Unfortunately, that didn't change the situation at all. In the end, neither woman was going to be able or willing to fill the hole in his life or erase the pain in his heart. He was still going to end up alone.

Enough! he mentally shouted in frustration. He was tired of whining and feeling sorry for himself. He'd had enough of all of it—the self-pity he'd been rolling around in for days was beginning to annoy even him. He couldn't imagine how Samantha had been able to tolerate it this long.

A moment later, the subway doors opened.

*   *   *

He walked onto the platform and started following the exit signs. He glanced at his watch and realized he was cutting it a little close. Their plan was to grab a meal before heading to the boat. As he emerged from the metro and headed toward the hotel room he shared with Samantha, he vowed to enjoy himself and really forget his problems for the afternoon. He owed himself that much. Thankfully—and surprisingly—he was able to do exactly that. He and Samantha met each other in the room as planned and headed out for a light lunch in a café next door.

She somehow managed to get him chuckling with a story about an angry French designer with whom she'd tangled earlier in the day. He loved how it felt to finally enjoy himself; laughter had been a stranger over the last few days. After they paid their bill, they headed for the metro that would take them to the dock. Their conversation was light and seemed to come easily for the next few hours—during the subway ride, the walk to the boat, and the cruise that afternoon, which took them past the beautiful sights and sounds of the city.

They talked some more about how they'd spent their mornings. John told her how enchanting *Sainte Chapelle* had looked in the early sun, and Samantha told him about a new fashion trend she was following. Then he explained the satisfaction he got from helping others and the experiences they would have if she joined him on the Habitat for Humanity trip. And she told him more about her family and her home.

The slow, easy pace of the day and the gentle lapping of the river against the boat had a calming effect on him. And so, he had to admit, did Samantha. He was relaxing for the first time in days and had to admit he didn't want the evening to end.

"Ready to head back to the hotel?" he asked her as the boat was docking. "Or would you like to experience a little nightlife?"

"Oh, let's go out!" she said with a flirtatious wink.

"Take me dancing, and I'm yours."

"Dancing it is," he said as he took her hand and led her toward the Seine.

As they walked off the boat and into the crowd, he thought again about how much he enjoyed the day, how easily he'd managed to finally block all problems from his mind, and how comfortable he felt around this new woman in his life.

Maybe things would turn out okay after all.

Chapter 39

The Turning Point

"OH WOW, sorry I'm so late," John said the next morning as he approached Olivia, who was perched on an overstuffed chair in the lobby of her hotel.

"Late night?" she asked as she stood to greet him, struggling to keep a steady, light tone that masked the annoyance and jealousy. "You look awfully tired."

"Yeah, you could say that, I guess. I'm too old for the night life."

"Oh, what were you up to in the wee hours?"

"Umm, it was nothing," he said, suddenly looking at her uneasily.

"You can tell me—I won't freak out and start crying again," she told him with a laugh that sounded a bit harsh, even to her ears. "I can chill out once in a while."

"Well, okay. Uh, Sam and I went dancing last night after the cruise and ended up eating dinner in a little Vietnamese place in *Montemarte*." This all came out a little stiff and awkward. "The food was really great."

"Wow, that sounds...uh, really good. I'm so glad you got to experience that." She was careful here not to say or do anything that would make him walk away again. "I don't know that I've never had Vietnamese food. I'll bet it beats the room-service dinner I had. And then it was lights out by nine like a senior citizen."

"At least you got some sleep," John added. As Olivia's face fell, John quickly added, "I got some rest, of course, but not as much as you did."

"Oh good," Olivia replied quickly, trying to erase the vision of John and Samantha spending the whole night having sex. She drew in a deep, shaky breath before continuing. "Listen, I'm truly sorry I've made you feel so weird about mentioning Samantha. This conversation couldn't be more awkward. Let's just start over, okay?"

"Sounds good to me," John said, smiling with what looked like relief. Then he took a deep breath. "Good morning, Olivia. You look lovely today. Shall we go muck around the piled remains of this city's entombed citizens?"

"Why that just sounds like a perfectly wonderful outing, John," she replied, a small smile threatening to dawn on her face. "Let's go."

*   *   *

That morning seemed to mark a new beginning in their post-breakup relationship—at least for her, and at least for a while. Of course, feelings between them weren't exactly where they had been before the wedding. But the comfortable friendship that had initially drawn them together helped them settle into a bit of a vacation routine. They'd meet each morning and investigate whatever sites they'd agreed to see. Then, after lunch, they would wander around the city together, smelling the unfamiliar scents, watching the fascinatingly diverse Parisians go about their daily routines, and taking in the amazing architecture, parks, and shops. Afterward, they'd agree where to meet and what to see the next day, and then they'd go their separate ways. But Olivia was careful not to mention the fact that he was returning each night to the hotel room he was still sharing with Samantha, and John stopped bringing it up.

One day, they took in the Impressionist and Post-Impressionist art at the *Musee d'Orsay*, which was housed in an old train station. They spent another morning trying to find the home of Victor Hugo and talking about how much they both loved his book *Les Miserables,* but how neither could get through *The Hunchback of Notre Dame.* Another afternoon they picked a random neighborhood and strolled around looking at street art and a small farmer's market.

In fact, she had been enjoying herself so much that, when they were together, Olivia was almost—*almost*—able to forget their problems. That is, until the day she suggested they go see the Eiffel Tower.

"I'm dying to see it," she said as they walked out of the little restaurant where they'd just eaten lunch. "I can't believe we haven't gotten over there yet—want to go tomorrow?"

"Umm, sure," John replied, suddenly looking uncomfortable. "Listen, do you mind if Samantha comes along? She mentioned this morning that she's got some free time tomorrow and wanted to know if she could join our plans."

"Of course. That'd be great," Olivia said, the falsely chipper tone in her voice giving away a very bad acting job. "The more the merrier."

"Great. Thanks for understanding," he said, clearly choosing to ignore that she was lying through her teeth. "Want to meet us in our hotel lobby in the morning?"

"Why don't we just meet at the tower?" Olivia suggested, hoping to minimize her exposure to the happy couple.

"Nah, I'd just worry about you," John insisted. "It's not in the best neighborhood, and it's a bit of a hike from the metro station."

"Oh, okay," she said, disappointed but willing to defer to his superior knowledge of the city. Besides, it was just nice to hear him say he would worry about her. "Your hotel lobby then. At...nine?"

"Let's say ten so Sam can sleep in a bit on her one day off."

"Of *course* she should sleep in!" Olivia chirped, biting back the cutting remarks that she *really* wanted to make about his little Sleeping Beauty. "What was I thinking? Ten it is! She's probably still trying to catch up from your long night of dancing."

John chuckled, and Olivia couldn't help wondering, *Wait, is he baiting me?*

"Okay," he went on. "We'll see you tomorrow morning, then."

"Sure, see you," Olivia said softly as he started down the stairs into the metro station to catch the subway back to his hotel. *Their* hotel, she corrected herself bitterly. She was close enough to her own to walk to it, so she continued down the sidewalk alone.

*　　　*　　　*

Samantha....

Why did that irritating woman have to pop into the picture again, just when they'd been making progress? Why did she have to be around at *all?*

Olivia spent the distance of a couple blocks angrily wishing the woman had never been on their flight. She didn't let herself think about the fact that he never would have left her side on the plane—and therefore would never have met Samantha—had she not broken up with him in the first place.

If it wasn't for Samantha, her thoughts continued, *circumstances would have prevented him from moving out of our hotel room, too....* He probably would have been forced to stay with her as planned, and she would have had that much more time with him to get to know him. And she really *had* been successful in that mission—the time she'd been spending with him all week had been priceless. They had so much in common, more than she'd ever realized. She knew without a doubt, for example, that there was nothing "boring" about him, as she'd mistakenly thought on their wedding day.

She had every reason to believe at that point, given the way their week had gone, that she really could have fallen in love with him had she been paying the least bit of real attention to him over the last year. Or, just maybe, she'd already fallen...?

She sighed as she sailed through the elegant lobby of her hotel and toward the tiny elevator. A hot flush colored her cheeks as she remembered that first day in Paris, when she and John had ridden this same elevator together, its condensed space forcing them close together. *What I would give to have him right here with me now!* she thought as she pressed the button for her floor and watched the doors groan to a closed position. But, no, he wasn't there with her. He was off riding in tiny Parisian elevators with Samantha instead.

Well, she'd just have to be a good sport tomorrow at the Eiffel Tower. She couldn't expect John to forgive all her mistakes if she kept piling them up by being jealous and spiteful at every turn. Despite how satisfying it would be to claw Samantha's eyes out of her smug face, Olivia had to be the better woman. John deserved at least that much courtesy, she thought as she entered the now-quiet and very depressing honeymoon suite. All she had planned was another lonely evening of room service and French television.

She kicked off her shoes and flopped onto the bed, her arms spread out straight while her feet remained firmly on the floor. She lay there for a long time, mindlessly staring at the ceiling as the clock on the nightstand ticked away the afternoon.

What a crappy honeymoon.

Chapter 40

Third Wheel

OLIVIA TOOK special care with her appearance as she was getting ready the next morning. She wanted to look her best, not only to catch John's eye but also— she had to admit—to try outdoing Samantha. Was it childish? Yes. But was she doing it anyway...?

Hell yes.

Of *course* she knew she was playing a child's game, but she didn't care. She wanted John to notice her and not Samantha, period. After much indecision, she decided to wear the yellow sundress she'd had on the day they went to the *Louvre*. John really seemed to like it. She left her curls down as well, knowing he especially liked her long hair.

After taking one last look in the mirror, she grabbed her sweater and purse, double checked to make sure she had her money, room key, and passport, then left the hotel confident that she was ready to take on her rival.

She stopped for breakfast along the way. She had plenty of time since she'd gotten up so early, a byproduct of having gone to bed at nine again. *Thanks, depression and boredom,* she thought as she walked into the lobby at the stroke of ten, only to be greeted by the sight of Samantha touching John's arm as she laughed at something he'd just said. Gritting her teeth, Olivia kept moving forward, determined not to let Samantha upset her.

"Olivia, good morning," Samantha said, spotting her first.

"Hi there," Olivia replied flatly. "Ready to go?"

"You really should have dressed more warmly," John said after looking her over. "It's probably going to feel cold and windy at the top."

So much for knocking him out with my sexy look, she thought resentfully.

"You could borrow a pair of my sweats, if you'd like," Samantha offered sweetly.

Not if we were spending the day climbing glaciers at the North Pole, Olivia thought even as she said, "I brought my sweater. I think I'll be okay, but thank you for the kind offer."

It wasn't until they were walking out of the lobby and onto the crowded sidewalk that Olivia realized she'd blown it. She had completely missed her chance to see their hotel room and get a real picture of what the sleeping arrangements were. She could have kicked herself, as it would have been well worth having to wear Miss Perfect's baggy sweatpants for the day.

Okay, so she hadn't gotten off to the best start. She'd set out to catch John's eye, yet he'd barely noticed her so far. She gave herself a few points for at least keeping her jealousy reined in. She didn't need the happy couple feeling sorry for her on top of everything else.

This day has to get better, she thought miserably as they made their way to the metro station, Samantha and John walking not just next to each other but well ahead of her. They both started laughing as Samantha referenced a funny moment in some French film Olivia had never seen. She rolled her eyes. *Did I really think this day was going to get better? Or that John was going to take notice of me again?* Not while Samantha was around. These two obviously had a million things in common—they were both well-traveled, they both spoke French, they both watched obscure foreign films...and the list probably went on and on from there.

How was she going to compete with that? She had barely left the United States before, choosing to throw herself with fiercely dedicated zeal into law school after college while the rest of her friends were happily backpacking around Europe. And she didn't speak any other languages. Oh sure, she'd tried taking Spanish in high school and college, but it just never stuck in her head. If they got into an emergency situation today in which someone desperately needed to ask, "Are there bananas in the marketplace?" in Spanish, then she was the woman for the job. Otherwise, she just wasn't going to be wowing John with her bilingual prowess.

And she'd never spent any significant time truly helping others. Certainly nothing to rival the years John had apparently spent building houses and bringing aid to the world's poor. And now Samantha was going to be joining him on yet another volunteer trip. Olivia had never even considered making such a huge sacrifice of her time. She volunteered to play in the charity softball tournament her company participated in each year, and she donated money each Christmas to the local animal shelter. But she'd never *really* helped anyone.

So, yeah...great. Just one more indication of how self-absorbed she'd become. Not only did she marry a man she'd apparently been too busy to get to know, but she never bothered to volunteer her time or money in any kind of significant way. She didn't even donate blood or buy Girl Scout cookies, for heaven's sake! *Well maybe things can change when I get home,* she thought as the trio descended into the metro station to catch the subway that would take them to the Eiffel Tower.

Yes, she thought, *most definitely yes*.... Regardless of whether she found a way to get to know her husband better, or to find out if she could have fallen in love with him, or even to perhaps one day reconcile with him, she was definitely going to be taking a personal inventory once this honeymoon was over. The old Olivia—the one who'd been so completely wrapped up in herself and her career that she hadn't found the time to fall for the wonderful man she'd married—was gone. She was a self-absorbed thing of the past.

The moment she got home, she was going to look into doing some pro bono work for starters. She could donate her legal skills to a shelter for battered women or something along those lines. And she was upping her monetary donations to the animal shelter to an amount that would actually make a difference. And not just at Christmas, either. Maybe now was the time to finally adopt the dog she'd always wanted but never seemed able to commit to. And perhaps she'd even take some Spanish classes at the local community college. Not being bilingual in today's world was inexcusable anyway.

"What are you so lost in thought about today, Liv?" John asked from his seat next to Samantha, which was across the aisle from her.

"Self-improvement," she answered quietly, a little shy about sharing her ideas about her personal makeover. But John needed to know she was capable of change, right? "I've been thinking about ways I could make some major life alterations when we get home."

"Like what?" he asked, actually looking interested in her reply.

"Well, like taking some classes at the community college, for starters," she confessed, wishing for the hundredth time that Samantha wasn't there listening and, no doubt, judging her.

"Classes in what?" Samantha asked.

"If nothing else, this trip has pointed out to me that I should have been more diligent in trying to learn a second language," she told them both, hoping to make a joke out of something that actually was really bothering her. "I was terrible at Spanish in school, and I've forgotten absolutely everything I ever learned, unless it involves ordering nachos at the Taco Hut."

John smiled at her attempted joke and nodded encouragingly. "That's a great idea, Livvie. Having a second language is such an advantage."

"So is having fourteen extra languages, huh?" she asked him with a teasing smirk.

John laughed and flashed her the first genuine smile she'd seen from him in a while. Olivia felt a little flutter in her heart as she beamed back at him—being the recipient of his smile felt like he'd given her a treasured gift.

"Oh, you speak more than just English and French?" Samantha piped in as she leaned forward to join their conversation. "Me too. What else do you speak?"

John turned back toward her and recited the laundry list of the languages he knew.

"Yeah, I speak those, too, although I've never gotten that comfortable with Italian," she said. "I know a lot of Latin, though. And some sign language."

"Oh, you know sign language? ASL? So do I!" John said, now fully focused on Samantha again. Olivia and her little community college classes in beginner

Spanish had been quickly forgotten already.

Unable to watch them connect in yet another fabulous way, Olivia turned her gaze elsewhere. This was just great news—these two worked with the deaf as well as the poor. Olivia was trying to compete with Mother Theresa for Saint John's attention. She closed her eyes tightly in frustration. When it came to being selfless and giving, she didn't even have the right to sit in the same subway car, she thought with exasperation and a little self-pity.

At the next stop, as the three of them got out to switch subway lines, John and Samantha carried on a long, laughter-filled conversation about their funny experiences when they were first trying to use their new sign-language skills. Olivia wanted to melt back into the crowd and then return to her hotel. Nothing sounded better at that moment than an afternoon of wearing her own baggy sweatpants, eating chocolate crepes, and wallowing in self-pity while watching BBC, the only television station in Paris that *she* could understand. But that was the coward's way out, she knew, and she wasn't about to add being a coward to her long list of faults.

She was still fiercely dedicated to her primary goal of getting to know John better. And if she had to put up with an afternoon of hearing these two yap endlessly about the summers they spent signing to orphans while deworming endangered chinchillas, then, by God, she was going to do it.

Chapter 41

The Eiffel Tower

BY THE TIME they reached the long lines of weary tourists at the Eiffel Tower, it was after eleven. Olivia was still trailing behind John and Samantha, unwilling to join another of their conversations. She figured she could learn about John just by listening and, as a bonus, she could avoid having to interact with Samantha, too. Perfect or not, the woman was annoying to no end.

There were two sets of elevators at the flared metal base of the monument, each with its own set of lines snaking around the plaza. The trio randomly picked the side to the right and agreed to buy the tickets that would take them to the top floor observation deck rather than just to the second floor.

As they reached the front of the line, they bought their tickets and then stepped to the side to let the guards inspect their backpacks and handbags. Finally, they crowded into an empty elevator that quickly filled to capacity, mostly with a teenage school group from the United States. Olivia was in the back corner. John was standing directly in front of her, facing the elevator doors. And Samantha was up by the panel with all the lighted buttons, a few spikey-haired teens separating them.

Olivia caught John's familiar, masculine scent, a simple combination of deodorant and soap. She'd always liked that about John—he wasn't one to drown himself in cloying aftershaves or colognes. When the elevator doors closed, Olivia found herself leaning toward him, lured by the comforting smell and the yearning for even the most innocent contact. Taking advantage of the situation, she rested her face against his back, her cheek cradled gently between his shoulder blades.

"Tired?" John asked, twisting slightly to catch sight of her.

"Mmm, yeah," she said, struggling against the urge to put her arms around his waist and go for a full embrace.

The elevator reached the first floor, and the attendant alerted them that the monument's restaurants were located there, but no one moved to get off. The doors closed again.

Olivia couldn't resist it another minute. This close proximity to John might not come her way again, she decided as she slipped her arms under his and around his waist, her fingers meeting in front of his flat stomach. John turned around then, looking a bit startled, and breaking her embrace.

"What was that for?" he asked, puzzlement written all over his face.

"I, uh, just wanted to give you a hug," she said lamely. "You just smelled so nice, and I've been really enjoying being with you and seeing Paris with you, and...." She trailed off then, unable to really explain her actions without embarrassing herself any further.

"Everyone has to get out on the second floor," the attendant said. "There is another bank of elevators that will take you to the top floor and observation deck if you purchased tickets to the top. Or you can stay on the second. The toilets, snack bars, and gift shops are here as well."

The group spilled out of the elevator and spread through the circular area, crowded with other groups of tourists lined up to use the bathrooms or buy something at the concession stands.

Olivia took a deep breath of relief as John abandoned their conversation, turning to follow the group. She followed mutely behind him and Samantha as they walked through the crowded area and then outdoors onto the observation walkway that encircled it. Their first sight of the city from that height was captivating. It was clear and sunny, providing a view of several miles, Olivia estimated, and her embarrassment and loneliness were temporarily forgotten.

John pulled out his phone and shot a few pictures as they walked around the circumference, trying to identify landmarks. They found the Paris Statue of Liberty, a smaller-scale model of the famous one in the United States, which was a gift from the French in 1885. And John pointed out the hilly *Montemarte* region of the city. At one point they stopped to gaze at the busy city below. The wind was getting a bit cold, so Olivia pulled her sweater out, hoping no one brought up her fashion miscues again.

"It *is* a bit cold up here," John said then. "Does anyone else want some coffee? My treat."

Samantha and Olivia both said they'd like a cup, too, then watched as John walked back inside, leaving them alone together for the first time. Olivia turned away from the door to continue looking out at the city, tensely unable to think of a thing to say. From her periphery, she could see Samantha turn to look at her, then take a deep breath, as though she was also debating whether to speak. Eventually, Samantha took the plunge and broke the awkward silence.

"You're wrong about half of what you're thinking about me," she began, adding, "but you're right on the money about the other half."

"What...I don't understand," Olivia said honestly as she turned to face her. "What are you talking about?"

"You're wrong. About Jed and me," she clarified. "We're just friends, you know—he's never so much as touched me or even given me more than a brotherly hug."

"Oh. I...how did you?...That's...." Olivia stammered, unable to form a coherent reply as waves of happiness crashed around her heart. *John hasn't been spending our honeymoon sleeping with her!* She was now delirious with relief. But she was also confused: How did Samantha know that was what she'd been thinking? Or that it would even bother her?

"Listen, I know this is absolutely none of my business," Samantha continued, shouldering the conversation again. "But we're both smart women, so let's not bother trying to lie to each other, okay? I just knew that was what you were thinking. It's not true, though, and for some reason I wanted you to know that I'm not a husband stealer."

"We're separated," Olivia finally managed to say. "I broke up with him. What makes you think I care what you and John have been up to—or haven't been up to—since then?"

"Oh, come on, Olivia. No matter what you've managed to make Jed think, anyone else watching you two can see that you love him. And I can clearly see he loves you right back. I don't know what's going on with you two or why you're both being so stubborn about this, but it's extremely obvious that you two are crazy about each other."

Stunned, Olivia said, "No, that's the thing. I think I might...but I don't *know* if I love John. I never took the time to really get to know him and find out. *That's* what I've been doing this week: Trying to learn all I can about him and figure out what my feelings are. I think I've completely blown it with him, but I owe it to myself to figure out if my instincts were right or wrong when I agreed to marry him. I *have* to know."

Samantha gave her a hard look, obviously not convinced.

"But you said I was right about something," Olivia added quickly. "That I was wrong about something and right about something. What am I right about?"

"You're right that I'm the competition," Samantha said after a pause and then a deep breath. "I want Jed, too. He's an amazing man with an enormous capacity for love and compassion, he's fun to be with, and, from what you just told me, he's available. I don't know if he mentioned this to you, but he and I are making plans to go on a Habitat for Humanity trip after we get back from Paris. Olivia, I'm not trying to be as much of a threatening bitch as this is going to make me sound, and I'm sorry if this puts a tight timeline on your little plan, but if you don't figure out what you want pretty quickly, I'm going after Jed. I'm backing off right now, but if we do end up taking that trip together, I'm going to consider him a free man and fair game."

"Thank you, then. I'll consider myself forewarned," Olivia said quietly, uncertain what to say or even think as John approached them with a cardboard tray laden with coffee cups, tubes of sugar, and small packages of creamer.

"Forewarned about what?" John asked, looking from Olivia to Samantha and back again. "What have you two been talking about?"

"Turns out that pink is the new color of the fashion season," Olivia said, gratefully wrapping her hands around one of the cups of coffee and grabbing a couple of the creamers. "So I'm going to have to stock up on basic black and ride it out. Samantha has been a wealth of information on the topic."

"Yeah, okay," John said, rolling his eyes and clearly not buying her lie.

"Believe what you want, it's true that Olivia *wouldn't* look good in pink," Samantha said, joining in on the conspiracy. "Thanks for the coffee, Jed. This is great."

"So, what? I leave for five minutes, and you two manage to team up? Is that it?" John asked, pulling the lid off his coffee and dumping most of the creamers inside the cup until the liquid turned a light mocha.

"Why don't you just order steamed milk next time?" Olivia teased.

John didn't say anything as he smirked at her, snapped the lid back on, pulled the tab open, and took a sip.

Samantha was right about one of the things she had said, Olivia realized—there *was* some sort of spark between her and John. But was it love? And if so, was it a strong enough love to be the foundation for an entire lifetime? She simply didn't know yet—she hadn't given herself time to get to know John and gather enough information about him to help her determine such life-altering outcomes. And until she did, she just couldn't take any chances by revealing her worries and questions to John or throwing herself into a catfight with Samantha over him. It was too much to risk, and it was too early to even consider taking such actions. So, despite Samantha's warning, she had to continue riding it out to see where this bizarre honeymoon would take them.

"Hey, you know, I don't think I'm going to go to the top after all," Samantha said. "I'll just meet you back at the hotel later, Jed. Okay?"

"Aren't you feeling well?" he asked, looking concerned now.

"Oh, no, it's nothing a little nap won't fix. Really, you two have a nice day together." She grabbed her coffee and purse, mouthed *you're welcome* at Olivia, and said her goodbyes.

Thanks to Samantha—who apparently really *was* perfect, Olivia thought in annoyance—they were finally alone together again.

Chapter 42

Getting Acquainted

OLIVIA BREATHED a sigh of relief as Samantha disappeared from sight. Then she turned back to John. He was sipping his coffee and studying her. She felt nervous and uncertain; suddenly the weight of Samantha's warning was pressing down on her.

"Hey," John said finally, "can I collect on that hug you started in the elevator?"

A tentative smile crept onto her face as she took the few short steps to where he stood. She looked up into his face and decided that the happiness currently flooding through her was mirrored in his gaze. After taking a deep breath, she melted into his outstretched arms. Nothing had ever felt more right than standing there in that moment, wrapped in his arms. Things that had appeared hopelessly murky, and questions that seemed to have no answers, were now very, stunningly clear. *This* was where she should be.

She'd been pummeling herself with doubts and questions and regrets since the day of the wedding. But now, there on an Eiffel Tower observation deck, she knew she'd found her answer. Yes, they still had problems and a lot to figure out. But none of that was truly important. No matter how hard the discussions and the soul-searching would get, she knew she had to stay right where she was—in John's arms and in his life. She could continue to beat herself up for not figuring this out sooner, but no pile of recriminations or even continuing doubts could erase one simple fact: Being here felt like *home*. And if that wasn't love, she didn't know what was.

"Ready to head up to the top floor?" John asked, pulling back from her to look at her face. "We aren't getting a whole lot of sightseeing done, are we?"

"No, I guess not," she replied with a smile. "But, you know, I'd kind of like to hit the gift shop first, if you don't mind. I don't think I've made a single purchase since I got here. I can't come to Paris and not at least walk away with an Eiffel Tower keychain or coffee mug."

"Sure," John said. "Souvenir keychains and coffee mugs it is."

They edged their way through the tourist crowd until they found a tiny glass-enclosed souvenir stand with the name *Les boutiques de la TOUR* on its door. Its racks of magnets, snow globes, pens, stuffed animals, hats, and t-shirts—all proudly displaying the name and likeness of the famous monument—were practically crowding the floor space to capacity.

"Wow, this is a tiny store," Olivia observed as she squeezed between two displays of postcards. "You couldn't fit three more people in here if you tried."

"Yeah, but it looks like there are several of these little stores on this floor alone. I'm sure no one who needs a stuffed Eiffel Tower goes away emptyhanded," John said absently as he toyed with a shelf of pencil sharpeners. "Where are those coffee mugs you were going to check out?"

"Hmm, I don't know. I don't think I actually want a coffee mug after all. I'm not sure what I want. Maybe a sweatshirt?" she said as she considered the stacks of shirts with the tower emblazoned on them.

She took a sweatshirt off the top of the stack closest to her. It was pink and had a large picture of the Eiffel monument emblazoned across the front. The words "My heart belongs in Paris" were spelled out in red sequins.

She wrinkled her nose at it, neatly refolding it and carefully placing it back on the shelf before pulling out a white sweatshirt from the next stack. This one displayed a cartoon tower with a little smiling face on it. The tower was sporting a black beret. With a laugh, she put this one back as well.

"I'm enjoying how seriously you're taking this purchase," he teased. "Take your time. Don't get hasty."

"Oh shush. Everyone needs a memento of their honeymoon," she said as she dug through the pile a while longer, then moved on to consider the t-shirts, tote bags, and umbrellas that were next on the shelves.

"Seriously, why would you even want mementoes?" John asked, bouncing a red rubber ball he'd found. "This hasn't exactly been the trip we'd hoped for."

"I'm starting to believe....," she started, uncertain how much of her newfound clarity should be shared just yet, "I...I just have a feeling I'll look back on this trip as...well, as the start of everything."

John studied her face for a moment, looking thrown. "What are you trying to say?" he asked cautiously.

"I...," she began, then trailed off as she spotted a small metal figurine of the tower. "Oh, this is perfect! I'm definitely getting this!"

They took it to the counter, where she rummaged through her bag and handed euros to the clerk. As she accepted her change and took the bag in hand, she said, "John, tell me about your volunteer work and all the time you spent in the Peace Corps."

"What's going on, Liv?" he asked as they started making their way out of the tiny store. "What did you mean back there? How could this trip possibly be the start of anything except maybe the need for therapy?"

"I've been getting to know you this trip," she said, looking directly in his eyes, hoping he'd feel the truth of her words. *Truly* know you. And what I've discovered is that the more I know, the more I *want* to know. The more I'm with you, the closer I want to be with you. Standing in your arms over there just now? It felt like coming home to me. This trip has given me the clarity that I couldn't find on our wedding day. I couldn't identify my feelings as love before, because in forty years I've never been as happy as I was when you hugged me just now. Or when you shared *Sainte Chapelle* with me. Or when we sat together on the floor of the *Louvre*. The more I know about you, the more I want you, and the more I want *us*. So please—please tell me about the Peace Corps."

John looked shocked by her words, turmoil and doubt chasing each other around in his eyes. Olivia continued gazing at him, praying he'd really, truly hear her and believe her, but wondering if maybe her words were way too little, much too late.

"Olivia, I don't even know how to process what you just said," he replied finally. "I think...I think I just have to pretend you didn't say it because I can't take this. I really can't."

"It's the truth, though," she insisted, quietly.

"Okay, so...the Peace Corps," he went on as though she hadn't just laid her heart out in front of him. "Well, to understand why I went and joined the Peace Corps, I guess you'd need to know about what led up to it—about my college years and my first marriage—and that's a story I admit I owe you anyway."

"Then back up and start clear at the beginning," she said, happy he was at least talking instead of walking. "I want to know everything."

"At the beginning? The very beginning? Yeah, all right then," John said, a teasing glimmer in his eye. "Well, some women are in labor for a really long time with their first babies, but my mom...."

"Not that far back!"

"Oh, okay, well then we'll fast-forward to the day I first saw Val...."

John dove into the story then, starting with the day when his sister Kate first brought Valerie home. He told her about his senior year, and how deserted Val had felt when he'd gone off to college. His doubts about getting married so young, and his secret desires to travel and see the world first. And he admitted that he'd blown it and made a terrible mistake by not heeding his fears and getting married anyway.

"So we have that in common, I guess, now that I think about it," he said with a shrug. "We panic before weddings and then get married anyway."

She nodded and waited for the rest of his story to unfold, not wanting to distract him.

He was, after all, opening up to her.

Finally....

Chapter 43

The Rest of the Story

HE TOLD HER all about that first marriage, the things about it that had worked, the things that hadn't, and the reasons it ultimately failed. Then he went into his travels around the world with the charity groups, and all he'd seen and done during those years. And he told her about how he'd come home, supposedly older and wiser, only to jump into another doomed marriage with the social-climbing Jackie. Then how that one drifted to its inevitable finish, and how he'd managed to move past it and forgive himself for yet another failed relationship.

Eventually the two of them got too cold and headed back to the elevators, then to the floor with the concession stands.

"Want to get some lunch?" he asked. "You've got to be starving, and you're probably pretty sick of this story by now."

"I'm not sick of it at all," Olivia replied. "But okay, let's grab something and find a place to sit if we can. I want to hear about the rest of your life right up until the day we were introduced at that party."

They bought sodas and hot dogs, but all the tables were filled with school groups and families. So they wandered to a corner and stood while they ate. When they were done, they tossed their garbage and walked back to the walkway to see the city again.

"So, keep talking," Olivia said, anxious for insight

into the parts of his life she'd neglected to ask about before. John told her about his life since his second divorce and what he'd been doing and where he'd been emotionally when he met her. And how after he met her, he'd just known from the beginning that he'd finally found his soulmate. He'd felt deep in his heart that he wasn't making a mistake this time.

"Big joke, huh?" he said with a shrug of his shoulders. "Clearly, I'm just not meant to be married."

"But you *are* married," Olivia reminded him. "There's still a relationship here that can be saved. We both have to want it, and we both have to fight for it."

"Livvie, I should have known. I should have, and yet I didn't have the tiniest inkling that something was wrong between us. It's just inexcusable. How could I ever trust my own judgment again?" He looked truly perplexed. "And do you want to hear the part that really gets me the most? I was warned."

"What?!" Olivia asked, startled. "What are you talking about?"

"Well, I don't want you to hate her for saying these things, but my sister came to see me right before the wedding ceremony when I was getting ready. Probably about the same time you were considering fleeing the church, changing your name, and going into hiding."

Olivia gave him a pained look but didn't interrupt.

"She asked me if I was sure about us," John continued. "She actually asked me if I was sure that you loved me. Looking back at that conversation now, of course, I can't believe how right on the money she was about the whole situation. But at the time I never even gave it a moment's thought. I just shooed her out of the room and didn't think about what she'd said until after."

"Oh John...you mean until after I said *exactly* what she was afraid I'd say to you?" Olivia asked.

"Yeah."

"If neither of us knew, how do you suppose *she* did?"

"Beats me. But Katie and I have always been close. However she figured it out, it was only because she was worried about me and loves me."

"And because she wants you to get back together with her friend Val," Olivia guessed. "They were very cozy at the reception."

"Yeah, that's probably a pretty accurate assessment," John said, then turned toward her with a puzzled look and short laugh. "How do you women *do* that? How do you figure that kind of stuff out about each other?"

"The way Kate knew about my feelings, or the way Samantha clearly knows I've been jealous of her?" Olivia asked.

"Yeah, that," he said with a short chuckle. "It's creepy."

"You've heard of women's intuition," Olivia offered. "That's all it is, although I don't seem to have too much of it. At least not when it comes to figuring out my *own* feelings."

"Speaking of you, it's your turn," John said. "Tell me your life story."

"Mine's not nearly so interesting."

"Yeah, well, you asked me, and now I'm asking you," he said. "So, spill it. What events formed my third wife?"

Olivia considered this for a moment. Then she took a deep breath and started telling him her story the way he'd told his. About the pain of growing up without a mother and how close she'd always been to her dad. She told him about the smattering of long-term relationships she'd had, all of which had ultimately gone nowhere, and about the way she'd thrown herself into studying the law with such abandon.

"And then I met you and ruined your life," Olivia said in a teasing tone. "Aaaand, that pretty much brings us up to present day."

That earned her a smile, which she slowly returned. Then they gazed at each other for a long moment.

"Let's get out of here," he said finally, reaching over and taking her hand. Olivia gasped as he gently threaded his fingers with hers, then she squeezed his hand in reply. They walked to the outer elevators and made their way to the plaza at the base of the monument.

Chapter 44

Moving Forward

"THAT WAS FABULOUS," Olivia said, looking sideways at John as they walked, still hand-in-hand, back toward the Metro station.

"Yeah, the views are amazing," John agreed lightly.

"No. Well, yes, the views *are* amazing," Olivia said quickly. "But I meant the talking. Finally filling in all the gaps for each other. Getting to really know my husband at last. It was just...it was great, John. Thank you for today and thank you for opening up to me about your first two marriages."

"Yeah, it was probably time, huh?"

"Definitely time. Way, way past time...."

Olivia trailed off as she tried to sort her jumbled thoughts into words that would truly convey all she wanted to tell him. As they descended into the Metro station, she said, "John, I've admitted to you that I messed up terribly by not really throwing myself into our relationship in the past year. I...I don't know. I somehow wasn't present enough in my own life to know what I was thinking or feeling on our wedding day. Now that I've taken the time to truly focus on us and learn more about you, I see what a rare, wonderful connection we have."

As they boarded the train and sat down, Olivia chanced a look at his face. She was disappointed not to see love and happiness radiating back at her. If anything, John looked stony and upset, and he took the opportunity to pull his hand from hers. She felt a sense of panic and impending doom then. He wasn't really hearing her. He didn't yet believe that they had a future. But since he was trapped in the subway car next to her for at least a few minutes, she decided to press on.

"So like I said, I've owned my mistakes in this. I messed up colossally. But John, after hearing your stories about your ex-wives, it made me wonder if...well, if maybe the part you played in this was in holding yourself back from *me*. I wasn't pressing for more, and maybe...well, maybe you were scared to truly open yourself up to me. You'd been burned before, and you could see that what we had was special and rare and right. Maybe...you didn't tell me all about yourself because it would leave you too raw and exposed?"

"I don't know," John admitted. "Maybe, I guess? But why does it even matter at this point?"

When they arrived at their stop and began filing toward the exit, John's words swirled wildly through her head. He was still convinced they were over! Panic bubbled through her. How could she convince him? What mix of words would prove that he needed to give them one more shot?

As they reached the sidewalk, Olivia decided there wasn't enough time left in their trip to chance leaving any words unspoken. His face told her everything she needed to know: While she'd been figuring out that she was going to fight for this marriage, he'd been deciding it was time to let it go.

"John, please just listen to me," she pleaded. She reached out and tried to take his hand, even as he pulled away from her.

"Don't," he said, grabbing the back of his neck, frustration coursing off him now. "Olivia, I hear what you're saying, I do. And, of course, you're right that I messed up by not sharing more of myself with you, obviously. I have no idea if it had anything to do with me being burned before or trying to protect myself somehow, but if that really was my plan, it failed pretty spectacularly. But even without me fully opening myself up to you, you still managed to hurt me more than any other women did cumulatively."

"That's because what we have together is so special," she replied quickly. "We have to fight to save it, John. This honeymoon has made that so crystal clear to me. You and me? We're *it*. We're forever. You're my person, and I know I'm yours. All you have to do is to allow yourself to believe what I'm saying. I know I hurt you, and I'd take every single word back if I could. I know it's going to take time for you to trust me again, and we have our whole lives to work on that. But I swear I've learned my lesson, and everything will be different now. I'll treasure you. I'll be present in our lives and dedicate every single day to proving to you that you did the right thing in giving us just one more chance."

She searched his face, desperately hunting for a clue to what he was thinking. But as he continued to assess her quietly, his lack of a reaction scared her.

"Okay, you can talk now," she said with a nervous laugh.

"Thank you," John finally replied. "I appreciate everything you just told me. I accept your apologies, and I really hope you accept mine. I believe that neither of us set out to destroy the other. Truly. But let's not continue to compound our mistakes, Liv. Let's just cut our losses and go home before this honeymoon kills us both."

"You're listening to me, but you're not *hearing* me. John, I *do* love you!" Olivia cried out. "Why won't you fight for us?"

"Livvie, honey," he began quietly, "you have to admit you don't have a sterling record with me when it comes to being in touch with your feelings. A month ago, as far as either one of us knew, you loved me and wanted to marry me. Then, on our wedding day, *poof!* Those feelings had magically vanished, and in their place were boredom, confusion, and apathy. Then along came Samantha, and suddenly you're jealous and, gee, maybe you just need to get to know me. Then also suddenly—like a genuine walking-on-water kind of miracle—you love me again."

"You're twisting everything," she snapped, impatient with him now.

"Baby, I'm not saying I don't love you. I *do* love you—with every fiber of my being. And, you know what? I'm not even denying that you might love me in return. But I learned a lot during this trip, too. For example, I learned that I've got terrible instincts when it comes to reading women. And I learned that maybe I need to take some time alone to figure out where I messed up and what I want the rest of my life to be."

Olivia reached for a tissue from inside her purse as tears started to threaten in the corners of her eyes. She didn't like where any of this was going.

"But mostly," he continued, "I learned that you need some time to figure out what it is *you* want. Maybe you genuinely do love me, and your freak-out at the wedding and everything afterward were just due to an overblown case of pre-wedding jitters. But, Livvie, *maybe they weren't.* Maybe you were right, and maybe you just saved us from a lifetime of wedded misery."

"No, John, no," Olivia begged, her pain overriding her pride. "Don't do this. Please."

"It's over Liv, it's just over," he replied, his eyes suspiciously wet.

"No, you're the one making the big mistakes now," she insisted. "I'm sorry I put us through all of this. I'm so sorry. Tell me what you want me to do to make it up to you, and I'll do it. But don't do this."

"No, Olivia. Come on now. Let's just make it clean and easy on everyone. We'll go home, we'll get an annulment or a divorce or whatever's easiest, and call it quits."

"No!" Olivia said, getting mad now. "I'll fight it, John! I love you, and I want this marriage to work with my whole heart!"

John turned away from her. "I'm sorry honey, but trust me when I say that I can't let myself believe what you're saying today. I know you need to take some time to think this all over, because I just can't go through that again. What if you're wrong? What if you change your mind again tomorrow, or next week, or next month? It about killed me to lose you once. I can't do it again. I just can't."

"Let me prove myself to you, then," Olivia said. "What can I do to show you how much I love you and how committed I am to our marriage?"

Her words hung in the air as people milled past them on the sidewalk, unmindful of the swirling turmoil. Finally, John turned his face back and met her gaze again.

"Okay," he said, a tenderness in his voice that hadn't been there before. "Let's give it a year."

"Oh, John, yes!" Olivia cried triumphantly. "*Yes!* I'll show you how wonderful our lives can be, and you'll forget all about separations and divorces and crappy honeymoons. I swear it!"

"I'm sorry honey, but that's not what I meant," John said with a wince and a sad look. "Not a year together. We need time *apart*. I need time to figure out why my judgment is so off-kilter, and you need to really search your heart and find out why you broke up with me and then suddenly wanted to save the marriage."

"No! No way. I can't do it," Olivia said, stubbornly shaking her head. "No."

"You may thank me a few months down the road," he argued. "You may realize you don't even *want* to save the marriage. But be honest about it with yourself and be honest about it with me when you see me again. I don't want you to feel guilty about everything you said here today. What happens on Parisian sidewalks *stays* on Parisian sidewalks."

Olivia couldn't stop a small giggle from escaping her lips before she started shaking her head again.

"No, I don't need a year," she insisted. "I don't want that."

"Listen to me," John said stubbornly. "These are your choices: I'll give you a year to think about it or I'll give you a divorce, but I'm not giving you my heart again. Not now. Not today."

She sniffed again and wiped her eyes with the pulpy tissue she'd been crying into. She nodded her head and finally looked up to meet his eyes.

"Fine, have it your way," she snapped. "I'll take the year."

"Good. And I'll make it easy on the both of us by doing as I'd originally planned and leaving New Jersey," he said. "I'm still going to take that trip I was telling you about."

"With *her*, you mean?" Olivia said as the warning Samantha had given earlier flooded back now. "That's what this is really about, isn't it? You're going to spend the year with Samantha! I'll be exploring my feelings, and you'll be exploring *her!*"

"Ahh, there's that little jealous streak of yours again," he said with a chuckle.

"This isn't funny," Olivia said. "*Nothing* about this is funny."

"Trust me, Liv. I'm not actually laughing," he said as the smirk faded off his face. "And I'm also not developing an elaborate plan so I can have a big old affair with Samantha. If I wanted her, I'd tell you and then I'd divorce you. But that's not what I'm saying or doing. I'll consider us married during this year, and I'll be faithful to you. I assume you can say the same."

"Of course," Olivia shot back.

"Fine. But I'm going to be brutally honest here and tell you that she might still come with me. She's been a fabulous friend to me, and if she wants to come, I won't stop her. She deserves at least that much consideration."

"No! She told me that if you go on that trip, she'll consider you fair game," Olivia revealed. "And that makes no sense anyway. How can you be grappling with your feelings for me during our year apart if she's constantly in your face? That's not exactly giving our marriage a fair chance!"

"I'm not grappling with my feelings for you, Liv!" John insisted. "I'm not the one who doesn't know how he feels here! I love you, and I've always loved you, almost since the moment I saw you. To recap, my year is for figuring out what's wrong with my radar; your year is about feelings and grappling."

"I just don't want you grappling Samantha," Olivia snapped.

"Stop saying *grappling!*" John said. "We're friends, and she's got nothing to do with this!"

"Right, well she thinks she's got a shot," Olivia reminded him, squeezing her eyes shut. She was tired out by their conversation and all the emotions it had drained from her.

"Well, she doesn't, okay?" John said. "You either trust me or you don't."

"So, this is it?" Olivia asked, happy to drop the Samantha subject. "We're just going to go our separate ways now and not see each other for a year?"

John nodded slightly. "It probably would be for the best. Doing this again would be too hard. And, to that end, please understand that I'm really talking about a year apart here. Don't call, don't text, don't ask my family about me. Just take this time for yourself. If you decide in a month or two to file for divorce, then fine just do it. But if you really want to try again, then we'll see."

"Where will we meet?" Olivia asked. "If we're not going to be in touch, we need a plan."

"Yeah, well, I don't think this is really going to happen, so whatever you think," John said with an indifferent shake of his head.

"Well, I *do* think it will happen, and when it does, it's going to mark the beginning of our new lives together. I want it to be big and meaningful and romantic...so how about we meet back here in Paris on our one-year anniversary?"

"Yeah, sure, why not?" John said dismissively. "At the *Venus d'Milo?*"

"Perfect!" Olivia said, offering him a tentative

smile. "I'll be there, you know."

"Right, well, like I said, please be honest with yourself, Liv. Don't show up to be stubborn. I'm leaving here fully expecting our next contact to be about the divorce."

"Yeah, well, I've got enough faith for both of us."

"Fine. Let's get you back to your hotel," John said, and they started walking again.

*   *   *

She was devastated that she'd been unable to convince him what they needed was more time together and definitely *not* a whole year apart. But if this time was what he needed as proof of her feelings, then she'd find a way to give that to him.

"Are you staying for the rest of our original trip?" she asked as they neared the hotel entrance. She could feel the dread blossoming inside her now. *How am I going to do this? How am I going to say goodbye to him?*

"I don't know," John replied, slowing his pace as they approached the door to the lobby. "I'll crash with Samantha until I figure out my next move, I guess."

"Right. Of course," Olivia said, desperately not wanting to fight about Samantha anymore. "I guess...I guess this is it."

"Yeah," John said with a sigh. "But it's going to be okay, you know, Livvie. *You're* going to be okay, no matter what this year brings us."

Olivia just nodded, unable to speak as the tears rushed to her eyes again.

"You won't reconsider?" Olivia asked softly, tossing out one last desperate attempt.

"You'll see that I'm right," John said. "It's for the best. You'll thank me one day."

"I love you, you know," she managed to reply.

"I love you, too," John said.

Olivia looked at him for one more moment, desperate to memorize every detail and feature on his face. Then she turned and walked into the hotel without looking back.

Chapter 45

A Call to Charlie

IT'S FOR her own good, John told himself as he watched her walk away—and take his heart with her.

If he thought even for a minute that Olivia truly loved him and wanted to spend her life with him, he never would have let her go. But he was sure what she was feeling was guilt and regret, compounded by her irrational jealousy about Samantha. And, by her own admission, her conscience had been eating away at her since their breakup, making her feel terrible for not getting to know him when they were dating. But he knew she didn't love him and truly want to spend her life with him. How could she, when a little over a week ago she'd broken his heart and dumped him so unceremoniously on the first day of their honeymoon? Feelings like that don't turn around over the span of a few days.

His mind wandered back to the horrible flight. He could still remember her precise words with cutting clarity, as they would be branded on his soul for the rest of his life—*That's the problem, John. I'm not in love with you. I don't think I ever was.*

What else had she said that day, John wondered as he headed for Samantha's hotel. He wanted to rip open those wounds and put himself through the pain again by willing the memories to come flooding back. Maybe if he focused on what she'd said, it would make forcing her to walk away easier to bear—

255

So, yesterday I got dressed and put my makeup on and had my hair done, and I went through the other motions of being a happy bride. But I wasn't. Happy, that is. So, I sat down and really thought about it, and I realized it's because I was making a mistake in marrying you.

John squeezed his eyes shut, embarrassed by how much power every syllable had over him. But thinking about what she'd said had exactly the effect he'd hoped: A woman who said those things was *not* ready to commit to a healthy relationship just over a week later, no matter how convincingly she stated her case.

But I didn't want to embarrass you by jilting you. It just seemed too cruel; you deserved so much more than that. So, I went through with it, thinking that I would just tell you after we got back from Paris and quietly divorce you then. It just felt like a much kinder plan, even though it meant having to lie to you and keep up an act in front of you and everyone we know.

Enough! John told himself. He couldn't handle any more memories of that day. Not now. Maybe not ever again. It was time to bury them as deeply as he possibly could. He had to get some distance before he could view them with any kind of perspective or clarity and really learn anything from them.

He was convinced that the path he'd chosen earlier was the right one. He would've been the world's biggest fool to believe what Olivia was telling him, that now she loved him and wanted to be with him forever. How long would their newfound happiness have lasted? A day? A week? Would it have been a month or six months before she was giving him another ruthless explanation about how she'd been wrong in thinking she wanted him?

No. He couldn't take hearing another one of her breakup speeches.

But what would he do if she really met up with him in a year and was still professing her love for him? Would he be able to believe her? After giving her a year to think it over...well, it would certainly be *tempting* to trust his heart to her again...

He shook his head, trying to shake the notion from his mind. Why torture himself with that scenario when there was no way in the world it was ever going to happen? She was gone and she wasn't coming back. All that lay between them now was the paperwork. He had to let go of all unrealistic hopes if he had any chance of healing and moving on. He'd been wrong about her before, but he was right this time. He had set her free, and that was the end of it.

Not that he wasn't planning to keep his word to her: He *would* spend the year trying to figure out why he'd been so wrong about her feelings for him. In order to move forward and trust his heart with anyone else, he definitely needed to understand that much.

He stopped for dinner before he got to the hotel and thought more about what he'd done and said. Yes, he truly believed they were over and that he'd done the right thing. But there was also a loose end that needed tying up before Olivia could be truly free. He pulled out his phone, bracing himself for the conversation.

"Hello?" the man's voice said. "John, is that you?"

"Yeah," John said, taking a deep breath. *Here goes nothing,* he thought. "It's me."

"Hello, son," Charlie said cautiously. "I'm surprised to hear from you. Is everything okay? Is Olivia okay?"

"Yes, we're both fine," he replied, mentally adding *physically anyway.* "She told me, Charlie. I know everything now."

"What do you mean?" Charlie said, obviously choosing his words carefully.

"Olivia broke up with me," John told him. "I know she never loved me now and that she just married me to save face in front of our family and friends."

"Oh. I'm so sorry to hear that." Charlie's voice bore the unmistakable tone of genuine disappointment. "I was so hopeful that she'd see what a mistake she was making and really work on saving this marriage."

"Well, no, it didn't quite happen that way. Actually, she told me everything on the flight over here."

"What?! What was that girl thinking?" Charlie's anger virtually bubbled through the phone line. "I thought she was going to wait until you got home or after a few days at least."

"No, the timing of her declaration was my fault. I could tell something was bothering her, and I basically dragged it out of her."

"John, I don't know what to say to you or how I can possibly tell you how sorry I am for everything. I thought I raised a woman with a solid head and a kind and loving heart. I couldn't believe that it was my Olivia acting that way and saying those things to me on her wedding day. She shouldn't have married you. I told her to go tell you right there and then, but she wouldn't listen to me. She just had to do it her way and look where it got the two of you."

"Charlie, I didn't call you to make you apologize or become even angrier with your daughter—just the opposite, actually. I wanted to let you know that a lot has happened since we got here. Olivia's feeling guilty and lonely, and she's even convinced herself that she really does love me and wants to save our marriage now."

"Why, that's wonderful news! That's the Olivia I know! She's a fighter, son. If anyone will work to make things right, it's my daughter."

John smiled despite himself. He knew Charlie couldn't stay mad at Olivia forever. In fact, he was counting on it.

"Well, it's not as easy as all that. I don't quite believe her, Charlie. She obviously doesn't know what she wants, so I convinced her that we need to take some time apart so she can figure it out. I can't sit idly by while she plays a game of 'I love him, I love him not,' with my heart, you know?"

"I'd love to argue with you John, but I can't say that I blame you."

"But don't blame Olivia either, okay? That's really why I called. She's hurting and she's alone, and she doesn't need to worry about fixing her relationship with her father on top of everything else. Please, Charlie, forgive her for what she did and be there for her while she heals. She's eventually going to realize that she's just fine without me, and I don't want you trying to convince her she's wrong or making her feel guilty about her decision. I know it's over, and it's just a matter of time before she realizes that, too. Don't interfere, just love her and be there for her. Will you do that for me, Charlie?"

"Are you really sure it's over, though? Sounds to me like you're the one who's not fighting to save the relationship. Don't give up on her now!"

"Charlie, I love your daughter with all my heart, and I always will. It's not about that. It's about me not believing *her* change of heart. It was only a handful of days ago that she was telling me she never loved me. Now she suddenly does? I'm sorry, but I don't believe it. It's just not true, and I don't want her manipulated into thinking it is. If by some miracle she shows up in my life again in one year telling me that she really does love me, I have to know that it isn't because she felt guilty. If she says those things, I want to know they're the truth. Do you understand what I'm asking of you?"

"You're asking me to be here for Olivia while she makes up her *own* mind. Yes, son, I understand, and I'll do it. Absolutely. But you're wrong. If my daughter told you she loves you, it's the truth. She won't need a year to figure that out."

"Well, honestly, I didn't give her much of a choice in the matter. And Charlie, just remember that she believed she loved me once before. Don't forget what happened that time." John turned from the phone for just a moment to fight back the tears that were forming in his eyes. "Support her and let her heal. And be there for her when she's ready to move forward without me. Take care of her for me, okay?"

"I will, son," Charlie said, sounding suspiciously choked up, too. "Don't give up on her."

"Goodbye, Charlie," John said. "And thanks for everything."

After he ended the call, he reminded himself that Olivia had Charlie to lean on. And that was good. In fact, he told himself, it was all he needed to know.

Now he could start the process of forgetting about her.

Chapter 46

Leaving Paris

OLIVIA FOUND she couldn't quite force herself to leave Paris. It felt too final, like she'd be abandoning John or leaving behind any small chance that he might change his mind. If there was even the slightest hope, she wanted to be here.

Of course, she was also dreading what was waiting for her at home. Returning to a job where focus would be a struggle and answering questions from well-meaning friends and family would be a nightmare. They'd no doubt wonder why she was home alone while John was off globetrotting with some new gal pal. And she couldn't even imagine how furious her father was going to be now that she'd bungled things with John so badly and hurt him so deeply.

So she called her boss and told him she was taking an extended leave of absence, giving a few intentionally vague "personal" reasons. Then she called the front desk and asked to make a switch to a cheaper room in the hotel and extend her stay if space became available.

After that, she spent the following week trying to relax and revisit the sites to which she hadn't done justice during her mock honeymoon. She went back to the *Louvre* and managed to see more than just one statue this time. On another day, she visited Notre Dame, really focusing on the tour of the beautiful cathedral grounds. Pulled by the memories and unable to stop herself, she walked back to *Saint Chapelle,* allowing the luxury of remembering the precious first visit and reveling in how much it meant that John shared one of his favorite places with her, despite how angry he'd been.

She even went back to the Eiffel Tower, drawn by the memories of the long discussions they'd had and the site of the hug that had finally snapped the pieces of jumbled confusion together in her mind.

When she got back to the hotel that evening, she decided to do the thing she'd been dreading the most: calling her father. If she didn't, he'd start to worry, and then he might call John in an attempt to find her. She had no idea what John would say to Charlie if that happened, but she wanted to avoid anything that would make her relationship with either man even more tenuous. At the very least, her dad deserved an explanation from her own lips. She knew he'd probably done nothing but worry since she made her confession on her wedding day. Charlie was getting old, and he certainly didn't need added stress or worry in his life.

Drawing in a deep breath to calm her nerves, she picked up her phone.

"Hi Dad," she said softly when she heard him answer.

"Hi there, baby girl," Charlie replied, sounding happy enough.

Olivia laughed in relief. She had half expected him to disconnect the call the moment he heard her voice.

"I'm not your baby girl anymore, Dad," she said lightly. "I'm a married woman now, remember?"

"Are you?"

"Yeah, I'm still married," she said. "Sort of. We're separated."

"I'm sorry, honey."

"I'm so sorry too, Dad. You're going to want to strangle me when you hear this, but I was wrong. I was *so* very wrong. I *do* love him. He's everything to me, only I figured it out too late to avoid hurting him or destroying everything we had."

"Oh, Olivia, honey, I wish I could have said something that day that would have helped you avoid this mess. I feel like I let you down."

"You did everything you possibly could that day," she assured him. "Believe me, you have no reason to apologize. This is all my fault."

"Other than beating yourself up about it, what are you going to do?"

"There's not much I *can* do, unfortunately. John doesn't want to see or hear from me for one year unless it's to serve him with divorce papers. He thinks I need time to figure out what it is I want."

"Maybe he's right," Charlie said.

"No, he's *not* right!" she fired back. "I love him, and I want to fight for this marriage! I know it sounds like an amazing about-face, but I really *didn't* know him before. And I think a big part of that was because *he* was holding himself back from *me*. I truly believe that was a big part of our problem. We talked a lot during this trip, and I learned so much about him that I never knew. He's an amazing man, Dad. If I'd known then even half of what I know about him now, I never would have convinced myself that I didn't love him, and I certainly wouldn't have hurt him the way I did. I just didn't know what a precious person I'd found until it was too late."

"Sounds to me like you need to find a way to make a convincing case for yourself," Charlie said. "You need a way to prove to your young man that you've really figured out what it is you want."

"How though?" she asked, genuinely confused. "If we don't see each other, how am I going to prove anything to him?"

"You're a lawyer, Olivia," Charlie pointed out. "Build your case. Find the evidence."

"Okay, I'll bite," Olivia said with a little smile of affection for him. He made it all sound so simple. "What kind of evidence?"

"Well, John doesn't have any reason right now to think you're serious. And other than the passage of time, he's not going to have much proof at the end of a year either, right?"

"Right, exactly. If he doesn't believe me now, what will convince him in a year?"

"You need to give him reasons. Write him daily letters or send him emails, letting him know what you're thinking about. Document all your emotions during this time. Also, go to a therapist and really explore why you didn't bother to get to know the man until it was too late. A note from your doctor couldn't hurt, right?"

"Okay, sure," Olivia said as her mind began whirring with possibilities. "Yeah...I get what you're saying."

"You just need to find enough evidence to make your case stick. Bury the kid with it. But truly take the time to think this through, Olivia. Don't just stubbornly spend the year with one eventual goal in mind. Truly dig deep and go through the hard work of honestly assessing everything. If you still want to save the marriage after a year, then you need for him to have no reason to doubt you."

"I do have some things I want to work on with myself anyway," Olivia told him, nodding as though he could see her. "I want to learn Spanish and find ways to work more actively with the animal shelter, for example."

"Then tell him about those things too, honey. It's going to be a lot of work, but you're up to it. I know I raised a fighter."

"Yes, that's right. I've got this. I'll just build my case. I love you so much, Dad."

"I love you too, Olivia," Charlie said. "Come home now, sweetheart, okay? It's time to start gathering that evidence."

Olivia said she would. Ten minutes later she had changed her return flight.

She left Paris the next day.

Chapter 47

Finding Clarity

One Year Later....

HE TURNED TO HER, *his green eyes studying her face in confusion.*

"You love me," he said. "So what's the problem?"

"That's the problem, John," Olivia replied as she watched the fiery fallout of her words etch pain onto John's normally relaxed face. "I'm not in love with you. And I don't think I ever was."

Olivia sat up with a start, her heart pounding wildly as the dream faded away. Slowly her surroundings became familiar as she worked to calm herself. The dim illumination of the moon revealed that she was, in fact, home, and alone in her own bed. She turned and looked at her phone. It was only 2:57. It was barely morning. She still had hours and hours to go before her flight.

She lay back down and tried to erase the lingering memories of the dream, but she knew it was a wasted effort. She would never escape the look of pain she'd seen on John's face, pain that she alone had placed there. That part *wasn't* a dream, unfortunately. It was a memory, as real as any other. And it had been haunting her ever since.

With a sigh she rolled onto her side and bunched the pillow under her head.

"Hey, I'm sorry I woke you up," she said as her

dog, Eiffel, climbed off his bed and padded over to investigate.

Absentmindedly scratching between his ears, she lay there lost in more memories as the time crawled forward. She was pretty sure she wouldn't be going back to sleep now. The nightmares had become a constant companion over the last year, despite all the work she'd put into improving herself and fighting for her marriage. The lack of sleep combined with the worry about where John was and what he was doing were a toxic combination.

Purgatory...I'm in purgatory, she thought. Not in heaven, not in hell. Not married, not divorced. Not in a relationship, yet not free. She was so very tired of the waiting and the not knowing, and of not being able to see John. She was tired of it all, and she found herself completely exhausted by the sheer force of will it had taken to survive. She hadn't let herself drown in pity and sorrow and longing, but it had taken every ounce of energy and resolve to make it this far. She'd spent the year resolutely trying to better herself and uncover the reasons why everything had gone so far off the rails. She was a fighter; she always had been. It was that determination alone that had helped her claw her way through this difficult year without him.

John.... She smiled as she pictured his face. Reaching over to her bedside table, she flipped on the reading light. Then she pulled open the bottom drawer to reveal a stack of photos. When the wedding photographer had sent the online proofs from the wedding, she couldn't bear to make any decisions about them on her own, so she just ordered one of everything. She practically could have bought a car for the amount of money she'd spent, but it had helped somehow to hold onto this connection she had to John and to those precious moments in time before she'd taken a flamethrower to their union.

She could see the love emanating off him in each picture. She had sorted out all the photos of just herself and kept only the ones of John in her bedside drawer. The pictures of her alone were incredibly painful evidence of how torn she'd been that day. She could see the doubt and confusion on her face in every shot. He had loved her so much, and she clearly hadn't deserved any of it. The pictures were a tragically haunting reminder of her mistakes.

But she still desperately wanted to make it all up to him, that much she knew for certain. He had been so right that a year apart would give her a clarity and an unblemished perspective that she just couldn't have possibly had while together with him on their honeymoon. But despite how beneficial the time had been, she missed him with an aching need that she just couldn't fathom. How could she not have seen it before? How had she ever seriously questioned her feelings for him? She had seen what was comfortable and had mistaken it for boring. She had seen dependable and had viewed it as dull. She had genuine love and threw it right back in his face with those two deadly sentences—

I'm not in love with you. And I don't think I ever was.

Those words hit like a punch in the stomach every time they replayed in her head, which, unfortunately, happened a lot. It was the way he had looked when he heard them, and the way their lives had unraveled from that point in time, that really stuck with her. Like ripples in the water when a pebble is tossed into a lake, the effects of those words had cascaded ever outward, on and on to every aspect of both of their lives.

But, in a way—as crazy as it seemed—she now believed that she had been right to do what she'd done. They hadn't been starting their lives together on a sturdy foundation, and she'd been the one who saw the cracks. If they were going to rebuild that foundation, they had to face those problems. A year's worth of therapy helped her acknowledge that the essential core of what she'd done was good even if there were an infinite number of better ways to go about fixing what was wrong. Most of them wouldn't have involved putting John's heart into a blender. She could have tuned into the problem earlier, for example, long before their wedding day. Or she could have asked John to go into couples' therapy with her. After all the bombshell things she'd learned about him, she knew she hadn't been the only one who'd made mistakes. Based on those revelations alone, she knew he would have been open to working on their relationship. But no, she'd just blurted out her doubts—and now here she was, one year later, alone, missing him, and so very afraid of what this trip would bring her.

She wanted to show up in Paris, leap into his arms, and never let him go. She missed him, she loved him, and she wanted to keep getting to know him better. Her year without him had cemented those truths for her, and there was no remaining doubt whatsoever. Reaching this level of deep confidence and resolve—really and truly knowing what she wanted—had come at the end of such a tough journey. Walking away from John that day had been one of the hardest things she'd ever done, and it hadn't gotten any easier from there. Everything inside her had been screaming that they were making a horrible mistake and foolishly throwing away precious time that could be spent together. But John had been adamant that this was the only option if she wanted even a small chance of spending her life with him. She was grateful he'd left at least this small door open, this tiny chance that they could, in the end, find their way toward a happily-ever-after type of scenario.

So, she'd taken his offer and, in the end, found—in spite of the nightmares and the lack of sleep—that the year apart had been beneficial after all. She felt stronger, more confident, and ready to fight for what she wanted.

But what had this year apart given *him?* That was the question constantly assaulting her. Was he now more convinced than ever that he wanted a divorce? Had he spent the year with Samantha, counting down the days, praying he'd soon be free of Olivia forever? Or would he show up at the *Louvre* feeling the same way she would: nervously hopeful and filled with a steely resolve to fight for their life together?

Would he show up at all?

She gave Eiffel one last pet, sighed, and rolled out of bed. Flipping off the reading light and turning on the overhead, she put the pictures back in the drawer. She had a trip to prepare for and—*please, God*—a marriage to save.

It was time to get started.

Chapter 48

Fragile Hopes

JOHN'S FEET BEAT a soft and steady rhythm that soothed him as he jogged down the beach. He'd been out here running along the ocean every morning, rain or shine, since he'd arrived after escaping the aftermath of the day his marriage had exploded somewhere over the Atlantic Ocean. The exercise and the physical exhaustion and the beauty of the waters off Puerto Rico had all played a part in helping him to survive this past year. They gave him a purpose and a reason to get out of bed each day.

And when he wasn't running, he was volunteering for Habitat for Humanity, which had really been perfect therapy, as it was yet another way to channel the pain. Working side-by-side with other volunteers, as well as the future homeowners themselves, had given him a sense of purpose and fulfillment that he just didn't get from his day job. No one's life was unalterably changed for the better by the hour or two they spent with their accountant. But helping a family build their home? There was just nothing else like it.

He hadn't simply been searching for a way to make a difference in the world, and he knew it would be disingenuous to claim it was his only motivation in coming here. No, what he'd really been doing was looking for a way to step out of his life, like casting off a dirty shirt. He just couldn't stay in his old apartment and work the same old job any longer. Not without

Olivia. So he walked away from it all and came to San Juan.

He had spent countless hours running on the beach, kayaking, and lifting weights at a local gym. When he wasn't helping put a roof on a new house or initiating a new batch of volunteers, he was relentlessly working his body. The exercise made him feel alive in a way that he hadn't since Paris. Not since that moment Olivia walked away, carrying his heart with her.

The net result was that he looked like a different person now. He was tan, his hair was blonder, and his muscles were hardened and defined in a way they'd never been before. He almost didn't recognize his own reflection. Oddly enough, it made him feel stronger inside as well as out, like maybe he was more able to deal with what his future might hold. If he was harder, stronger, leaner, faster...maybe he wouldn't hurt so badly when his marriage came to its inevitable end.

He couldn't believe it hadn't ended already. He had fully expected to receive divorce papers by now. Every time his phone rang, every time a text arrived, and every time he opened his mailbox, he was sure that would be the day Olivia let it all go. But the papers never came. She'd stayed true to her word and gave him a full year alone without even the tiniest trace of contact.

So now what...?

He stopped running and leaned over, hands on his knees as he worked to catch his breath. As usual, even thinking about her left him feeling off-kilter. And still very much in pain. The year was over, but now he was at a fork in the road, and he wasn't sure which path he wanted to take. He could go home and try to rebuild his old life without her. Or he could start fresh somewhere new. Or....

...I could go down the toughest road of all and go back to Paris to face her, assuming she even makes an appearance.

Even thinking her name still made him feel so raw. And vulnerable. And exposed. He had been the one who insisted they take this year apart. *Genius idea....* It really wasn't his most brilliant moment. He was the one who was totally in love and knew what he wanted, whereas she was the one who needed the time to think and then decide. He was supposed to use the year to figure out how she'd been able to blindside him, and why he hadn't realized that they didn't truly know each other well enough to get married in the first place. But the year hadn't really given him much clarity about any of those issues. All he knew was that he still loved her and felt completely lost without her.

The truth was that he wanted her back. Right now, she was just a beautiful ghost haunting his dreams. A memory that was paralyzing him at this crossroad in his life. He wanted to move forward with her in his heart completely. He wanted a real marriage, not just the world's most painfully drawn-out honeymoon. But in order to get those things, he would have to take a huge gamble.

He could go to Paris, show up at the *Louvre*, and end up standing there alone all day like a complete chump, desperately scanning the crowds and wondering when to give up and admit she wasn't coming. Or maybe she would show up, but only to offer him the courtesy of asking for a divorce in person. *Panic and last-minute waffling had made her refuse to end things with you the first time,* he reminded himself. But maybe the year apart gave her the clarity she needed to make her realize what a good idea it really was. She was a lawyer. She could easily waltz into the museum and hand him the divorce decree, along with a pen and a book to lean against so his signature would be super clear when she filed the paperwork.

He was a total fool. Once again, he'd just served up his heart on a platter to her, and now she held all the cards. *Wait, I'm mixing metaphors now....* He's holding his heart on a platter while she's playing a game of cards? *Yeah, okay, that actually checks out,* he thought miserably.

He tried to let his jumbled thoughts fall away as he straightened up again and started walking. He passed a couple other joggers, but mostly the beaches were still empty at this early hour. It was the perfect place and time to think about what to do next. He needed to pack the few belongings he'd brought to San Juan with him. Then he needed to decide where he would be going. Home? And just not bother to give Olivia the opportunity to rip his heart into a million pieces again? It was tempting to go that route.

If he went to Paris, he would be acknowledging that he still had hope, and it would mean giving that hope wings to fly. He didn't really want to put himself in such a vulnerable position again. He didn't want to feel the way he'd felt the day she told him she'd never loved him. If he went to Paris, there was a chance—a *big* chance—that it would happen a second time. He didn't know how he would possibly survive that. He could just hear her now: *Hi John! Thank you so much for giving us this year apart! Wow, to think that I almost decided to stay married to you! Whew, what a close one, huh?*

He exhaled slowly and walked on.

It doesn't have to go that way, though.

Maybe she was still committed to trying. Maybe she'd walk up to him and say, "Hi, I love you. Let's start over." Or maybe she'd fly into his arms, and the year of separation would simply melt away. That was probably just wishful thinking. Even if he did show up in Paris and she did, too, it would be the first step in a marathon. They still had to sort through all their issues and figure out why everything had blown up the first time around.

He spotted something by his feet and bent over to pick it up. It was a sand dollar, cracked but otherwise beautiful. He slowly applied a small amount of pressure to it and watched as the two halves separated, and the tiny white pieces in the middle fell out. They fluttered onto the surf and floated there until the next wave lapped them up and carried them off. That was precisely how fragile his hopes and dreams for the future felt—like there wasn't any way to repair the damage. It wouldn't take much pressure to make them crumble and disappear.

He started walking again, thinking that he had to make a choice now. It was time to pack *and* time to decide where he'd be flying. Was he ready to put himself out there again? Was a chance for a life with Olivia worth the possible pain of a second rejection? He didn't know, but he needed to figure it out fast.

Tomorrow was their one-year anniversary.

Chapter 49

Returning to the Louvre

OLIVIA STOOD in the *Louvre* while the crowds milled around her. She was looking into the face of the *Venus d'Milo,* but she really wasn't seeing it. The statue had moved her so much when she'd seen it a year ago. But now it was only John's face she wanted to see. *Please let him come, please let him be here.*

She scanned the room, searching the faces of the other visitors. She'd arrived before the museum even opened today, not wanting to take any chances that they'd miss each other. And if she didn't find him, she still wouldn't give up. She'd search the world if she had to. He wasn't pushing her away again. Not this time.

She tried to imagine how their reunion would go, but the vision was elusive. Would she run to him and throw herself in his arms? Would they be awkward and aloof, unable to start up the countless conversations they needed to have if they were going to make this work? Would he even be open to taking the journey with her? Had the damage she'd inflicted been too deep to ever heal?

Okay, now I'm starting to make myself panic. And that wasn't helping the situation. She walked away from the front of the statue and went to a corner to better view the actual spot where they'd been sitting that day he'd read about the statue to her. *Please let him show up today. Please, please, please....*

She reached into her bag and dug around to make

sure she had plenty of tissues, because this could easily turn into a waterworks situation. When she looked up again, she still didn't see him. But there was a man standing in their spot now, his face turned away from her toward the entrance of the room. His hair was shorter than John's, but it was the same basic color. No...this man's hair was lighter, like he spent a lot of time in the sun. He was John's basic height, too, actually. But this man was different in every other way. His darkly tanned skin was rippling with muscles, his t-shirt snug and leaving little doubt about just how cut and defined his body was. His arms were bulging, and his jeans looked molded to his form, showing a narrow waist and the promise of strong, defined legs to match the glorious arms. It was like a male model had crossed genes with a Greek god.

Okay, what was wrong with her? She was supposed to be searching the crowds for her husband, not mentally undressing strangers. But if she was going to pick a stranger to undress, he was definitely the one she'd choose. His body was just beautiful, as if one of these masterpieces had come to life and decided to take a stroll through the halls of the museum. She kept watching him. She couldn't help it; she felt almost drawn to the man, entranced by him. He seemed to be watching the entrance, scanning the crowds the same way she'd been for the past hour. He searched the faces of strangers, considering each momentarily then dismissing them one by one. *Who is the Greek god looking for?* she wondered. *His date? His wife?*

He turned as though he sensed her eyes on him. Then, almost in slow motion, his eyes locked with hers and she gasped.

John!

She couldn't breathe. She couldn't react. She just stared. It was the same face she'd been studying in her wedding photos all year, but he'd clearly been busy making some changes, and those changes had made him *beautiful.* While she had been sitting around mooning over pictures and obsessing over how she was going to get him back, he had been...what? Power-lifting Volkswagens in a tanning bed? The change was unbelievable. He was so lean, so tan, and so....

Okay, now she was acting like a love-struck teenager who just met her celebrity crush—and it was *not* one of the ways she had seen this reunion unfolding. She felt unbalanced and even more unsure of how to go about winning him back than she had been before. And, given her mental yo-yo'ing of the past year, that was saying a *lot*. She needed to get a grip. Time to stop gaping.

She gave herself a mental push forward, and her feet tentatively followed suit. Slowly, she willed herself in his direction, one quiet step at a time, never breaking eye contact. If she did, she might snap the spell that had fallen between them. Finally, she was there, stopping a step away and still lost in his gaze. A lot might have changed, but his beautiful green eyes—those eyes that always radiated kindness and love—were the same. Yes, it was still John in there, still the man she intended to fight for. And she clung to that knowledge like a lifeline.

He was the first to break the silence.

"You came," he said quietly.

"You did, too," she answered, offering him a tentative smile. "Or at least I think it's you. You've changed so much I didn't even recognize you at first."

"Oh, yeah, that. Uh...I had a lot of free time on my

hands, and I basically spent it in the gym." He ran his fingers through his hair in the same fidgety way she'd always loved. She felt comforted to see this. It helped her feel like he wasn't a complete stranger after all.

"I can't wait to hear all about your year," she finally replied, realizing she'd been staring again. *I seriously need to snap out of this*, she reminded herself. She was fighting for her life here. A little bit of focus would help.

"Yours too," John was saying. "I want to know what you've been up to."

"Well, nothing, really, compared to you," she said with a laugh. "John, seriously, you look amazing."

"Thanks, you too. Although you look like you've lost weight, and you didn't have any extra weight to lose. Are you feeling okay? You're not sick, are you?"

He seemed genuinely concerned, and she thought that was a good start. He also seemed happy to see her. A positive step in the right direction.

"No, no, it's fine. I'm fine," she said. "I just...I had a hard time adjusting this past year. I couldn't really eat. I wasn't sleeping right. I didn't...I didn't feel like myself."

"I didn't, either. I think that's why I ended up working out so much. It gave me something to focus on, something to wrap my mind around that wasn't you." He ended this sentence with a sad smile. "We're a pair, aren't we? Can't be together, can't be apart."

"It's the 'together' part that brought us both here today, though, right? Oh, and speaking of which, I have something for you." Olivia finally broke their eye contact to look down at her purse. She rummaged around for a few seconds, then pulled out a large brown envelope and handed it to him. "Here, I want you to have this."

John's mouth fell open, and the color drained from his face. He looked shocked, like she'd handed him a bomb instead of a letter. What was wrong?

"Dammit Olivia! Why didn't you just hand that to me to begin with? You let me think...is this some sort of game you're playing?"

"I...what...?" she stammered as he snatched the envelope from her hand and stalked away.

What just happened?

Chapter 50

The Envelope

OLIVIA FROZE for a moment, rooted in place by panic and confusion.

This museum is a relationship curse, she thought angrily as she located her equilibrium and started to chase after John. This was *so* not one of the ways she thought this reunion would play out.

"Wait, John! Please!" she called as she sprinted after him. As she caught up to him, she said, "What is it you think I just handed you?"

"I knew it!" he snapped, turning to face her. "I knew I shouldn't have come! I was so close to not showing up at all. I didn't want to give you the chance to do this to me again! But, no, like an idiot I came anyway! And now here I am, a year later, willingly letting you dice me up a second time. But it won't happen a third, I can guarantee you that."

"John, did you hear what I just asked? *What do you think I just handed you?*" She tried reaching for his hand but missed as he flinched backward. "Talk to me!"

"Didn't you just hand me divorce papers?" He waved the envelope for effect.

"No! Seriously? You think I flew all the way over here to serve you with papers?!"

"Yes, actually, the thought had occurred to me," he said, yet the anger was slowly vanishing from his tone. "When you handed me an envelope out of nowhere, it was pretty much *exactly* what I figured you'd do. You're a lawyer. It wasn't the world's biggest jump in logic."

Olivia reached for his hand again, and this time she grabbed it. She looked down at it as she collected her thoughts and gently ran her thumb over his roughened palm. It felt so good to be touching him again. Then, in a surprising gesture, he lifted his hand and gently pulled her chin back up so their eyes met again.

"I'm sorry about the hair-trigger reaction," he said softly. "I didn't mean to jump to conclusions. Okay, let's start over. Hello Olivia, it's good to see you. You look beautiful. Here I am making charming chitchat. Oh, and I see you have an envelope for me. What's in it?"

She smiled as he used his thumb to wipe away a tear that was starting to trail down her face. "Okay, yes, I can make human conversation, too. Hi, John. I barely recognized you back there. You're looking especially handsome. Guess what? I wrote you a series of letters this year to document my journey and prove my dedication to fixing us."

"It's *letters?*" he asked, the last traces of his anger visibly falling away. "What kind of letters?"

"Well, when I got home last year, I just didn't know what to do and where to start. I felt like if I didn't approach the year the right way, we'd be stuck in the same spot forever, with you not really knowing whether you can ever trust me again. It was actually Charlie who helped me figure out a plan."

"Charlie?" John asked, a soft look sweeping across his features. "How's he doing?" Olivia had always been touched by how much love John clearly had for her father.

"He's great, and he was a huge help to me. He was the one who really helped get me out of my funk and get proactive. He suggested that I approach the past year like I'm in lawyer mode. He said I should build my case and present you with the evidence. Bombard you with it. He also thought I should write you emails all year, but you asked me to give you space. So I figured spamming your inbox probably wasn't the best idea...."

She paused to take a deep breath. She knew she needed to slow down and make sure she said all of this just right. It was her big chance to state her case, and she didn't want to mess it up with poorly chosen words.

"So, instead of sending emails, I just started writing you letters. Documenting the changes I was making and the ways I was working to better myself and find my way back to you. To *us*. Then I figured I'd start off by giving you the letters and letting you witness our year apart through my eyes."

"Oh, yeah, that's...um," John took a deep breath and then released it slowly. "Thank you, Liv. That was a great idea. I'll start reading them tonight."

"Great," she replied, beaming into his face. *He's going to read the letters, and then he'll start to understand and believe!* "No more misunderstandings between us, no more uncertainty, John. Cards fully out on the table: I came here today to fight for you. To fight for *us*. That is absolutely the truth, and I can only hope you'll grow to believe me when I tell you that. The only questions I have right now are about what you're thinking and feeling and what *you* want now. All I know is what you just told me, that you almost didn't come here today. Why *did* you come? What do you want to happen between us?"

"I had no idea which way things would go today," he began. "When we split up last year, it was so you could go figure out why *you* broke up with *me*. I truly had no clue which way you were going to go, but I was pretty sure I'd be receiving divorce papers long before this day arrived. Then the year was over, and I was left wondering what I'd find if I came here. Would the woman who married me just to be nice be the one to show up? Or would the woman who begged me not to divorce her come instead? After everything that went down between us, well...it wasn't hard to assume the worst." He reached out and touched her hand just then, and she laced her fingers with his in response. "But in the end, Liv, I decided I'd take any risk in the world to be with you, even just to see your face again one last time. I came because...nothing could keep me away, I guess. No matter how small our chances of ending up together, I had to at least show up and find out."

Relief flooded through her with the strength of a tsunami. "I'm so glad you took the risk," she said. "It'll be better this time. I promise you that much. I want this marriage to work, and I'm not going to give up, ever."

John smiled and squeezed her hand gently. "Okay, then you should know one thing."

For just a moment, fear fluttered in Olivia's stomach again. "What's that?"

"I think I've spent as much time in the *Louvre* relationship room as I can possibly take. How about we walk around and see exhibits we missed the first time?"

Olivia couldn't hold back a smile that lit her whole face.

"Sure, let's do it," she said, and they began to walk toward the nearest hallway.

She glanced over at him and found nothing but hope on his face. It felt wonderful to see him so happy. She hadn't seen that carefree look—except in their wedding pictures—since that horrible flight one year ago. She needed to make sure it stayed right where it was, and that he never had another reason to doubt her again.

She'd make sure of it.

Chapter 51

The First Letter

JOHN LAY DOWN on his hotel bed, tired from the long day he and Olivia had spent exploring the *Louvre*. His exhaustion mingled, however, with the relief and happiness he felt at the way everything else had turned out. It so easily could have gone differently, and almost all of those options were extremely bad. Yet somehow that hadn't happened. Except for the misunderstanding about the envelope of letters, it had been almost perfect. Almost as though he'd scripted it. She had been there, and she still wanted to work on the marriage, just as she promised. It was almost enough to make him forget the last time they'd been at the museum together.

Almost...but not quite. The truth was, he wasn't quite ready to jump back in with both feet. They still had a long way to go, and his default setting—which was to doubt her intentions—was deeply ingrained. Was she really in tune with what she wanted this time, or was this all guilt over last year's spectacular meltdown, driving her to say the words he so desperately wanted to hear? Was it all still an illusion? He just couldn't tell. That was the biggest problem and what was really holding him back, keeping his guard up and firmly locked in place around his heart. How could he ever really know? He sure hadn't known what she was thinking and feeling on their wedding day. Now he continued to doubt his ability to read her at all.

That was why he'd been so quick to assume the worst when she'd handed him that envelope. Believing she'd flown all the way to Paris to serve him with papers immediately? That was easy. Believing she'd spent the entire year concocting a master plan to win him back? That was tougher to accept. Much tougher. It meant trusting in her. Trusting in their future together. Letting go of the pain of rejection and all the doubts that had been planted on that plane.

With a sigh, John reached up and flipped on the reading light. Then he leaned over and grabbed the envelope off the bedside table. It was time to start reading her letters. He slid his finger under the flap, loosening the seal, then pulled out the stack of pages. He flipped through them briefly. He could see each letter ended with her familiar script signature at the bottom. *Love, Olivia*, she'd signed them. That was encouraging...wasn't it?

Exhaling slowly, he went to the start of the first letter, which was dated about a week after the last time he saw her—

Dear John,

I flew home from Paris yesterday and landed safely this morning. I went to visit Charlie first thing. You're not going to believe this, but he's not mad at me! I was so surprised, but our relationship is right back to what it used to be, which is a greater relief to me than I can express.

I know you don't want to see me, but if we're apart, how can I ever convince you that I'm taking our separation seriously and truly working to save our marriage? So please, I beg of you, read my letters, and keep your mind and heart open to learning about what I'm doing in the coming months. If you don't, I'm not sure how I can make you understand and believe and trust me.

I know you're feeling beaten up and abused, and that you've got no reason to ever trust me again. But I have to try, both for you and for me. So, with self-improvement on my mind, I called a therapist and made an appointment for the day after tomorrow. I'm going to start seeing her regularly so I can work through what happened. And, like I mentioned to you, I want to take some Spanish classes. I'm also thinking about volunteering at the animal shelter.

Anyway, I'm not going to bother trying to convince you with mere words how I feel about you or how committed I am to this marriage. Clearly, words alone won't work, or you wouldn't have asked for this time apart. Instead, I'm going to let my actions do my pleading and convincing for me. I'm looking deep inside myself and making some changes, but always with the goal of being with you again. You'll see the proof.

Love,

Olivia

John read it three times before setting it down. He flipped off the light again, leaned back on the pillows, and closed his eyes. *She wrote that letter, and the others in the stack, on Charlie's advice...?*

He smiled. He was so glad Charlie had listened to him and hadn't stayed mad at her. She'd really needed her dad's support when she got back from Paris last year. Knowing that Olivia had him to lean on was pretty much all he had for comfort in those early days of the separation. It had made him feel like she'd be all right, and then he could be free to move forward and forget about her.

Now it was a year later, and he hadn't moved forward at all. And he certainly hadn't forgotten about her or his feelings for her. They were as strong as on their wedding day, when he pledged to love her forever. But it seemed like Charlie had played a big part in helping her devise her campaign to convince him of her feelings. Had Charlie lied to him about staying out of it? Had he actually been twisting Olivia's arm this year, making her act out of guilt more than anything else? It was hard to tell. He didn't think so, though. It didn't sound like it in that first letter.

John flipped the light back on and reread it, analyzing the words she'd chosen. No, she hadn't said anything about Charlie convincing her. She just talked about counseling and self-improvement. That didn't seem so ominous.

Then he decided he wasn't going to pick her words apart any further. If they were going to move forward, he had to put some effort into this, too. The first step was working to let himself believe her and take her words at face value. If he could do that, then maybe things just might work out this time.

He could believe at least that much.

Chapter 52

Carefree Afternoon

THEY DUCKED INTO a café for an early lunch, then walked back to Notre Dame. They stopped in the plaza out front so Olivia could take some pictures of the famous façade.

"Did you read any of my letters?" she finally asked.

"The first one," John said, a half-smile tentatively appearing on his lips. "Repeatedly, in fact. Thank you for...I don't know. For really taking this year seriously, I guess. And for looking for ways to make this—make *us*—right again. It gave me hope that we're really on the right path."

"Oh, John, I've got it, too! Hope, I mean. I've got *lots* of hope. I feel like this is all very tenuous and fragile, but it also feels right. And I wanted to tell you that I am absolutely blown away by the strength you showed by coming back to Paris."

"You don't have to—" he began, but Olivia cut him off again.

"No, please let me say this. Hearing you explain things yesterday from your perspective and knowing that you came here almost totally convinced that I was going to break your heart again, I...I am completely in awe of you. Maybe I didn't know lots of details about your many talents and your likes and dislikes and all of that, but I always knew what a strong man you were. And I always knew how forgiving you were, too. I can't express to you how important those qualities are to me.

I showed up yesterday just as scared as you were, and then I got tied up in knots when you appeared so different. But I looked into your face, and I could still see it all there. The kindness and the generosity of spirit. It's what draws me to you. I *adore* those qualities, I really do. And I know that's what brought you to the museum yesterday. I'll be grateful for the rest of my life that you gave us this chance."

"Liv, let's find a bench and sit down," John said in reply, lightly taking her hand and leading her through the crowd. He continued until they found a place to sit. Once they did, he kept her hand in his own, swirling his fingers lightly across her palm, seemingly lost in thought.

"Did I say something wrong back there?" Olivia started. "I really did mean those things I said."

"No, I appreciated all of that," he assured her. "And reading your letter last night made me think about this situation we find ourselves in. It *really* made me question how we're ever going to be able to fix things."

"Oh John, please don't ask me for more time apart. I can't take living my life in this limbo any longer. Don't say it."

"No," John said quickly. "I agree that there's no reason to drag this out any longer."

"No! You're breaking up with me, aren't you? John! I am so serious about working hard on this, but you've got to give it longer than a day! I—"

"Livvie! Geez already, let me get a chance to string two sentences together," John said, laughing now. "You aren't in court, Liv! You don't need to object constantly!"

"Okay, yes, sorry," she replied, trying to rein in her

zigzagging emotions. "I don't know what's wrong with me. I'm so jumpy. Okay, yes, go on...."

"I understand why you're so jumpy," John acknowledged. "I was, too, yesterday when you pulled your letters out. We're both really in a vulnerable spot right now, and obviously we're both quick to assume everything is falling apart again, given even the smallest bit of evidence. We both seriously need to calm down. Like, a *lot.*"

"Yeah, I agree. I definitely am...unsure about what to say to you," Olivia said, nodding. "I don't know how to handle this. I feel like I'm negotiating a minefield without a map."

"Do minefields come with maps?" he asked, a teasing glint in his eyes.

"They should. At the visitor's center?" Olivia's smile slowly fell away. "I'm serious, though. This...isn't easy."

"I know, and that's what I was trying to say before. We have to make a plan for our time here and try to promise each other that we will work not to jump to conclusions or give up easily. Let's spend a few days talking and getting acquainted again. Like we're dating and doing it right this time."

"That makes sense to me," Olivia said, thrilled that he was suggesting it.

"I think it'd be a big mistake if we jumped into being together and didn't use this time to face or deal with things," he continued. "We have pretty solid evidence that says when you and I get together, we get super comfortable and unable to see any issues between us. We dated for a whole year on cruise control, Liv. That's how we ended up standing at the altar with a world of problems that we'd never even acknowledged.

I feel like if we go home with things still unspoken and unresolved, we're going to slip right back. It's so easy for us to be together. Too easy. We know that we can pull off the day-to-day stuff. It's the deeper connection that we messed up the first time around."

"I still want you to keep reading my letters," Olivia told him. "I offer up my every thought and emotion to you in them. I really do think they're a huge step toward getting this right."

"I will," John said with a nod. "Of course. But I want to sort of take my time with them, not race through them in one sitting. I'm trying to rebuild my ability to trust you. But it's not going to happen in a single afternoon."

"Oh, no, of course not," Olivia said, feeling a little frustrated. Hadn't the fact that she'd spent a whole year working on ways to save the marriage rebuilt any trust already? She felt weary, like the jangling nerves and emotions and worries had taken all her energy for a whole year, and now the terrible thought that maybe all she'd done might still not be enough was sapping any remaining strength she had. "I was wondering...could we perhaps have a completely carefree afternoon together today? I don't want to talk about any of this for the time being. I'm weary, John. Do you think, maybe, we could slip into our old comfortable zone until tomorrow? I'm sure all the heavy stuff will be right there waiting for us."

"Sure, okay," John said, taking her hand again. "I can make that deal. One completely carefree afternoon together? I can do that. No guilt or accusations, and no worrying that anything we say will send the other person running in the opposite direction."

"Yes. It'll feel so good to just be a normal couple

again, even if it's only for an afternoon."

John stood then, gently pulling her up, too. She squeezed his hand back, happy to follow him wherever he decided to go. He started toward the Notre Dame cathedral, which was perfectly fine with her. A normal, stress-free day with her gorgeous husband was *exactly* what she needed. She hadn't felt like herself in such a long time.

*   *   *

They spent the next several hours wandering around the exterior of the cathedral and the surrounding neighborhood, including a stroll along the pedestrian walkways that lined the Seine River, which was dotted with painters and performers. And when John confessed that he was starving and asked if she'd have dinner with him, she was delighted.

They found a restaurant nearby that didn't need reservations, *La Brasserie de l'Isle Saint-Louis*. They feasted on steaks and wine and a shared caramel-custard dessert while John told Olivia about the houses he'd helped build that past year and the joy he'd felt when families were able to move into them.

"Now why don't you tell me something more about *your* year," he said as he took another sip of wine.

"I...no, that's okay. This is my free day, remember?" she replied. "I just want to forget about anything that doesn't have to do with you being here with me right now, in this moment. Just for tonight?"

"Sure, Liv. I'm not trying to push you. I'm just curious about the journey you've been on."

"That's what the letters are for," she said, smiling again. "Read more of them when you get back to your room tonight. Unless...you want company?"

Oh God, no....

Olivia couldn't believe she'd just blurted out that suggestion. So much for taking things slowly. The peace between them was fragile. She needed to keep reminding herself to be cautious.

John looked at her, a sad wistful smile flickering on his lips. "Oh, you have no idea how badly I want to take you back to my room tonight, Liv. But that wouldn't help us get all our issues ironed out. In fact, I think it'd have the opposite effect. If we spent the night together, I don't think we'd leave the bed again for two weeks."

Olivia didn't know if it was the wine, the mental picture John had given her of the two of them happily spending two weeks together in bed, or some combination of the two, but she was suddenly burning up. She put her palm against her cheek and could feel the heat radiating there. Good thing she had a dark complexion, or she'd be bright red.

And now he's looking at me as though waiting for a reply. Wait...what did he just say?

"Uh...yeah, that would be terrible if we spent our time here in bed," she replied, hoping that was somehow connected to his last comment. "Horrible outcome, really. The worst."

John laughed.

Olivia smiled back at him in spite of her growing unease.

"We'll get through this, Liv," he told her. "I'm more sure of it with every passing moment. Let's just hash all of this out so we can put it behind us, okay?"

"Okay, sure," she agreed. "Like I said before, I'm all in."

They shared a cab back to Olivia's hotel. John paid the driver, then turned back to face her. She was hesitating near the door. He reached over, took her hand, and held it for a moment as he studied her face. Finally, he squeezed her hand then let go, dropping his arm back to his side as he took a step back.

"I'm not even going to kiss you," he said, "or my resolve will completely melt away."

"You're sure?" Olivia asked, then mentally gave herself another kick. *Honestly!*

"You said you were in!" John reminded her with a laugh, rubbing his temple like he was trying to ward off a headache. "Get out of here already, and we'll meet back here at nine for breakfast."

"Okay," she said with a tiny smile and wave, "See you tomorrow. Good night." Then she turned and headed for the elevator as happiness surged through her. She'd had a terrific time, and he'd talked about them making it! This was it. It was happening.

They were finally about to finish weathering this storm.

Chapter 53

The Second Letter

JOHN WALKED all the way back to his hotel, which was probably about a mile away, but he was grateful for the exercise. It helped take his mind off what he really wanted to be doing that night instead of returning to his empty hotel room.

When he finally got there, he kicked off his shoes, flopped back on the bed, and turned on the reading light. He was filled with curiosity about what else Olivia's year had brought her and took the next letter in hand—

Dear John,

You wouldn't believe what I did today! I went to the animal shelter and signed up to volunteer on the weekends. It's not glamorous work; I'll be taking dogs for walks, sifting through kitty litter, cleaning cages, those kinds of chores. But it feels marvelous. Other than tossing a check at the shelter each Christmas, I've never done anything to support or care for homeless animals, which is a cause I supposedly believe in very deeply. It's just one more indication to me of how self-involved I've somehow let myself become. The biggest indication of that, of course, was how I was so wrapped up in my own head that I didn't learn much about you during the year we were dating. I soon realized I'd barely even begun to peel back the layers and uncover the real you. I think sometimes about how over the moon I would have been for you on our wedding day if I'd spent a whole year getting to know you in the right way.

I took another huge step today and adopted a puppy! I think having another living, breathing being in the house, and one that is totally dependent on me for its survival and affection, will be a good way to help me this year. And he's just so adorable, John! You're absolutely going to love him. He's a shepherd mix, and I'll bet he's going to be 70 or 80 pounds when he's done growing. He's tan with black markings on his face and tail, but his feet are white like he's wearing little socks. I can't wait to introduce the two of you. Anyway, I named him Eiffel, which is one of many sites I want to visit with you when we meet again in Paris next year. He's sitting on my lap right now and says to tell you hi.

Well, I'd better wrap this up. I've got to go buy Eiffel some toys and food and treats and whatever else a growing boy needs. Please take care of yourself.

Love,

Olivia

He read the letter twice, then set it aside. The first one had made him so hopeful, but this one had left him feeling a little...worried? Her life had changed so much, and so quickly. Was there really room in it for him? And probably what bothered him most was that she'd gotten a dog without even considering him. He happened to be a huge dog lover, but since this was Olivia he was dealing with, really, what were the chances that she had any idea whether he liked dogs or not? He could be allergic to them, and she would've had no idea. Had fitting him permanently into her life really been her goal? Was building a real marriage what she was after, or was getting rid of her guilt the objective? How could she honestly want a life with him when she barely knew him at all?

He was tired of the uncertainty. He got up, tossed the letter on the stack, and dug around for his sweats. Hopefully the gym was still open. Working out was what he needed. Nothing else felt more real than pushing himself to the limits of exhaustion.

He needed that now more than ever.

*   *   *

He woke up the next morning still feeling depressed about the situation. On the one hand, she was here and saying all the right things, the things he had barely let himself believe she'd ever say to him. On the other hand, she obviously wasn't planning to live her life with him if she was making huge decisions like adopting a dog without taking him into consideration. Had they ever talked about getting a pet together? He couldn't remember for certain, but he didn't think so. And if he didn't remember them talking about it, Olivia likely didn't, either. *Come on, face it—she probably doesn't even know I have brown hair and green eyes.*

He rolled those eyes now and sat up, rubbing his face with his hands. Lying here feeling annoyed wasn't going to solve anything. It was still early, though. He wasn't due to meet her until nine. Plenty of time for a run. He did all his best thinking while running. There was no better way to clear his head and gain a little perspective.

Twenty minutes later he was jogging along the Seine, happy to be out of that hotel room. He was tired of the way things were. Tired of living alone. Tired of being in exile from his home and family. But mostly he was tired of hurting. He needed to get past this new annoyance he felt after reading the second letter— which, really, in the ocean of problems between them, was nothing more than a tiny drop—and find his focus again.

Stay methodical. Meet her today. Get everything out on the table and then, please God, just move past it.

He would love to be able to live in a world where every conversation with his wife didn't somehow head right back to that devastating moment on the plane when she told him she'd never loved him. Finally being able to bury that memory would be the most fantastic gift of all. He had to keep moving forward on this journey with her if he wanted to get to that place. One step at a time, just like his morning run. He could do it.

By the time he returned to the hotel, showered, and changed, he was at least resolved to stay on the course they'd agreed to the day before, if not exactly in the best of moods. *Oh well, how festive do you really need to feel to work on a mountain of problems with your estranged wife?* he asked himself as he entered the elevator. This wasn't going to be a ton of fun no matter how he was feeling. Hopefully, they could just get it over with quickly.

*　　*　　*

Outside her hotel, she looked more chipper than he was feeling as she stepped out of the front entrance. *Good, maybe she'll keep things light,* John thought, forcing a smile as he greeted her.

"Hi," he said. "Let's go get this over with, I guess."

"Now there's the attitude," Olivia replied, looking a little less certain as the smile on her face haltingly disappeared.

Oops, how grumpy did I just sound? he wondered. "Sorry Liv, I'm just not...I don't know. Wrong side of the bed this morning, I guess. I don't mean to be snapping at you. Let's just go have breakfast and see where the day takes us."

As they entered a nearby café a short time later, an uneasy quiet settled between them.

"Okay, we've got a billion problems, and we've got the time," Olivia said in an obvious attempt to diffuse it. "So how are we going to fix this? What do we need to do or talk about to be able to move forward?"

"I'd say the biggest thing is that we didn't know each other. More specifically, you didn't know me," John said, sounding churlish even to his own ears. "Maybe we start there?"

Olivia shook her head in frustration. "All right, just spill it. What's bothering you? You're not yourself this morning. What changed? We had a great time yesterday, and I thought we were both feeling so hopeful. Don't you want to do this anymore? I thought we were both resolved to try."

"Yeah, I know. Sorry. Okay, well, if you really want to know, it's this exact topic. You didn't know anything about me, right? But you adopted a dog? Really?" He stopped to ask the waiter for coffee, then they both placed their order. "Did you stop to wonder if I like dogs?" he went on. "If I even wanted one? That maybe I'm a cat person? And that, if we were going to adopt a dog, maybe I'd want to pick it out *with* you? It made me feel like you don't actually have a place for me in your life or any intention of moving forward as a real married couple in a functioning relationship. It's stupid, I know, but it seemed symbolic of how far off course we are."

"I hear what you're saying," Olivia answered slowly, being very deliberate with every word. "Totally my fault. I obviously messed up again. But, well, since you had a dog as a kid, I guess I just assumed you wouldn't mind."

"Wait, what?" John asked, astonished now. "You knew I had a dog growing up?"

"Yeah, you told me about it, don't you remember? We were watching something on Netflix at your place, and you said something about the dog in the show reminding you of your dog when you were a kid. Don't you remember saying that? And I made some dumb joke about how maybe someone would get us designer dog dishes for our wedding."

"Wow, yeah, okay," John said, nodding as the memory came back to him. "I do remember that."

"Wasn't it an Irish setter?" Olivia continued. "No, wait, golden retriever!"

"Yellow lab," John said with a smirk, pausing to accept his coffee from the waiter, then looking back at Olivia in amazement. "That's right. Wow...."

"Your parents got it for you and your sister for Christmas one year, and I think...didn't you name it...I want to say...Lucy?"

"Lucky."

A smile crept across her face, along with a slow dawning of excitement.

"Do you see what just happened here?" she asked him.

"Yeah, I think so. Did you actually just now realize that you knew one small detail about me before you married me?" he asked with a laugh, setting the cup and saucer down with a light clink.

"I think I did! I knew you liked dogs! Yes!" Olivia said, looking triumphant now. "See? I wasn't being *completely* thoughtless when I adopted Eiffel. Would I rather have had you there with me to help pick him out? Of course! But you didn't exactly give me a lot of options for our year apart, John. You didn't want to see me and presumably you didn't want to adopt animals with me. You wanted space, so I was working hard and using every idea I could come up with to survive the year and find ways to prove to you that I was changing. Taking care of Eiffel was a huge part of that healing process for me. He's essentially my therapy dog."

"I'm glad you got him, Liv, I really am. And I'm sorry that I overreacted about it. This is all such uncharted territory, and I never know how I'm going to feel from one minute to the next. It's hard to figure out if we're going to navigate our way through it, especially when every little thing keeps setting us off."

"John, here's the thing," Olivia continued cautiously. "You've got to stop wondering *if* we're going to make it. The question is *how* we're going to make it. Stop saying or thinking 'if'. You and me? This is it. We're happening. Get used to it."

John took a sip of his coffee as he contemplated her words. They sounded great, but...he just wasn't there yet. She might not want to hear it, but part of him still wondered if this was all going to work out the way they hoped it would.

"I'll try, Livvie," he said finally. "I really will try."

Chapter 54

Another Day Together

"WHERE TO?" John asked after they'd finished breakfast.

"Let's just walk a while," Olivia suggested, and they started down the sidewalk in companionable silence. She tentatively reached for his hand and was happy when he accepted it, wrapping it snugly in his own.

She felt bad about the way he had reacted to her letter about Eiffel. Adopting that dog had been nothing but wonderful. He loved her completely and without question, racing to the door to greet her every single day as though they'd been separated for years instead of hours or minutes. Not much could rival the affection of a loyal dog, and she had desperately needed that acceptance and love during the past year. Surely John could understand that. And she knew that Eiffel and John would immediately fall in love with each other. Eiffel would probably switch his allegiance to John within the first ten minutes.

It was easy to see it from John's point of view, though, considering it evidence that she wasn't really planning a life with him. But it was still frustrating. If he didn't view the letters as proof that she'd made changes for the better and wanted to stay married to him, then they would never be able to rebuild the trust. And if he could never believe her and trust in her love...well, then this was all a colossal waste of time.

Now that's a depressing thought. Was there really a chance they could go through all this and still decide to go home and file the divorce papers? The thought spiked through her heart like an icy spear. There really still was a huge chance this wasn't going to work out. Suddenly she realized John had stopped walking and was watching her, his face wary.

"What is it?" he asked. "You look like you're about to hyperventilate."

"I...I'm sorry," she said. "I was just having a bit of a panic attack."

"About what?" he asked, gentle concern emanating from his face as he reached up to cup her cheek gently in his hand. She closed her eyes and leaned into the warmth and comfort he was offering.

"About...about all of this, I guess. I was just thinking that if my letters weren't helping you to believe that I really am dedicated to working on us, then I don't know how I'll ever prove it. And if I can't prove it, then this is all going to end the same way it did last year, with you pushing me away. Only this time you won't give me a year, you'll just want a divorce, and...."

"Livvie?"

"...and I don't want a divorce, John, I don't. I worked all year to make sure you really understood how much I don't want it, but...."

"Liv, honey, please just stop."

"...then you still don't believe m—wait, what?"

John reached down then and grabbed both of her hands, gently pulling her toward the façade of the building they were standing in front of. "What's this really about?"

"I—I'm just...," Olivia looked down for a long moment, trying to gather her thoughts. What did she want him to say? Nothing. Nothing could ever really fix this. "You scared me before. I'm just...petrified I'm going to lose you. And I'm terrified that there's absolutely nothing I could ever do to take away the pain I inflicted that day on the plane."

"Liv, with all the time that's passed and with everything that's happened...well, I'm just going to ask this: Did you ever forgive *yourself* for everything that happened? You need to, sweetheart. If you can't let it go, neither can I. And I seriously want to just let it go. Please forgive yourself already."

"Okay, I've never understood that," Olivia said, shaking her head as she looked up at him. "*You* were telling me within days of our breakup that you forgave me. But that's just crazy. It makes no sense. You should hate me for it. In some ways, *I* do."

"That's what I thought was eating away at you. You've got to stop it, Olivia. Let. It. Go. I wasn't lying when I said I forgave you. I get why it happened. I understand. Please honey, just forgive yourself. Didn't you cover this in all that therapy you've been in all year?"

"Yeah, well, obviously I might have a lingering issue or two," Olivia said with a small laugh as she leaned into him, wrapping her arms around his waist. "How do you do it? How do you have such a forgiving heart after all the craziness we've been through?"

"I don't know, it's just in my nature, I guess." He smiled then. "Don't tell anyone, but forgiving ex-wives is actually my secret superpower."

"Oh, come on, that's just sad. You need to demand a refund. Try to exchange it for the ability to fly or, I don't know, X-ray vision or something more useful," she teased. "I mean really, how often is the mayor going to need to signal you with that lame superpower?"

"I think it's come in pretty handy," John said, hugging her back now. "At least about three times that I can think of off the top of my head. I'd be pretty miserable right now if anger had been eating away at me all these years."

"And I'd be pretty miserable, too, if you hadn't forgiven me. Thank you for that."

"You're welcome."

Olivia tightened her hold on him and tried not to think anymore about the possibility of ever having to let go.

Chapter 55

Filling in the Gaps

THEY WANDERED around with no destination the rest of the afternoon, mostly stopping when window displays caught their attention. Eventually they decided to get some coffee, sitting down under the umbrella of an outside table.

As Olivia stirred hers, watching the swirl of the cream, she said, "I know you've said repeatedly that you're not hanging the exclusive blame for everything on me, and that you're not keeping score. But it's been hard for me not to keep score and blame myself. That's a lot of what I talked to the therapist about this past year. I think some of the issue is that I lost my mom so young. I never knew her, which of course meant I was raised by a single dad. He's the best father anyone could ever ask for, but under those circumstances...." She trailed off, pausing to take a sip, while John watched and waited. "He never got remarried. He never even dated really. So, although I always knew theirs had been a happy marriage, I never got to see it up close."

"A lot of people are raised by single parents," John reminded her.

"Of course, and I'm not saying that if you are raised by a single parent, then you automatically don't know anything about love and marriage, of course. And I know there are thousands of people out there who *were* raised by two parents who were miserable in those marriages. No one's childhood is going to be perfect."

"Of course not."

"All I'm saying is that I really do think in my particular situation, it made things harder for me. I wasn't as self-aware as I could have been about the things I wanted in a marriage. I don't think I knew what I was looking for. Does that make sense?"

"I guess so," John said with a shrug.

"So, I don't know, I dated and dated for years without finding anyone I even remotely wanted to marry, and I eventually ended up doubting myself. By the time I got into my late thirties, I think in a way I had given up trying. You reach a certain age, and part of you thinks that maybe your standards are too high, that you've been dismissing perfectly wonderful partners for silly reasons. But you don't want to just take any old guy who happens to still be single. Like, am I being too quick to overlook this man's faults? Am I latching onto the first guy who comes along and doesn't have a travel store worth of baggage?"

"So, what?" John asked, "You married me because you thought I didn't have baggage?"

"I think that I knew you were someone I could depend on. Someone who would love me and be good to me," she replied cautiously. "And I think beyond that, I had so fully given up trying to find a Prince Charming, and I was so tired of being let down by the whole dating process, that I was completely blind to the fact that, duh, my perfect match was standing right there in front of me. And...oh, I'm not explaining this well at all."

"Yeah, I'm not sure I'm hearing what you're trying to tell me," John said. "I'm no Prince Charming? Is that your point?"

"No! John, you *are*, that's what I'm trying to say.

You totally are. But I doubted *myself*. I didn't really trust that I knew what I was looking for. And if you don't know what you're looking for, then how will that search ever end well? How can you see that you've found what you're looking for—truly realize that it's right in front of you—when you have no idea what it is that you've been seeking? Does that make more sense?"

"Well, I guess so. In fact, I may have been doing the same thing, only I was dumb enough to marry a couple of the 'close-but-not-quite-right' people I met along the way. It's not like my journey to find you was much smoother. But maybe it's because I'd lived through those failed marriages that I had such a clear vision of precisely what I wanted. When I met you, it absolutely clicked into place for me. I just knew it. You were the one, and I had no doubts. Maybe I was so certain of our future together that I just bulldozed us into it. I never even formally asked you to marry me, which I can see now was incredibly stupid. Maybe if I had, it would've forced you to analyze your feelings before the actual wedding. In the end, I guess I was just so certain that I pushed us forward without realizing you hadn't caught up to me in that place of total certainty. It's like I was so convinced about it that it never occurred to me to question it."

"This is the part I could never figure out while I was sorting through everything this past year," Olivia replied as her fingers began idly playing with the sugar packets. "I thought people are supposed to get wiser with age. Getting married at forty should have given me so many advantages, right? I should have had more clarity, more insight into life, more...wisdom, I guess. But I honestly believe that it made everything worse. It made me question things in a way I wouldn't have if we'd gotten married straight out of college."

"I tried that route too, though, remember?" John reminded her. "With Val, we were just too young. I don't think there's a *perfect* age, and it's really all about timing. Finding the right person when you're both at the time in your life where you're equally ready for the commitment, I guess. I think there's a lot of luck and chance and perfect timing involved too, along with the clarity and wisdom."

"Yes, I guess so," Olivia said. "It's amazing anyone ever figures this all out and makes it work."

"Every journey is different. For a variety of reasons, and due to the things you just mentioned, you just weren't ready. It wasn't our time yet. Let's accept the premise that we definitely got married too soon. If we'd just taken a little more time, this might not have happened." John paused here, looking thoughtful. "That's probably where our ages really come into play. When you're young you want to wait until you finish school or save up enough money or get established in your career. But we had our degrees and our careers and our savings accounts. So there was nothing standing in the way, forcing us to take our time. I think the older you are, the less you want to wait around and delay the next stage of your life, even if you really should."

Olivia nodded in silent agreement.

"Look Liv, I think the most important thing for you to remember is that we both did dumb stuff that got us to this point. Stop looking at it like we're on a mission to discover exactly how many ways *you* messed up. That's not what this is about."

"Okay, okay," she said, eager for a topic change. "I have a request."

"Name it."

"We passed by a music store a block ago or two. Can we walk back to it?" she asked, looking hopeful.

"You mean like old vinyls?"

"Not that kind of music store. It had instruments. I'm dying to hear you play guitar. I have been all year, since you first told me you played."

"Oh, well, sure, I guess. It's been a while," he said. "And trust me, you didn't exactly marry Eddie Van Halen."

"Jimi Hendrix?"

"Oh yeah, well sure, I'm way better than him," John teased. "Hendrix had nothing on me."

*   *   *

They found the music store, which had a small sound booth for trying the instruments. John picked out an acoustic guitar, but they had to wait. A boy who looked to Olivia like he couldn't have been more than twelve was practicing his chords.

"I'm not much more advanced than he is, you know," John said as the boy started producing a particularly discordant tune.

"Oh stop. I just want to hear you play," she said. "Even if you can only do...what's the guitar equivalent of *Chopsticks?*"

"I don't know. Chopstrings? Oh wait, here he comes," John said as the door opened and the boy walked out, looking self-conscious that he'd had an audience.

They went into the booth and John sat on the stool, perching the guitar on his knee. He tried a few chords to get the feel of the instrument. Then with a smile he said, "Okay, you asked for it. Here it goes."

She sank to the floor and wrapped her arms

around her legs, closing her eyes in anticipation as John began to strum. He played some songs she knew, both rock classics and more recent hits, as well as a few she didn't. Then he finished with *More Than Words* by Extreme—one of her favorites.

"Oh John, that was beautiful!" she said, her eyes sparkling. "I've always loved that last song!"

"Yeah, I know," he said. "I thought about playing it for you at our wedding reception, but I chickened out."

"It means so much to me that you thought about it, though. I guess in a way I'm glad you didn't. I don't know if I would have appreciated it like I should have. I was such a mess that day.... But seriously, why didn't I know you played? I've never seen a guitar at your apartment."

"Oh, it was there. In a closet. I don't know. I taught myself when I was pretty young. I used to play all the time and then I just, I don't know. Stopped." He got up then and reached out to help Olivia do the same.

"When we get home, I want you to serenade me every day for the rest of our lives. That was just so beautiful."

She leaned toward him and wanted to kiss him, something she'd been dying to do since he picked up the guitar. *There's nothing sexier than a man holding a guitar*, she thought.

John looked down at her and seemed to be leaning toward a kiss, too. But a knock at the door startled them both, causing her to jump backward awkwardly.

"I guess we've outstayed our welcome," she said.

"I guess so," he agreed.

They returned the guitar to its hanger and headed back outside.

"Do you want to go get something to eat?" Olivia asked on the sidewalk, looking at her phone to check the time.

"Nah, you know, it's been a long day. Why don't we just quit while we're ahead? You still game to keep doing this? We'll meet again tomorrow?"

"Yes, definitely," Olivia said, suddenly feeling awkward again.

When will things between us just be comfortable? *Will they ever???*

John walked her back to her hotel and said goodbye, then headed back to his own hotel. Olivia smiled as she watched him go. The more sides she saw of him, and the more time she spent really getting to know him, the more she wanted to save the marriage.

It was all going to be worth it in the end, she reminded herself.

Chapter 56

Montmartre

THE NEXT DAY they decided to take the subway to *Montmartre*, not far from the Basilica of the *Sacré Cœur.*

"The basilica's on the highest point in the city," John offered cheerfully. It felt good to just be with her. "There are amazing views from the dome, if you want to go there."

"It's really beautiful," Olivia admitted. "I wouldn't mind taking some pictures of the outside of it. But I'm not overly motivated to climb a ton of stairs, I guess. I seriously should have been working out this year, too. So...I guess let's just wander around. I think it would be hard to top the view at the Eiffel Tower anyway."

"Okay, sure," John said. "Pick a direction."

As they walked along, they watched the crowds of busy people milling around them.

"It seems strange to see people busy working and going about their lives," Olivia observed after a few blocks. "We're sort of stuck in an artificial state of suspended animation right now. Not quite on a vacation. Definitely not back in the real world. Sort of stuck in the past and yet moving forward. And we're surrounded by people just going about their normal lives. Working, pursuing their dreams, raising their families."

"Speaking of families," John began, "we should talk about kids. Do you still want them after everything that's happened? That's like the one thing we *did* talk about before we got married—we both wanted kids."

"Yeah, I do. I still feel exactly the way I felt back then. If we're lucky enough to get pregnant, that would be fabulous. But another year has passed us by. I have no idea if I can even get pregnant or if I'm too old now or what. I don't want to end up getting my hopes up for no good reason. I want to just see what our future holds and to keep spending time getting to know each other. Anything more would be...." As Olivia trailed off, John turned and looked expectantly at her, waiting for her to finish the thought.

She took a deep breath and started again. "I feel so blessed to be getting a second chance with you. I don't want to tempt the fates by asking for even more good fortune on top of that, you know?"

"We've been given a huge gift here," he agreed. "Feels greedy to want more?"

"Right. How much more good luck could I possibly hope to have?" Olivia squeezed his hand for emphasis. "I feel like I used up every ounce when I showed up at the *Louvre* a few days ago and found you standing there."

"I hear what you're saying. I think it's smart for us not to jump from this mess straight into a panic about whether we can start a family. Just remember, though, that our ages are working against us. If we were younger, we'd have time to get through this and then leisurely figure out the family thing."

"Timing," Olivia agreed. "We are absolutely awful when it comes to timing."

John looked down at her with a swell of affection. "Oh, I don't know. I'll forever be grateful for the timing involved with us both going to that same work party where we met. We got it right that day, anyway."

Olivia nodded. "Yeah, me too."

"And by the way, I don't know if I can, either," John said. "Have kids, that is. I never tried with Val and Jackie. Never had any scares or near-misses with anyone. I was always careful."

"Well, we'll just see," she said. "It's a fresh canvas for both of us. We can see what happens together. And, of course, we could consider adoption or fostering, too. We do have options."

"Yep," John said.

Then Olivia gasped.

"What is it Liv?"

He followed her line of sight and discovered that they'd stumbled across the familiar red windmill of the *Moulin Rouge*.

"Phone!" she squealed happily, reaching in her bag. "I need my phone!"

John watched as she made her way across the street to gain a better angle, then take what appeared to be a few million pictures. Then she turned and took a few of him standing on the sidewalk waiting for her.

"Let's go see if they still have tickets for tonight!" she exclaimed when she came back.

"Are you a big cabaret fan," he asked, "or did you just like the movie?"

"I think it's mostly about Ewan McGregor," she replied with a smirk.

*   *   *

After they got their tickets, Olivia said there was no way she could wait until show time to eat. So they found a Thai place a few blocks away.

"This place is fabulous," Olivia said as they sat sipping their post-meal tea. "Thank you. Today was wonderful. I feel freer than I have in a long time. Things are getting more comfortable between us, I think."

"Yeah, I think so, too," he said, sitting back and considering her words more carefully. It was true, he thought. He was feeling more comfortable with her again.

"Where's your wedding ring?" she suddenly blurted out, breaking through his reverie. "I haven't seen it again since that day on the plane. Did you flush it down the airplane toilet? Use it to fund your trip to San Juan? Donate it to the poor?"

"Nah, I've still got it," John replied. "But no, I never put it back on again. It was burning a hole in my hand that day, or at least that's how it felt. I walked down the airplane aisle away from you and yanked it off and crammed it in my pocket and...I don't know. Not much else to say there. I didn't pawn it or anything. But, well, of course I haven't been wearing it. I was serious when I said that almost no part of me actually believed you'd come back to the *Louvre* wanting to reconcile."

"And where's the rest of your stuff?" Olivia went on. "I know you moved out of your apartment. In a moment of complete weakness, I showed up there once after I got back from Paris, and a little girl I'd never seen before answered the door. That was not...that was a definite low point for me."

"I wasn't doing so great, either," John said. "I packed all my stuff and put it into storage. That's when I gave up the apartment. My truck's parked at my parents' house. I came home for about a week to deal with all of that and was practically catatonic at that point. I just couldn't deal with any of it. Kate came over to see me. She was absolutely beside herself with worry, and she kept grilling me about it. But, I don't know. I refused to talk to any of them about what was going on with us, which was driving them all crazy. I don't know if they thought we'd broken up or I'd had a nervous breakdown. Maybe both. Then I finally went back to San Juan. It was too hard to be there. I don't know how you did it, I really don't. But I was strong in my resolve not to see you. I didn't even let myself drive anywhere near your apartment or office. So....yeah, that was a great trip. I haven't been home since, although I've at least taken the time to reassure my family over and over that I'm going to be okay."

"Wow, I'm sure they're going to be thrilled to see me," Olivia said.

"They just might," John replied. "I'm serious when I said I never told them anything. And I never will. It's not any of their business, especially if we can actually work through everything and go home together. Trust me when I say they'll be so glad I came back that nothing else will matter. They'll probably erect statues of you in the front yard."

Olivia laughed, then shook her head sadly. "I can't believe what we've been through, the two of us."

"Well, we're not going to spiral into depression today," John said, cutting her off before she could travel too far down the path of regrets. "We've got a can-can show to look forward to, remember? Gotta meet Ewan McGregor."

They paid their bill and walked out onto the street again.

"This is my favorite day," Olivia said, tucking her arm around his as they went along.

"Since we got here?" John asked.

"Since forever. I'm just really happy to be right here, right now, with you. It's good. More than good, in fact."

John wrapped his arm around her shoulder, then leaned over and kissed the side of her head.

"I'm happy to hear that," he told her, "because it's my favorite day too."

Chapter 57

Walking Away

THE NEXT DAY at breakfast, Olivia was stirring her coffee, lost in thought and worry, because she knew there was one more topic they hadn't touched on since their return to Paris: Samantha.

"What's got you looking so deep and reflective?" John asked, taking a bite of whatever egg dish he'd ordered. Olivia had been too distracted to hear what he'd told the waiter. She wasn't even sure what *she* was eating.

"Uh, well, to be honest, I was trying to figure out the best way to bring up something we haven't addressed yet," she said, looking up at him now. "And I still don't know the answer really, because—like a lot of them, I guess—this topic is an extremely touchy one."

"Oh, just jump in," John said with a sweep of his hand. "We've talked about a lot of touchy subjects. What's one more?"

"I guess. Okay...." She drew in a deep breath to steady her nerves. "The thing is, you haven't told me about what happened between you and Samantha this year."

"Are you serious?" John said, the look in his eyes immediately turning steely and fierce as he leaned toward her. "How many times do I have to tell you that *nothing* happened between us, and nothing was ever *going* to happen between us before you believe me?"

"I *do* believe you, but I don't know the details,"

Olivia pointed out. "I don't know if you ended up spending this entire year with her. You can remain faithful and still form an emotional connection with someone, you know. And that floats into a gray, fuzzy area that really might be interpreted as a *form* of cheating. You're a good guy, and I know you wouldn't have set out to fall for her. But, hey, maybe if I vanished, you'd have Samantha right there waiting for you with open arms. And maybe, in the end, you wouldn't think that was such a bad outcome."

"I didn't fall in love with Samantha this year!" John said, his voice a quietly furious hiss. "She showed up in San Juan for a few weeks, then she left. End of story."

"Really? That was it?" Olivia all but hissed back. "Just a casual wave across the building site crossbeams?" *How can he be so dismissive about this?* she wondered as anger started to take root in her chest. "She told me that day at the Eiffel Tower that she was going to consider you fair game and make her move once you left Paris. You're telling me now that she was just messing with me?"

"Well, maybe her big move was so subtle that I didn't pick up on it," John said, sitting back again, the intensity of the moment dissipating somewhat. "She asked about you, I was super vague and said that we're still working on the marriage, and that was it. We had dinner a couple times, but that's all that happened. I've told you she was nothing but a friend to me in Paris, but you still can't let it go, can you?"

"It's a little hard to just drop this subject as though it didn't matter, or as though it didn't have huge butterfly effects on our whole honeymoon. Yes, you're right! You got me! I *hate* the fact that you ran into Samantha and that you spent your honeymoon nights in her hotel room when you could have been with me, trying to sort out our issues. I hate it with the heat of a million suns. All the hotel rooms were full. If it hadn't been for her offering you an easy out, you would have been forced to come back to our room and talk to *me* and deal with this mess! Maybe the year-long separation never would have happened in the first place! Maybe we could have worked everything out, by ourselves, without her interference. I think we needed that time, and she *stole* it from us!"

"Stop it, Liv. That's a fairytale, and you know it. I would have slept in the airport until I could get another flight. Or I would have camped on the grounds of the American Embassy. Or found a youth hostel. Or slept under a bridge. Maybe rented a car and driven to Luxembourg. Anything. I would have done *anything* other than go back to our honeymoon suite. No way would it *ever* have happened the way you described. In fact, Sam might have done us both a favor. Her having the room for me gave me the space I needed to cool things off and make it possible to see you again."

"Oh great," Olivia snapped, shocked at his words. "So now you're saying that I should feel *grateful* that you turned to her?"

"Yes, actually, I think that I could successfully make that argument," John said. "But I didn't 'turn to her.' I just crashed at her place. Those are two totally different things."

Olivia pursed her lips and considered what he'd said as she worked to push back the anger that was trying to take control of her.

"Maybe you're right," she decided to concede. "Maybe it did keep you around. But the whole thing was still awful. Why did every single room in town have to be booked? It would have been so much less painful if you could have just gotten another room in our hotel, or if we could have moved to an actual suite with separate sleeping spaces."

"I think you're overlooking the real positive of the situation," John said, taking a sip of his coffee.

"All the money we saved by you staying with her for free instead of paying for a second room?" Olivia suggested in a weak attempt at humor.

"No. That your jealousy of Sam was the catalyst that turned you back around to maybe wanting me again. You couldn't have cared less what I did until you thought I was interested in another woman. Or, maybe even more accurately, that another woman might be interested in *me*. Then suddenly you were looking at me differently and wondering if you might really have feelings for me. None of that would have happened without Sam. Seriously, we should be thanking her."

"That's not funny," Olivia said, pushing her plate away. She was quickly losing her appetite along with her temper. "You accused me of not being able to let go of the Samantha thing, but you're one to talk. You can't let go of any of it, can you? After everything that's happened, and everything we've talked about or tried to do to fix this mess, it's impossible because you've still got the things I said to you on the plane clanging around your head. You claimed that you forgave me, and I do think you want that to be true. You're a great guy with a forgiving nature, and I really do think you've tried. But it's not working, is it? You still don't believe me when I tell you that I love you. You don't believe that I'm sorry for not understanding my own feelings and for not realizing until it was too late that I loved you all along."

"Me?" John asked when Olivia stopped to take a breath. "You think *I'm* the one who can't let things go? You're still focusing on the Samantha issue, which was never a factor in any of this to begin with! How are we even pretending we can move forward when you don't understand that I would never even think of looking at Samantha or any other woman? That's not who I am, but hey, that's only a drop in the bucket of the things you didn't know about me, right?"

John's words hung in the air as Olivia studied his face. The anger inside her was abruptly gone now, and deep despair was flooding in to take its place. In that quiet moment, Olivia suddenly understood everything she hadn't puzzled out before: It was over. The marriage was done. It wasn't ending in that café, though. That was the part she hadn't fully grasped until that very moment. What she now knew with complete certainty and clarity was that it had died a year ago. What she had been desperately holding onto was nothing more than the corpse of what they could have had together if she hadn't killed it.

"And there we are, right back to you still throwing everything in my face because you can't forgive me, and you definitely can't forget," Olivia said as John sat silently studying her, too. The regret and sadness were cascading through her now, making the words sound like they were struggling their way out of her throat. "You never even finished reading my letters, did you?"

"No," John said, expelling a long breath as he appeared to gather his thoughts. "I don't know why, exactly. I mean, you know I *started* reading them."

"Right, you started. The same way you started to fight for us. But then you gave up."

Olivia felt like all the emotions that were crashing

around inside were like waves threatening to pull her under. "You didn't get any counseling this year, and you didn't do a single thing to try to understand or deal with your feelings, right? You told me you spent the year assuming we were getting a divorce while you spent all that time working out."

John gazed at her for a long moment, and Olivia wondered what he was thinking. He wasn't exactly jumping in to deny her claims, which further strengthened her understanding about how little there was left for them to save.

"No, I didn't go into therapy or work on us," John admitted with a slow shake of his head. "It felt too much like I was setting myself up to get annihilated again."

"You're still stuck there in that same headspace, unwilling to make the leap and truly trust me or open yourself up to all the uncertainty that comes with being in a relationship," Olivia told him, finally understanding that what she needed to do now was acknowledge that it was over and set him free. "You're still not wearing your wedding ring. You didn't bother to read all of my letters. You're still throwing my mistakes back at me. I didn't see it before. I didn't truly understand. But I get it now."

"You get what?" John asked, his eyes narrowing with suspicion.

"The words that I said to you on the plane—the same words that have been haunting me all year long in my dreams—were something that can't ever be taken back or forgiven." Tears fell from her eyes and trailed down her face. "You gave me this year because you're a loving person, and because you didn't want to be the one to truly end things and hurt me. I took the year as a time of hopeful change. But you? You took the year to grieve and move on. I finally see it, John. You were right when you said it was over last year. There's nothing left to save."

"No, I don't think that's true," he replied, shaking his head. "And don't put this all on me like we could have saved our marriage if only I'd chanted *I think I can* a little harder."

"I'm not pointing fingers," Olivia said, wiping away her tears with her napkin. "Obviously, when the blame gets all tallied up, I have to take most of it."

"No, I'm not trying to throw blame around either," John said, shaking his head and then offering a reply in French when the waiter approached. After the waiter was gone, he continued with, "I don't think you're right that I've given up or that this can't be fixed. We've just got to keep talking and see where that takes us."

"It's not taking us anywhere except in circles," Olivia said, her resolve strengthening. *This is it,* she truly believed just then as she dug in her purse and pulled out some cash before looking back into John's green eyes. "I know you don't believe me, but who knows, maybe you will someday. Please, though, try to just accept that I love you deeply, and that I always will. I hope you'll be able to love and trust again. I hope I didn't destroy that for you the way I destroyed *us* that day on the plane."

"Wait, Liv, what are you saying?" John asked, looking frantic now. "We're still spending this time together, right?"

"No, I can't do this to you anymore," Olivia replied, gathering her things and standing up. "I'm done now, too."

John studied her a moment, then pulled out his

wallet and added to the money she'd already left on the table.

She started toward the door, pulling it open and stepping out into the gray, cloudy weather. Without any thoughts about a destination, she started walking. Then she heard John jog up behind her.

"Olivia, hang on a minute," he said, anger and confusion wrapped tightly together in his voice. "What's going on here?" You're just giving up? Leaving it all behind without another word?"

"I'm done fighting alone for us, John," she replied as she turned to face him. "Please don't think I'm mad at you or that I blame you. I love you with my whole heart, but the words I said to you on that plane can't ever be unsaid. They're still right there, wedged between us, no matter how hard I try to erase them. I tried to prove it to you, but you won't even look at the proof. I understand now that you already let go of us a year ago, on the day you asked for a divorce. Now I have to let go, too."

"Don't do this, Livvie. You're acting like you're doing me some kind of favor here, but you can't decide what it is I want or how I feel." John reached up to wrap his hands around her arms, the intensity now coursing through his body language as well as his words. "It's ridiculous to give up after we've come this far."

"That's exactly my point!" Olivia said as she pulled back. "We haven't made any progress! No matter what you say, your actions are telling a different story. You haven't come far at all—you're still on that plane!"

"So what? That's it?" John said, running his fingers through his hair in a show of frustration. "You're giving up and asking me for a divorce?"

Olivia shook her head sadly at him as his words echoed around them.

"No, I'm letting *you* give up," she said.

She looked at him through a long, tense moment, watching the mixture of anger, frustration, and sorrow battle across his face before, finally, she turned and walked away.

Chapter 58

Trying to Apologize

ANGER PROPELLED John back to his hotel before he consciously realized that's where he was going.

He went to his room and immediately started digging around for his running clothes. Just like the day he'd gone running on the beach before he left Puerto Rico, he felt as though he was at a crossroads and in need of the therapy that running gave him. He quickly changed, put his card key and phone in his pocket and, with a final look back at the stack of Olivia's letters, he turned and left.

Soon he was in the park, letting the thumping, rhythmic beat of his shoes soothe him. He tried to sort through his jumbled thoughts and emotions while snippets of Olivia's earlier words bounced around in his mind.

She was just walking away *now?* After everything they'd been through? He was so frustrated with her actions and the finality in her words. But what really was fueling his anger was that she'd somehow managed to flip everything around and make it seem like *he* was the one who gave up and wanted out. Like she was doing him some sort of favor by letting go and walking away. But she had it all wrong. It was *her*, right? She was the one who didn't trust him. That was the real problem. He'd told her a million times and in a million different ways that Samantha had absolutely nothing to do with their problems—past, present, or future. If Olivia had known him at all when he met Samantha, she never would have had any reason to doubt him.

He slowed as he came up to a family with small kids darting around the path, then veered off, circled around them, and resumed his former pace.

Okay, so where was I? Olivia...oh, right. She didn't trust him because she didn't know him back then. That was the original problem. It was their own personal Patient Zero in the epidemic of jealousy and pain that had spread through every part of their relationship. So yes, that was a huge issue. But...well, she'd already, *repeatedly*, owned the fact that she hadn't really known him at all. And they *had* talked it out, right? They'd been working to hammer out that issue, and he'd forgiven her...but then why was he beating her over the head with it now? Why was he, in one breath, accepting that she hadn't really known him well enough to get married, and in the next breath losing his mind over the fact that she hadn't known him well enough to really trust him?

He exhaled and shook his head in frustration. He was an idiot. He kept telling her he forgave her, acting like he was some kind of hero about it. But, clearly, he *hadn't* forgiven her yet and let it all go. The pain and heartache were still right there, threatening to devour him.

So, wait, does that mean Olivia was actually right this morning...?

Was his stubborn refusal to let go of the pain of her words on the plane holding him back from trusting her and truly working to move forward? Was *he* the reason they hadn't managed to resolve their myriad issues?

Her words echoed in his mind just then—*We*

haven't come far at all! No matter what you say now, your actions are telling me another story...you're still on that plane.

No, he thought. *Enough.* He was weaving together memories of the time they'd spent this week and the hopes he allowed to take root inside of his heart. His own actions were the very poison that was killing those hopes and preventing them from becoming reality. Olivia was right—he hadn't been ready to let go of everything. To move forward. To *believe.*

He was going to lose her. *Hell, I probably already have.* If he didn't dedicate the same amount of work and effort and reflection that Olivia had, he was going to be the reason that the love of his life walked away forever. He needed to let go of all of the negatives—the pain, the beating his pride had taken, the frustrations—if they were going to save this marriage. Take the leap of faith and finally, fully, believe in the love they shared and the future they could build together. Olivia had told him that he needed to stop saying *if* and start believing *when.* She was so right then, too. *Not if, but when....*

And that *when* needed to start right now.

He was suddenly overwhelmed by the need to see her. To hold her again, and to reassure her that he wasn't giving up. He'd promise her anything: he'd go into therapy, either solo or couples. He'd read all her letters. He'd never again mention the mistakes she'd made or dwell on her words on the plane or her jealousy over Samantha. Anything. Whatever it took, he was going to make this right.

*   *   *

He changed course and started running toward her hotel. He went down the trail, out of the park, and onto the sidewalk, keeping his pace as long as the crowds would allow.

By the time he got to Olivia's hotel, he was beyond convinced that he was doing the right thing. *First, I'm going to promise to read those letters today*, he thought as he repeatedly pushed the button for the elevator. By the time he got up to her room, he had a huge smile on his face. He hadn't felt this happy since their wedding day. This was it. They were finally going to get it right.

He knocked on her door with anxious anticipation. When she didn't answer, he knocked again. Maybe she was napping. He knocked a third time, a little harder.

"Liv, it's John! Open up!"

When he still received no response, he stood back from the door and double-checked the number.

No, this is the right one. That's the room number she gave me.

He tried calling her then, but it went directly to voicemail.

Finally, he turned and headed back to the elevator, surging with disappointment. He wondered where she'd gone, praying she was still in Paris and not at the airport boarding a flight out of town.

He took a deep breath as the elevator returned him to the first floor. *Okay, it's not like this is the end*, he thought. He'd find her eventually, and he'd make things right with her. Still...he was hurting. Again. Now that he'd decided he was more than ready to start the rest of his life with her, he wanted that life to begin immediately.

They had definitely wasted enough time.

Chapter 59

The Rest of the Letters

AS HE WALKED BACK through the lobby of Olivia's hotel, he debated what to do next. The letdown of not finding Olivia had drained his energy and focus. He could go back and hit the gym at his hotel, since a good workout was his preferred method of therapy. He was already dressed for it, too. Then again, the dash from the park to Olivia's hotel had been long. He was already exhausted.

Still uncertain, he left her hotel and simply walked the mile back to his room. Then he showered, changed, got his wallet, fully intending to go back out and keep searching for her. That's when he glanced over and saw Olivia's stack of letters on the bed.

He paused a moment as he considered them. Why *hadn't* he read them already? He'd told her that he wanted to take his time with them, and that reading them in a single afternoon wasn't going to instantly heal him and help regrow his trust in her. But was that the full truth? Maybe he'd known deep down that if he read her words and saw inside her true feelings—by reading thoughts that were coming straight from the depths of her soul—that maybe, just maybe, he wouldn't be able to hold onto his lingering fears and doubts anymore. He would be forced to let all of that go like the security blanket it had become. As long as he held onto the hurt, he wouldn't be able to open himself up again. His heart would still be safely guarded.

He needed to do this. If he really wanted to save his marriage, he had to let her in and fully allow her to stitch back the threads of trust between them.

He went to the stack of letters and picked them up. What had she called them? Her evidence in the case she was building? She had remained committed all year long to saving their relationship. She'd spent the entire time, while he was in San Juan trying to escape their past, making sure they'd have a chance at a future.

He sat on the bed and studied the pile, noticing that she'd numbered all of them so they could be easily kept in order. She'd clearly given this a lot of thought. He'd already read the first two, so he pulled up the one she'd numbered with a three.

Dear John,

I did a really dumb thing today. I know you asked me to stay away, but I just couldn't anymore. I needed to see you so badly. So I went over to your apartment, but your stuff was gone and someone else was moving in. A little girl answered the door, and I thought I was going to fall to pieces right there in the hallway in front of her. It felt like, I don't know, like a vision of what could have been for us had opened that door. We could have had a family together. We could have had a lot of things together. But right now, we have nothing. Okay, I'm sorry. I just can't write anymore today. This is too hard.

Love,

Olivia

He blinked as his eyes became suspiciously damp and pulled out another letter, this time randomly from the middle of the stack.

Dear John,

It's New Year's Day today, so I guess I need to wish you Happy New Year. I hope that you're happy and safe wherever you are. I can't help but wonder what this year will bring us. My resolution, of course, is to continue to bombard you with proof of how much I love you and how much I want to save this marriage. I can only pray you'll want the same thing.

Love,

Olivia

The sadness that emanated from her letters was really painful to absorb. It was very clear to him, though, that she'd been telling the truth. She'd really spent her year thinking about him and doing everything to prove she was serious about their future.

He sat down on the bed then, leaned against the pillows, and proceeded to read the entire stack.

*   *   *

Olivia revealed *everything*. From tiny details about mundane errands and problems at work to longer letters detailing the topics she was covering with her therapist. He let the feelings and emotions that she poured into her writing wash over him and settle into his heart. He could feel her regrets, her loneliness, her frustrations, and, yes, her hope. Throughout the year, while he'd been sitting around anticipating divorce papers, she had firmly held onto hope, using it as the sail to guide her through the storm. He wished he'd done the same.

Finally, he was holding her last letter—

Dear John,

I'm flying to Paris tomorrow. I plan to get to the Louvre *first thing and wait for you there. I'll wait all day if I have to. And if you don't show up, then I'm going to search forever until I find you. We're going to finally have our chance at getting this right. I know we are; I can feel it deep in my heart. Everything we ever wanted or could possibly be together is right there waiting for us. We just have to grab hold of it together. I desperately want that future with you, John. That vision of what we could be is so clear in my mind. I guess I can only hope that you'll feel the same way, and that you'll want to reach for it too. No matter what happens, though, please know that I'll love you into eternity.*

Love,

Olivia

Yeah, he decided in that moment, they were going to have another chance. And another and another until they got it right. He wasn't going to be the one who gave up. She was reaching out for their future, and he was finally going to reach out for it, too.

He got up and headed back out. He had to find her. He'd turn Paris upside down if necessary, or he'd search the world looking for her.

Their story wasn't over, not by a long shot.

*   *   *

She still wasn't answering her phone, so he took a cab back to her hotel room, even running up the stairs to avoid waiting for the elevator. But for the second time that day, he found himself knocking on a door that wasn't opened.

Where could she have gone? The possibilities were

endless. Would she want to go somewhere they'd been together and think about their journey? Notre Dame? *Sainte Chapelle*? *Montmartre*? Or would she want to be somewhere that held no memories of him, their marriage, or their problems? Had she really given up altogether? Was she at the airport at this very moment, booking a flight home?

Could all of this pain and longing and hard work all be coming down to this final test that they just hadn't been able to pass? Was their second chance at happiness going to end before it ever really began?

He didn't know what to do or where to go now. With no idea where to look for her, he started walking back to his hotel. Maybe it really was time to leave Paris and hunt for their happily-ever-after life once they were home. *If that's how it has to be, then that's fine*, he thought. He wasn't giving up on finding her and making things right regardless. *Never.*

He prayed Olivia felt the same way.

Chapter 60

Finding a Way Forward

OLIVIA WAS LOST, emotionally as well as literally. Ever since she'd walked away from John that morning, she'd just kept on going. She'd spent the entire day wandering aimlessly through the city until she realized she had no idea where she was or how much time had passed. All she knew for certain was that she was in pain.

All her dreams of a future with John had died that morning, and she couldn't even begin to imagine how to move forward without him. She'd come to Paris so hopeful, and so certain her letters would show John one truth above all others: that she loved him. If he would ever trust her with his heart again, she'd guard it like the priceless treasure it was. Clearly none of that ever had the slightest chance of happening now, no matter how desperately she wanted it.

Coming to the stunning realization that John had never seriously entertained the thought that they could save their marriage had been devastating. Part of her was furious with him for not throwing himself into the salvation of the marriage the way she had. But another part—the part that could still see the devastation her cruel confession on the plane a year earlier had caused him—totally understood. She'd ripped his heart right out of his chest and destroyed whatever trust he could ever have. Yes, part of him would always love her. She understood that. But without a foundation of trust, well...it was clear to her now that they'd never had a chance after that flight.

She sighed as she continued onward, deciding she didn't really care if she was lost. *Eventually I could catch a cab or turn on my phone and use the GPS*, she thought as her mind immediately went back to John. She pictured his handsome face and the kindness that was always evident in his eyes. She'd really missed him this past year. Like he'd said earlier, they had fully mastered the art of being comfortable. She missed those easy conversations filled with laughter and love. They'd always fit together like puzzle pieces, whereas without him, she was just a series of jagged edges.

At that thought, an avalanche of regret swept through her again. Why? Why hadn't they been able to work through their problems? Why had their marriage been so impossibly difficult to save when their relationship always had been so incredibly easy and natural?

Why couldn't they escape the tidal wave of pain, despair, and mistakes that had been drowning them since the day they got married?

Suddenly, an idea came to her. An epiphany! Like her earlier clarity that she needed to let him go, she had a perfect vision of what they'd done wrong. All this time they'd been working to save their marriage, but that marriage had been dead on arrival when the plane landed in Paris a year ago. They shouldn't have been fighting to save the marriage; instead, they should have been trying to rewind to the beginning and start over. Maybe what their relationship actually needed wasn't a saved marriage at all. Perhaps what they needed *was* a divorce! And from there, a do-over and a fresh start! Their marriage started off with mistakes that had proven irreparable. Their wedding album would always have horribly sad pictures that Olivia would *never* want to frame and put on the walls of their future home. At the wedding, she hadn't meant the vows she was saying. And John hadn't worn his ring in more than a year, so he clearly hadn't found a way to trust her or move forward. Thus, the marriage had been an utter disaster—but the love between them *was still there.* Despite everything, she knew that was true. They just needed to start over. They could date for however long it would take him to trust her again. Hell, she'd date him forever, if that's what it took. Because in the end, all she really wanted was to be with him—*married or not.*

She crossed the busy street and found herself on the pedestrian pathway along the Seine. She stood there a long time, watching the water swirl as the memories and thoughts chased each other through her mind. The more she considered this unique solution, the more she liked it. *If any situation ever needed a fresh start, it's ours,* she thought. Then a familiar voice pulled her out of her reverie.

"Olivia!" John was calling. "Olivia!!!"

She turned and saw him hurrying toward her. In that instant she felt love and relief like never before.

Stopping short of where she stood, he said, "Where have you been? I've been looking for you all day!"

"Oh," she said simply. "I didn't mean to make you worry. I've been doing a lot of wandering...and thinking."

"I've been thinking, too," he replied. "Thinking and reading—all your letters, Livvie. Every last one. And I know how hard you've been fighting for us. I get it now, I really do."

"Yeah, I did fight," she said with a nod. "But I can see now that I was going about it the wrong way."

"No, no, clearly it was *me* who didn't do things right this past year," John told her. "You were working hard to save our marriage while I was just sitting around waiting for it to be over. I was an idiot, and the things you said this morning made me see that."

"I see things differently, too."

"That's great!" John said. "So, we agree that it's not too late. Despite what you thought and said this morning, I'm not ready to give up, and I know you aren't, either. This marriage is worth fighting for, and this isn't over between us."

"Well, no, that's not quite the same conclusion I came to today," she continued with a wince. Then she paused to consider how to say this so he'd understand....

"What do you mean?" John asked, looking uneasy now.

"I don't think our marriage can be saved at all," Olivia said finally, her words coming out stronger than she actually felt in that moment. "In fact, I think we should get divorced."

Chapter 61

The Do-Over

HE STOOD and stared, awash in confusion as her words moved clumsily around his mind.

What did she just say?

"A divorce?" he finally choked out. "Are you serious right now? After everything we—"

Then he stopped when Olivia threw her arms around his neck. She stared deeply into his eyes for a long moment, and he studied hers back, lost in confusion at the mismatch between her words and her actions.

She wants a divorce and yet...

Olivia leaned forward, her lips a mere breath away from his, and whispered, "Don't you get it? This is a do-over, John." Then she gently touched her lips to his.

Unable to maintain control any longer, he captured the kiss back in a greedy response. Relief and love and hope and every other wonderful emotion poured through him and flowed into their embrace as they tested and tasted and connected in ways they hadn't in over a year...or maybe ever. In that instant, the hurt and the pain and the doubts didn't seem quite so insurmountable anymore. This connection they had, this remarkable chemistry, was everything he ever wanted. It was all his questions and all his answers wrapped up in a blistering meeting of two souls who had been kept apart for much too long.

Finally—and more than a little regretfully—he

pulled back and leaned his forehead against hers, his eyes closed now.

"Divorce, did you say?" he asked, a part of him suddenly worried that she'd simply been saying goodbye to him via one emotionally charged kiss.

"Yeah, I know it sounds drastic," Olivia said, "but I started thinking today that maybe killing off this marriage is the way to *save* our relationship."

"Okay, I'll bite," John said, pulling back to read her facial expressions and body language. "How does getting a divorce help us to stay together?"

"Well, I don't think we need to take the time, money, and paperwork that would be involved with an actual divorce," she explained. "I'm talking more of a symbolic thing. Like...I don't know. I'm an officer of the court. I'll issue us a citizen's divorce."

"Okay," John said cautiously, feeling the worries start to loosen their hold on his heart. "So, we get divorced but not really. Then what?"

"Then we start over, and this time we do it right. We could go back home and date again, for a year or two or twenty. Whatever it takes for us to build back the trust and the love. Or we could fly to Vegas and get married all over again. Whatever you want. Whatever it takes. But I want a complete do-over, John. This marriage right here, the one we're currently frustrated with? It's never *not* going to be completely awful. We've talked, and we've gotten to know each other, and we have laid out all our issues. I bared my soul, and you bared yours, and look where it brought us. That marriage was damaged in ways that are irreparable. Our wedding album will always be a painful reminder of how spectacularly we messed up the first time around."

"If it's new pictures you want," John said, "we

could easily get back in our wedding clothes and stage a few."

"Yeah, I guess we could do that. But isn't that still sort of sad and pathetic? I want a fresh start, not a weird reenactment."

"What else do you think a new wedding will fix then?" he asked. "I'm open to the idea if you think it'll help us, but I wanted to find you to tell you I'm all in. I read the letters, and I'll do whatever it takes to save what we already have. I'll go see a therapist. I'll see a whole *team* of therapists. I'll adopt multiple dogs. Like you said before, whatever you want and whatever it takes."

"Yes, we can do all those things. But I still want to start over, at least symbolically. Don't you see how perfect this idea is?" Olivia started to talk more animatedly now, her face bright with excitement. "At the original wedding I didn't mean the vows I was saying. At the time, I was plotting a way to get out of them. Now I want to say them and have you know how much I mean them from the bottom of my heart."

"That would be great, of course," John replied. "I'd love to hear those words again, knowing that you actually mean them this time."

"And you haven't worn your wedding ring in a year," she pointed out. "I want to put it back on your finger knowing that it means as much to you as it does to me, and that this time it'll stay there."

"That sounds good, too."

"And don't forget—in this current marriage, we never had a real honeymoon," Olivia continued. "We've never even slept in the same bed since our wedding night. We didn't actually sleep together that night, either. And you spent the next night, the first night of our honeymoon, with another woman!"

"Yeah, about that...I was thinking more about that night and about our earlier fight, and I don't think I ever told you one minor detail that might really help you get past that. Did I ever tell you that Samantha's hotel room had two beds? That we never actually slept in the *same* bed?"

"You...no, you never explained that. Jeez, John, you were totally burying the lead. Knowing that *definitely* helps. I totally had a mental image of the two of you spooning away my entire honeymoon."

John smiled sadly at her, then turned to look at the river for a moment, temporarily lost in thought. When he turned back, he said, "I understand what you're saying about how this marriage is never going to provide a happy starting point for the rest of our lives. The wedding memories are sad, the photos bring you pain, the honeymoon memories are pathetic, and honestly the whole first year is something I just want to forget."

"That's exactly what I'm saying! We're not sweeping anything under the carpet, either. We've put in the work, and we both know there's more work to be done. But we're ready to face it together. We took our time and didn't rush into any decisions. I don't think we're kidding ourselves that we can honestly have a fresh start. But let's make it a real one. Let's fly to Las Vegas and find one of those tacky wedding chapels. Just the two of us. I want someone to snap a bunch of pictures so I have happy wedding photos to frame. I want to celebrate the anniversary of *that* ceremony going forward instead of the first one. I want to smile my way through our vows and laugh and hold your hand and exchange rings and just be happy. I want to remember the days that follow as the real honeymoon. Let's just wipe the first marriage out and put a shiny new one in its place. I think we owe it to ourselves."

John studied her face as his love for her wrapped itself tightly around his heart. "I think it's a great idea. You've got a deal. But on one condition."

"Anything. Just name it," she answered, looking hopeful.

"We've got to stay at the Paris hotel in Vegas. The one with the big cheesy replica of the Eiffel tower. The symmetry is too good to avoid."

"I'd marry you in Paris, Texas, if that was what you wanted," Olivia replied, smiling back. "But yeah, we kind of have to go to that hotel, don't we?"

"Come here," John said, reaching for her. She accepted his hand and walked into his arms, smiling up at him. He studied her happy face for a long moment before saying, "Olivia Marie Conte, would you do me the incredible honor of divorcing me?"

"Oh John, I thought you'd never ask," she told him before burying her head into his shoulder and wrapping her arms around him.

"Do we have to do anything more official than that? File mock papers?" he asked. "I know, we could go back to the *Louvre* Relationship Room of Doom if you wanted to really achieve symmetry."

"Oh no, please. I can't take anymore drama in that museum. I think it's enough to just declare that it's done and over. That marriage is officially, without a doubt, dead and buried."

"Huh. I feel like we should do something a bit more official to mark the occasion," he said. "Maybe burn something in effigy?"

Olivia nodded, a flirty look on her face now. "I

have an idea. Like I was saying before, we never consummated the marriage. But I think we *definitely* should consummate the divorce."

"You just keep having one good idea after another today, don't you?" John observed, laughing. "That's really how you want to celebrate? You don't want to go see some more sites? Analyze an artifact or two? Have another fight?"

"No, I do not," Olivia replied with fake haughtiness. "I want to go to whichever of our hotel rooms is closest right now, and I don't want to leave it again until it's time for our flight. Think you can handle that, Mr. Daux?"

"Hmm, yeah, I could probably move a few appointments around and make the time," John said, all traces of laughter gone now as he leaned down and touched her lips with his own. The kiss quickly deepened, ignited once more by the pent-up frustrations that had been building in both of them for what felt like an eternity. He couldn't believe how happy he felt in that moment simply to be with her and finally moving forward together.

This divorce was the best thing that had happened to him in a really, really long time.

Chapter 62

The Next Morning

THE NEXT MORNING, John was up before the sun. He glanced over and could make out the silhouette of Olivia's head on the next pillow, her hair fanning out and brushing against his arm. He reached over and touched a silky strand of it, gently running the curl through his fingers for a moment. Then he smiled before turning his gaze back to the ceiling, lost in thought as he crossed his arms behind his head.

He couldn't believe they were finally reunited after all the garbage they'd been through. The countless misunderstandings and hurts and frustrations...it was all finally and truly over. They were together, committed, in love. *And divorced.*

He smothered a small laugh. *Okay, so maybe I really did need to add a third divorce to my list of failures to get to this point.* It was worth it, he decided. It was all worth it. He'd slog through all of it again if he had to, if he knew that he'd eventually wind up right back here in this bed, with this woman, and in this city at this moment. They were just so happy now. So in love and closer by far than they'd ever been before. All it had taken was a year of pain, loneliness, doubt, and uncertainty. *So if it wasn't the record holder for the world's most meandering path to happiness that anyone had ever taken, it at least had to be a runner-up....*

He smiled as Olivia scrunched up her nose, itched it, and rolled over, all while she remained asleep. He was never going to spend another night without her, that much he knew. He was anxious to get started on their new life together. Maybe today they could ditch one of their hotel rooms to save money and start making plans for their upcoming wedding.

He felt a little bad that the wedding she was going to treasure and remember forever would be held in a tacky Elvis chapel. But the thought of it seemed to be making her so happy—and from that day on, ensuring her happiness was his number-one goal.

"Hey," she said, looking a little shy when he glanced over at her.

"Hey," he replied, getting onto his side to face her. "How'd you sleep?"

"Great. You know, I can't believe it, but I had the first deep, dreamless sleep I've had since we got married. And the nightmare...it didn't come."

"What nightmare?" John asked, reaching over to gently push an errant strand of hair out of her eyes.

"Every night I've been transported back to that first flight we took to Paris. Not sure if you'll remember the one I'm talking about. I might have said something to you about not being in love with you or something?"

"Uh, I don't know. Maybe it's starting to ring a bell?" John gave her a sad little half smile. "Those words have been haunting you?"

"Yeah. Well, not so much the words as much as the look on your face when I said them. I see it over and over and...." Olivia closed her eyes, looking sorry she'd brought it up again.

"Livvie, don't be afraid to talk to me. That's all behind us now, remember? Those are scenes from the old marriage, the one we threw away yesterday. It's all gone now; it can't hurt us anymore, right?"

She nodded and sniffed, and it looked like she was going to cry. This certainly wasn't how he thought this morning was going to go.

"As happy as I am that we're finally moving forward, let's not make the mistake of building glass walls around those memories either," he said. "We got through it, and we're putting it behind us and starting over. That part is all great. But let's always be honest about it. Let's be able to talk about it if we need to, face it, and admit if something from that time is still bothering us. If you continue to have nightmares about it, I want to know. Don't worry about dredging up the old hurts. I think if you do, it could have the opposite effect and turn that time into some sort of slowly building resentment, which could harm us. Let's not give it the chance. I never want to let it hurt us again."

Olivia sniffed as she considered everything he'd just said. "You're right. We always need to be able to talk about that time and what happened. All right. Here's the truth: Every night I wake up in a cold sweat from that dream. In it, I turn to you on the plane, and I tell you that I wasn't in love with you and that I never was. And then you...look...." She exhaled slowly before starting again. "I can see the devastation on your face, and I see it every night, over and over."

"I'm sorry, honey. Come here...." John pulled her into his arms then, and she cried. It was slow at first, but eventually the tears became sobs. "Hey," he went on, "you don't have to do that. It's over, remember? It's all over now. You said the dream didn't come last night. Even your subconscious knows we're the world's happiest divorced couple."

Olivia nodded as the sobs began to slow, and John reached down to gently kiss their trails away. "Liv, I told myself this morning that I was going to make your happiness my top priority from now on. You're already making me look bad."

"I'm sorry. Those tears had nothing to do with us as we lie here today in each other's arms. We're so happy, and we're so in love, and I seriously can't wait to marry you again. But I guess I needed to grieve over that first marriage and cry over those mistakes one last time. I don't think I was ready to really let go of all of it until this moment."

"Whatever it takes," John replied. "Whatever you need. That's what we'll do to make this right. Anything you need."

"I just need you," Olivia told him, pulling his face to her own and claiming his mouth with kisses.

Chapter 63

The Dress

LATER THAT MORNING, they wandered to a nearby café for a breakfast of crepes and coffee, then back to Olivia's hotel so she could pack her suitcase and check out. After the suitcase was relocated to John's hotel, they got lunches to go and walked to a park bench overlooking the river, where they sat together enjoying the newfound ease in each other's company. Olivia tucked her knees under her chin as she alternately watched the river and John's profile, smiling each time he turned and caught her loving gaze.

"We should go shopping," she said finally. "We may be planning a quickie wedding, but I was serious about wanting nice pictures from it. Let's go find a new dress for me, and we can get you a suit, too. That is, of course, unless you happened to bring one along for whatever reason. But I want to do this right."

"Do you want to take some time to look for the dress alone?" John asked.

"No! What, you're not up for an afternoon of dress shopping?" she said with a laugh and a nudge of her elbow in his side. "Trying to weasel out of it?"

"I'd be happy to sit down and do our taxes as long as I'm with you," John replied, "but no, I just thought you'd want to stick with the old superstitions about the groom not seeing the bride in her dress before the ceremony."

"I can't help but think we've drained our entire

reserve of bad luck already," Olivia pointed out. "Look at it this way: You didn't see my dress before our first wedding day and, well, look how *that* turned out."

"Hmm, good point, counselor. All right then, dress shopping it is." John stood up and offered a hand. "Shall we?"

*   *   *

They walked until they found a queue of available cabs by a hotel, then secured one and asked the driver to take them to the *Champs-Élysées*. If they really were going to go dress shopping, this trendy district seemed like a good place to start.

The driver brought them to the street near the *Arc de Triomphe*. There, they stood on the sidewalk letting the crowds flow around them while they studied Napoleon's famous arch.

"What a perfect place to come when I'm feeling so wonderful and happy and...triumphant," Olivia said with a smile. "That really is a great word for it. Okay, so where's your phone?"

Taking it in hand, she shot a couple pictures of the arch, then urged John, always a grumpy model, to pose in front of it. "C'mon, smile!" she commanded. "Look triumphant, John! We've got a lot to be smiling about!"

Her words worked in finally securing a carefree grin from him, and she was so grateful to capture that moment. There really was a lot to smile about lately.

After that they started walking, popping in and out of stores that caught their eye. Eventually, they wandered off the main street and spotted a little dress boutique.

"Oh John, look at that one!" Olivia stopped to peer through the front window. "I have a good feeling about it."

"Then why don't you go ahead and take a look?" John suggested. "I know what you said about us already using up all our bad luck but, well, I just don't want to take a single chance that we might be taunting the wedding gods by breaking the rules. Too risky."

"Oh, okay, I guess. But...you're sure? You know, we really don't have to do this at all if you don't want to. I could just pick something up when we get to Nevada."

John shook his head. "No, please, go ahead and find a dress you really like, and we'll meet back here later. I'll wander around and see if I can find a suit, or at least a jacket."

"Hmm, okay, then. I'll be missing you, though," she added. "I'm not ready to be apart from you yet."

"We'll have the rest of our lives together, honey. This isn't a dream or an illusion. It's real, and we're finally together and happy. You're not going to suddenly wake up alone."

"I know, I know," she replied, although she knew deep down it would take some time before the thought of being separated from him would stop being a source of fear. "I just have to keep pinching myself. Okay, off you go. Back here in an hour?"

"How about ninety minutes?" John suggested.

"Even better."

Olivia gave him a kiss goodbye, then opened the door of the little boutique and wandered happily among the colorful racks. She wasn't exactly sure what she was looking for. It didn't have to be white or an actual wedding dress. Just something beautiful that wouldn't be too hot for a Nevada summer.

She tried on a couple, although most of the styles were a bit short. They looked like they were intended for someone half her age, which deflated whatever good feelings about this shop she'd initially felt.

She left then and peeked into a few more, but nothing was catching her eye. Mildly discouraged, she rounded the corner and walked on, though she didn't want to get too far away from the spot where she was meeting John. She was so absorbed with thoughts of him at that moment that she almost walked by a pink dress in the window of a little odds-and-ends shop. Was it a consignment place? She wasn't sure. But the dress was precisely what she'd been looking for. Perched on an old-fashioned tailor's form, it was a simple gown with spaghetti straps like her original wedding dress, but also a soft petal pink with a long, flowing skirt. The kind a little girl might wear to twirl around and feel like a princess. So simple, but so beautiful.

She pushed the door open, sounding the tiny bell overhead.

Twenty minutes later it rang again as she emerged with the dress in question, tucked in a bag that swung from her arm. It had been an almost perfect fit. If she had more time, she probably would have had a few alterations made. But really it was close enough, and it was perfect for her fairytale second wedding. She would absolutely become the princess who had finally found her prince. Beaming, she turned the corner and headed back to where she'd be meeting John.

Everything was finally falling into place.

Chapter 64

The Ring

JOHN FELT a little guilty being so secretive, but he needed time alone if he was going to surprise Olivia at the wedding.

He wanted to find a jewelry store. Sure, they already had their rings. And he didn't think either one of them wanted to exchange them for new ones. Yes, they definitely needed a new start, but the reminders of where they'd begun and what they'd been through were important, too.

That didn't mean he couldn't surprise her with *another* ring, however. Maybe something to wear on her right hand or one that could be stacked on top of those she already had. He wasn't sure.

But he did know he wanted to give her this present so she'd see how seriously he was taking this do-over. This wedding really was going to be a brand-new start, and the ring would be a reminder and a symbol of their new life together.

As he walked along, he passed a few storefronts that had jewelry in the windows. But most of it looked like vintage jewelry to him. He wanted something brand-new that was only for his beautiful bride and had never been worn before. So he kept walking.

He passed by a fancy store with a designer name he recognized, but no, he wanted someplace smaller and more personal. So he kept walking....

He soon realized he'd already passed by the bulk of

the stores and was running out of time. Olivia was going to be standing around waiting for him soon. So, deciding to try his luck on the next street, he turned the corner and eventually took another right so he could ultimately loop back around to where Olivia would be.

After a block or so of heading back in the direction from which he'd already come, he finally found a little store that was exactly as he'd been imagining. Small, maybe family-owned, certainly not a chain. And probably full of beautiful, unique rings worthy of Olivia.

He had a big smile on his face as he walked in and was greeted by a clerk who eagerly showed him their wedding collection. But they all looked too much like the one she already had. Either traditional bands or solitaires or more ornate sets, but not something that would coordinate with the current set. Their engagement, their first wedding, and now their second wedding—he still liked the idea of having them all stacked in a row.

"Do you have something that would stack with an existing wedding set?" he asked the clerk in French.

"You mean like an anniversary band?" the man asked, leaning under the counter, unlocking the case, and pulling out a tray of slim bands. Each featured sparkling diamonds that looked like they were standing at attention in their neat, single-file rows.

An anniversary band!

That sounded perfect. They'd already had their first anniversary, which was when the real work of their marriage had begun. The first wedding and the whole first year weren't the important parts of their marriage. No, the important part was all they'd accomplished *since* their first anniversary.

"What's the price on that one?" John asked, pointing to a platinum band. The size was right, and the price was around what he'd been guessing he'd spend. Plus, it was time to get back and meet Olivia. Yes, that was the one. He could feel it.

He made his purchase and took the box in hand, turning down the offer of a bag. He wanted to surprise Olivia right there at the wedding. He certainly couldn't show up with a bag in his hand.

Satisfied, he headed back to the sidewalk and hurried to meet her. His face broke into a huge smile when he saw her waiting on the corner with a store bag of her own in hand.

"You found a dress, huh?" he asked.

"Yes! I'm so excited to wear it!" she said, her happiness contagious as he reached out to pull her into a hug.

"You weren't as lucky?" she asked, looking up into his face. "No suit?"

"Oh no, I am very, very lucky. The luckiest man alive," he said. "Well, at least the luckiest man alive who still doesn't own a new wedding suit."

"Oh well," she said, looping her arm around his waist and snuggling into his arm. "We can always just look for something when we get to Nevada."

"Yeah, I'm not worried," he said as they strolled down the sidewalk. "I've got everything I need right here."

Chapter 65

The Eiffel Tower Again

TWO DAYS LATER, their cab pulled to a stop in front of the Paris Hotel and Casino in Las Vegas. As they got out, a bellhop greeted them while the cabbie popped the trunk.

"Hello and welcome to Paris!" the bellhop said with a smile.

"Thanks! We've got reservations for a honeymoon suite," John told him.

"How wonderful! Congratulations! And is this your first visit to Paris?"

"No. Well, yes," Olivia said with a wink at John. "It's the first time we've been here in Vegas. But we've been to the other Paris. Actually, I went there on my honeymoon with my first husband."

A look of confusion quickly chased across the bellhop's face before he turned with a slight shrug to grab their suitcases and load them on the wheeled cart. As John pulled money out of his wallet to pay for the taxi, the cabbie leaned over to him with a whisper, "Her first husband took her to Paris, France, and you bring her to the knockoff Paris in the middle of the desert? Nice one, buddy." Then he took the bills from John's hand before getting back into the car and driving off.

Olivia covered her mouth to hide her laughter as John looked over at her with a mock roll of the eyes.

"Great, yeah, I guess I didn't really think that one out, did I?" he asked as he pulled her in for a kiss.

"Come over here. I've got to start working on making sure you forget about that lousy first honeymoon with that jerk ex-husband of yours. *This* is the trip to Paris you need to remember."

"Of course I'll forget all about that other guy," she replied, relief and happiness mingling inside her as she thought about how wonderful it felt to simply be able to tease him and be silly. *How far we've come since the last time we arrived at a honeymoon hotel,* she thought.

They walked hand-in-hand into the luxurious hotel and checked in, then headed to the large queue of elevators.

"Look at the size of these, John," she said, astonished as she made some mental measurements. "They're like ten times bigger than the elevators at our first Paris hotel. Do you remember?"

"Yeah, we were standing there, squeezed in so tightly in that little deathtrap, and I was so mad and miserable," John replied. "Despite everything, though, I wanted nothing more than to reach over and hold you. But I couldn't, of course. That's when we were pretty much at our lowest point. And now look how far we've come. Even the elevators are an upgrade."

"I don't know," Olivia said, putting her arms around his waist, "I kind of liked the close quarters."

"Yeah, good point."

They found their suite, and John smiled at her as she flitted around, admiring the whirlpool tub and the king-sized bed with its padded headboard and crisply folded linens.

"Oh, this is just beautiful," she said, returning his smile.

"I think so, too," John replied as he turned away to answer a knock at the door. The bellhop briskly carried in their luggage and showed off the features of the room before John handed him a tip and sent him off.

"Okay," he said. "Now what? Do you want to head right out and find a chapel?"

"Let's go tomorrow," Olivia told him as she started to open her suitcase. "I think we've got a pretty long to-do list today. We still need to go find you a suit, and maybe we can send my dress out to be pressed. And I know this is silly, but I absolutely want a marriage certificate from this wedding to officially mark our new anniversary date. We probably have to apply for it at the courthouse, don't you think? And then let's just enjoy the evening. We can have dinner, and then I absolutely *must* go to the top of the Eiffel Tower again with you. I want to see the lights of the city."

With their plans set, they spent the rest of the day together, checking off all the preparations for the ceremony. They took a cab to a men's store and found a wedding suit they both liked. Then to the courthouse, where they filled out the necessary paperwork for a Nevada wedding license. Back in the suite, they dropped off John's new clothes and made arrangements to have Olivia's dress pressed. Finally, it was time to relax and see the famous row of casinos from the view high above their hotel, on the Eiffel Tower's observation deck.

"Look, John! You can see the Statue of Liberty from this Eiffel Tower, too!" Olivia said, pointing to the New York, New York hotel. "They really pulled out all the stops in bringing the realism here!"

John smiled back at her. "I'm glad they worked so hard on it. Everything has to be perfect for my beautiful bride."

"It is," she said, wrapping her arms high around his

neck. "Everything is absolutely perfect in every way."

They had supper that night in the Eiffel Tower Restaurant.

"Let's order some wine to celebrate," Olivia suggested.

"What's the occasion?" the waiter asked as he handed them the wine menu.

"We're getting married tomorrow," she answered.

"In the chapels or the tower?" the waiter asked.

"In the...oh, wait, what do you mean?"

"Are you getting married here at the hotel? Did you talk to the wedding coordinator? There are two chapels to choose from, or you can do it poolside. You can also get married right here in the tower, up on the observation deck."

Olivia turned to John, delight flooding through her now.

"Get...out...." he said, smiling back at her.

"It just keeps getting better," she said with a laugh.

They thanked the waiter for the information and placed their order. Then Olivia turned back to John and said, "We absolutely *must* get married at the top of the tower. You know that, right?"

John reached for her hand across the white linen tablecloth. "I definitely agree. The only thing that had sort of made me feel bad about this whole idea was the thought of taking you to a tacky drive-through chapel. I want our wedding to be something beautiful, so much so that you'll love and cherish the memory of it forever, not have it be some goofy joke. So yeah...this is so much better."

"I would marry you at a gas station if you wanted, and I'd still cherish it," she said emphatically. "But yes, this is going to be so great. I can't wait! Let's ask the concierge how to arrange it as soon as possible."

"Absolutely."

*   *   *

After dinner they wandered down to the concierge's desk.

"Oh, I'm sorry," the man said, "but those wedding packages book up pretty quickly. You didn't book it when you made your room reservation?"

"No. This has all been pretty last-minute," John replied. "And when I said I wanted a honeymoon suite, I suppose they assumed we were already married."

"Oh. Well, yes, we *do* often hold weddings on the observation deck in the mornings. But I'm pretty sure we're booked solid for a few weeks now."

"That's *so* disappointing," Olivia said, as she felt the smile on her face wilting. "We were so excited to get married up there. It would have been so perfect."

"Actually," John said, squeezing her hand. "We technically *are* already married. We don't really need a license or a minister. We could just walk up there and exchange our vows on our own, you know."

"So...it's a vow renewal then?" the concierge asked.

"Yes, sort of. Seriously, it's a complicated story," Olivia said before turning back to John. "That would work, I guess. We already got our license. We just need someone to sign and file it. But it seems like maybe the ceremony would be lacking something if we're standing there trying to hear each other while crowds of people jostle around us."

The concierge tapped a pen on his desk for a moment, lost in thought. Then he pointed the pen in the air for emphasis. "I think I have an idea. The observation deck doesn't open until nine thirty, but people will be up there much earlier getting ready for the day. I'll pull a few strings and get you there around that time, too. Before the sun's even up, if that's what you'd like. If all you need is a little privacy, we can arrange it."

"Oh, thank you!" Olivia exclaimed as relief flooded through her. "That would be wonderful!"

"The name's Andre, by the way," he said, extending his palm and shaking each of their hands.

"Thank you, Andre," John said, the relief very evident on his face. "You have no idea how much you're helping us out here."

"Just meet me at the elevators at, say, seven tomorrow morning, and I'll take care of the rest."

As they turned to make their way out of the lobby and back to their suite, Olivia felt a bubbling rush of happy gratitude welling up inside her. Happiness about this day. Gratitude for John and for this opportunity to marry him all over again at the top of the—well at the top of *an*—Eiffel Tower. It couldn't have been more perfect if they'd scripted it.

"I think those wedding gods you worried about us offending are actually smiling down on us right now," she said fervently, giving his hand a squeeze for emphasis.

"You know," John said, looking down at her with a look of love mixed with amusement, "I think you just might be right."

Chapter 66

The Second Chance

THE NEXT MORNING, they crept out of bed in the dark and got ready. John showered and shaved, then Olivia stepped into the bathroom when he was done. She wanted to put on her dress in private and surprise him, another affectionate nod to John's worries about superstitions and wedding gods. She swept her hair into a loose bun, letting a few curls fall free, then carefully applied her makeup. It was a far cry from the professional styling at her first wedding—for which she'd paid a small fortune—but she was too happy to care.

Wow, what a difference from a year ago, she thought as she applied her mascara. She'd been so miserable in the hours before the first one. And conflicted. And alone. But now here she was, absolutely giddy to be getting the chance to do it all over. Life could sure surprise you sometimes.

When she was done, she stepped back and surveyed her work. She looked precisely the way a bride should look on her big day. Radiant. Happy. Excited.

She stepped out of the bathroom to find John dressed and ready, his back turned as he looked out the window and down at the lights of the Strip.

Then he turned back to see her standing there. She smiled before twirling once, the pink material billowing around her legs.

"What do you think?" she asked. "It's so simple,

but it kind of reminded me of my first dress, too."

"You'd marry me in a gas station, and I'd marry you in a burlap sack," John said, crossing the room and taking her hands in his. "But seriously, you look absolutely amazing in that dress. I don't know how you managed it, but you're a thousand times more beautiful than you were a year ago. And a year ago you already could take my breath away. I might need oxygen when we get up on the observation deck."

Olivia laughed, then stood back to inspect his new suit.

"I still can't get over how different you look, too," she said. "All the exercise and the time spent in the sun. And your hair's shorter. But even more than all of that, I'm looking at you with so much love and adoration. Absolutely everything has changed this time around. And all of it is for the better."

John responded with a series of kisses, first on the forehead, then the tip of her nose, and finally her lips. He lingered on the last one for a moment, both of them lost in the happiness of the moment, before he pulled away.

"We better go so we don't keep our new best friend Andre waiting," he said.

"Don't forget your phone, because I want pictures," Olivia told him as she grabbed her purse and tucked the room's card key inside. "Okay, let's do this!"

"Oh wait, one more thing," John said as she paused by the door. "You might need this during the ceremony."

Olivia looked into his outstretched palm. In it was John's platinum wedding band, the one she hadn't seen since he'd taken it off a year ago on the plane.

"You have it!" she cried, the delight making her

eyes sparkle. "Oh, I'm so glad you brought it with you when you came back to Paris! It really proves that, despite everything else, some part of you must still have believed we could make it to this day!"

She reached out to accept it, then slowly removed the matching band of her own. "This is the first time I've taken off this ring since our *other* wedding."

"And you'll never have to take it off again," he said with a smile as he took the thin band from her hand. "Now, are you ready to do this?"

"I've never been more ready for anything in my life," Olivia said, giddy excitement starting to thrum through her now.

"Me either," he said. "Let's go."

*   *   *

As promised, Andre met them at the bank of elevators that led to the top of the tower. They stepped in one of the cars, then Andre pressed the button for the observation deck.

"You two look great," he said.

"Thank you so much," Olivia replied. Then she took John's phone and held it out. "I hate to keep piling on the favors, but would you mind taking some pictures of us up at the top? I desperately want some wedding photos. I know it's just a phone, but it really takes great pictures."

"Of course! It's no problem at all," Andre replied.

When they got to the observation deck, the light was breaking across the horizon. Andre cheerfully took pictures from many different angles. When he finally handed the phone back, he said, "I'll be over by the elevators when you're done." Then he walked away, leaving them alone.

"It's finally happening," Olivia said. "And right at

sunrise. Oh John, this is the happiest moment of my life."

"Mine too," John said, a look of intense contentment on his face as he took her hands in his own. "Olivia, I have loved you without question since the first time I saw you at that party. Life and the many crazy circumstances it threw our way have tried their best to test that love. But it's always been there, and it always will be. And you can count on it every day for the rest of our lives. I'll love you and support you in whatever you do, and I'll never stop being thankful that we both hung in there and fought for this chance to start our new journey together. A year ago, we promised to love each other for better or for worse. And Livvie, we've finally found our way to the 'better' part of that. But even when we hit more rough spots, we've proven that our love will help us weather any storm as long as we do it together. Today, here at the top of the faux Eiffel Tower, I swear to you that I will cherish and love you forever."

Happy tears started to slide their way down her face. "That was beautiful, John, but I think you missed a real opportunity to call it the 'Ei-faux Tower'."

"Ugh, you're so right," he said with a smirk. "Yeah, sorry."

Olivia laughed back. Then, switching to a more serious tone, she said, "I love you too, John. I'm sorry it took three trips to two different Parises, two weddings, and one divorce for us to make it to this day. But it's all been so worth it. I don't know that I would have ever cherished what we have if not for the journey through fire that brought us here. Now I want to put this ring back on your finger where it belongs and, finally, go home and start our lives as husband and wife. I want to buy a house with you, make some sort of family with you, and finally introduce you to our dog. But mostly, I want to grow old with you." She slid the wedding band on his finger then. "I swear I will never forget the tough lessons we've learned about how precious our love is or how hard we should always fight to stay together. And yes, John, I promise that I will love and cherish you every day for the rest of my life."

From the inside pocket of his jacket, he took out Olivia's ring, and slid it in place. Then he reached into his pocket again.

"I've got a surprise for you," he said, showing her the diamond anniversary band. "I bought this for you as a symbol of our second wedding and the fresh start we've been given."

Olivia gasped, inspecting the ring with pure delight as he slid it onto her finger until it was neatly stacked on top of the others. "When did you find the time to buy this? It's gorgeous."

"When you were busy buying this dress. I felt like we needed something new to help us remember this day."

"Oh, John, I'll remember it and cherish it even without the ring," she said, "but it's absolutely perfect, and so are you. I love you, and I'll spend the rest of my life making sure you never have any reason to doubt it again."

And she did exactly that.

Epilogue

JOHN AND OLIVIA returned to Paris, France, the following year. They had staged a do-over of their wedding, so they decided to do the exact same thing with their honeymoon. It was important to return and create brand-new memories as a way of erasing the first two trips completely.

"Are you sure this is a good idea?" Olivia asked on the flight as she laced her fingers together with his. "It hasn't exactly been the luckiest city for us in the past."

"Absolutely—Paris is my favorite place in the world," John said, turning to look at her. "Paris is where my gorgeous, adoring wife first realized she was in love with me. I can't wait to get there. We're going to create memories that will erase the bad ones for good. I promise you that, honey. This will be the fabulous honeymoon we never had the first time. Or the second, for that matter. Plus, I think there was one residential street in a southern suburb that we haven't seen yet."

"So, wait," Olivia said, with a teasing glint in her eyes, "you're not going to abandon me in our honeymoon suite while you traipse off with some other woman you pick up on this flight?"

"Oh, yeah, I am absolutely going to do that," John said, laughing as Olivia jabbed her elbow into his side. "But the other stuff will be completely different."

"That's not funny, you jerk," she said, her smile belying the harshness of her words.

"You know I'm just teasing you, Livvie. There is no other woman on the planet for me. Plus, I'm a little afraid of that jealous streak you've got."

"Yeah, you'd *better* not forget it!" she said, leaning in to give him a long, passionate kiss. "You're all mine."

"But I do hear what you're saying about this being the final chapter in our Paris story," John eventually went on. "Next year, let's go anywhere else in the world. Africa. South America. Canada. The North Pole. I don't care. Any place that *doesn't* have an Eiffel Tower."

Olivia nodded. "You've got a deal. And who knows, maybe someday our vacations will consist of pushing strollers through amusement parks and zoos and water parks with our kids, if we're lucky enough to have them."

"Absolutely. With kids or just the two of us, island resorts or playgrounds—it doesn't matter Liv. Let's just see what happens and enjoy the ride, no matter where our journey takes us."

After they landed, John made sure all his promises to Olivia came true. They revisited all the sites they'd toured before, but this time they held hands, kissed, teased, and laughed their way through all of it. They returned to *Sainte Chapelle*, Notre Dame, and the Eiffel Tower. They walked hand-in-hand along the Seine and went shopping on the *Champs-Élysées*. They took their time viewing the treasures of the *Louvre* and the *Musée d'Orsay,* and they finally got out of the city to tour a vineyard.

But mostly they enjoyed each other's company, amazed that they had managed to come so far in two short years.

* * *

"It makes me so sad to think about our first honeymoon," Olivia admitted one night as they strolled along a busy sidewalk near their hotel. "I can't help but remember the pain we were both in, and the fights we had, and how alone we were feeling. And then that miserable year we spent apart and alone, not knowing if we'd lost each other forever. It was such a terrible time. Isn't it some sort of bad omen for us that we got off to *such* a rough beginning?"

John took Olivia's hand and pulled her gently toward the nearest building so the crowd could continue flowing by.

"Olivia, at that first wedding I promised to love you for better or for worse. I didn't know then that we were already in the middle of the 'worse' part. But that's why we started over with the second wedding, remember?" John tucked her hair behind her ear and smiled. "And it's all going to be smooth sailing from now on—look at everything we went through, and still we were able to emerge on the other side as better people with a closer and stronger relationship than we ever dreamed. Livvie, I thank God we went through those terrible times. Without them, we wouldn't be able to enjoy, appreciate, and treasure what we've found together in the same way. So remember—they weren't the world's worst wedding and honeymoon, sweetheart. They were the world's *best.*"

Olivia smiled back and then wrapped her arms around his neck before pulling him in for a tight hug.

"Nice try, honey, but that trip was crap, and we both know it," she said, and John burst out laughing.

"Yeah, it was pretty bad," he said, hugging her back.

Finally, they ended their embrace with a kiss,

joined hands again, and continued walking toward the hotel, both simply happy to be there, creating and sharing their new honeymoon memories—together.

Thank You!

THANK YOU for reading John and Olivia's story! I would appreciate it so much if you took a moment to rate or review it on your favorite site.

This book is part of trio of books I wrote about women finding love on fabulous trips. The first book is *Curveball: A Love Story*, in which Emma travels to Dublin and runs into a sexy American bartender who's in hiding from the mistakes he made and the life he left behind. That one is available in paperback and ebook formats.

The third book of this informal trilogy is still upcoming in paperback and ebook (although, like *The Honeymoon*, you can find it now on Kindle Vella). *The Bridesmaid* is about Julianna, an American on vacation in London who falls into love—and danger—on the trip of a lifetime to England.

Here's a sneak peek of *The Bridesmaid: An Insta-Love Romance*—

2003

"OH, HONEY, you're gonna look gorgeous in that dress! You *sure* you don't want to try it on again?" the seamstress asked as she fluttered around, obviously dismayed.

"Nah, I trust you," Julianna said, carelessly shoving the dress into the garment bag she'd just been conned into purchasing so she could safely transport the dress back home.

"You're going to wrinkle it!" the seamstress cried, nudging Julianna out of the way with her hip as she tried to gently ease the dress into bag, straightening and smoothing as she went.

"What do I owe you?" Julianna asked, patiently stepping back from the garment bag and bracing herself for the inevitable bad news.

"Hmm, let's see," the woman said, as she slowly zipped the bag, stopping constantly to ensure she wasn't catching the dress's abundant tulle in the zipper's teeth. "The dress was over $300, and the alterations were another $100 or so, the garment bag was $40, and then there's the sales tax, of course."

"Of course," Julianna said with a silent sigh. *Stupid, ugly, overpriced dress*, she grumbled to herself as she dug her wallet out of her purse and handed the woman her credit card.

"Thanks, hon!" the woman chirped as she finally finished worrying about the dress and turned her attention back to Julianna and the monetary transaction at hand.

Julianna signed the receipt, grabbed the heavy, awkward white bag, and made her way out of the seamstress's shop. At a final price tag of almost $500, as painful as the expense was to her and her bank account, the final tally wasn't so bad compared to what she *could* be paying in a city boutique.

Finally out of the seamstress's disapproving sights and out on the sidewalk, Julianna folded the bag in half so she could carry it more easily. As she struggled with it, a cab pulled up in front of her to deposit its passenger. She hadn't planned on taking a taxi, but since there was one right there, she also had no intention of ignoring fate's little present.

It's about time something went my way today, she thought as the cab's passenger finished paying the cabbie and got out of the car. Julianna pitched the garment bag into the backseat then crawled in after it.

"Port Authority," she called up to the cabbie as the polite ex-passenger closed the door behind her.

"Thanks," she called through the glass, finally glancing up to acknowledge the man who'd just vacated the backseat.

As the cab pulled away from the curb, she caught a glimpse of the curly-haired passenger's bright blue eyes.

*   *   *

The taffeta confection swirled over her head in a Barbie-doll-pink cloud, as she groped around trying to find the armholes, her arms pinned awkwardly over her head.

"You'd think I'd be able to figure these stupid things out by now," Julianna muttered in frustration, torn between ripping the dress off her head and struggling awhile longer to wiggle into it. Knowing she had to succumb to it eventually, though, she sighed and gave in. With one final stretch, she found the left armhole, then was able to target in on the other. Glad no seams were popping, she tugged the dress over her head and smoothed it over her hips. Turning around, she looked into the full-length mirror.

"Oh, give me a break! Megan, I look like Glinda the Good Witch!" she said, only half joking.

The dress WAS completely wrong for her. The length, which hit her in the middle of her shins, did nothing to accentuate her 5'10" height. The very full skirt, topped with tulle, shot off her rounded hips, creating more of a shelf than the bell-like ballerina effect the bride had promised her. And the color was just, well, too "little girl" for a 30-year-old to pull off.

"If I were eight years old and four-feet tall, this dress would be the one I'd pick," Julianna sighed.

Her sister just laughed.

"Well Jules, it's not like you didn't know what you were getting into," Megan said. "What is this, like your tenth wedding?"

"Yeah, you're really helping. It's *only* my ninth," Julianna said, laughing as she caught her sister's eye in the mirror. "I know, I know. I seem to be going for some sort of warped world record. I don't know why I can't get out of this cycle."

But she did know why—and it didn't have anything to do with being a romantic sap who dreamed moodily about her own wedding while conning her way into other women's big days.

No, Julianna was quite happy with her life just the way it was. When other women, during and after college, had been actively open to finding their life partners, she had been just as busy, but she had spent her time studying and cultivating friendships. She loved hanging out with the girls. Shopping, going to the movies, hitting the flea markets, going out for after-work appetizers and frothy drinks.

But it seemed like one day she was surrounded by all her single friends, laughing and dishing on the latest gossip, and the next day they were all suddenly paired up with their mates like they'd gotten a call from Noah and were headed for the boat. But she hadn't gotten the same call.

It wasn't that she had anything *against* dating or falling in love, really, but she just didn't ever seem to have the time these days. Between her full-time job at the hospital—a registered nurse, she worked three 12-hour shifts a week—her time spent with girlfriends and family, and her voracious movie habits, her life was a full and happy place to be.

Yes, dating and love would be okay if they fell in her lap somehow, without taking up too much of her time. But the wedding whirlwind she'd gotten sucked into had started souring her on the idea of weddings and the institution of marriage itself. It seemed the more she saw of the whole mess—friends morphing into bridezillas, fighting in-laws, outrageous expenses, goofy traditions, and ugly dresses—the more it all seemed to be a big waste of time. Why bother being in the spotlight of one of these ridiculous affairs? She'd seen enough from the sidelines to last her a lifetime.

It hadn't started out that way. In fact, wedding number one had been pretty great—standing up for a girlfriend who got married their junior year of college.

That bride, bless her forever, had asked Julianna to wear any dress she wanted to wear, since she was the only attendant. As a poor college student, Julianna had just pulled out the dress she'd worn to her high school graduation. It had fit, no minor feat considering the midnight pizza orders and diner runs, and the style hadn't gone noticeably "out."

So that wedding ended up being painless and stress-free—a trip to the justice of the peace at the town hall with a few friends. No expenses for the maid of honor, really, other than whatever she had spent putting together a scrapbook for the newlyweds of various pictures and mementoes from the past few years. It had been perfect, from Julianna's point of view. No parties, no fittings, no forced trips to a hair stylist to find a perfect updo. Just friends and love and a certificate. And since the couple was still married, she figured she wasn't the only one who thought so.

As a result, it hadn't even occurred to her to say no when another friend, this time from high school, announced he was getting married. Julianna, although she didn't really know his bride that well, was still honored and happy when they asked her to be a bridesmaid—friends, love, happiness, what could be better?

But that was when things started to slide downhill. She wasn't the only bridesmaid; in fact, she was one of *twelve*. And the dress choice wasn't exactly debated and voted on democratically. The woman had been a nightmare, picking out and insisting on this yellow number that warred wildly with Julianna's blonde hair and pale complexion, giving her a waxy look and making her feel like a big, frumpy lemon the day of the wedding.

And after all the money she'd spent on that day— between the dress, shoes, accessories, hair, makeup, and present—the couple hadn't even managed to stay married for two years. What a waste.

And it had just gotten worse after that. The funny thing was, none of the weddings started out big and none of the brides started out evil. It was always the same, "No, no, really. I promise. We'll find a simple, cheap dress that looks great on all of you, and you'll be able to use it again. Trust me!"

Every single time, no matter the type of wedding, indoors or outdoors, formal or informal, that was always the promise. And every time, she ended up wrapped in ruffles and bows and tulle and fabric roses.

"Use the dress again—hah!" Julianna burst out, making both of them laugh. Megan knew exactly what she'd been thinking about. It was a well-covered topic between the two, and the subject of much debate. Just how *could* those dresses be put to good use? Blocking drafty doors was the winning entry so far, although tire traction in a snowstorm was a serious contender.

"I hate to say this, Meg, but I can't wait for this stupid wedding to be over with," Julianna sighed. "And after this, I'm hanging up my bouquet. I'm just sick of the schmaltz," she said, with an added and overly dramatic sigh.

"Oh poor baby!" Megan teased, flopping down on the bed. "So many friends who love her and want her in their weddings! Life is so *hard!*"

"Oh shut up, you know what I mean. I'm just in a rut, I guess. I've spent so much time being in my friends' lives. I think I forgot to live my own," she said, making one last, futile attempt to flatten the tulle. "I need a vacation. When's the last time we went anywhere?"

"Hmmm...was it the family summer trip to Niagara Falls the year before you went to college?" Megan offered. "After that vacation, you always stayed home each summer working."

"Yeah, I think that was my last trip. Wow, that's really depressing," Julianna said, sort of absent mindedly, as she started the struggle to get back out of the pink concoction.

"Well then let's go somewhere! You've got time coming, and my semester will be over in May. Why don't we just pick a spot and price tickets before we change our minds or chicken out?" Megan suggested, eagerly. "Oooh, how about somewhere tropical? An island in the Caribbean maybe."

"Nah, you know I can't take vacations in the sun. Ten minutes on the beach, and my pasty white skin becomes radioactive," Julianna said, finally pulling free of the dress. "Nope, no sun. Oh, hey, what about Europe? London, maybe? I think I saw a commercial about an airfare sale."

"That's a great idea!" Megan easily agreed. "Perhaps I'll take a lift to my flat and stop in the loo after riding in a lorry," Megan babbled with a horribly affected accent.

"Yeah, okay, there Princess. Might want to bring it down a notch."

"Fine, but can't you almost taste the scones and tea now?" Megan asked with a happy smile before she took off for her computer to check the prices. Julianna draped the dress on a hanger, shoved it into her closet, and sighed. One more wedding to suffer through, then she was cutting loose—it was definitely time for an adventure of her own.

Acknowledgments

JUST AS OLIVIA AND JOHN have to follow a long, twisting road to find their second chance, so did this book. I wrote the first draft of *The Honeymoon* about twenty years ago. I tried to shop it around to many different publishers, and I had a fair amount of interest in it. But a couple editors asked for big changes, so I kept rewriting and changing it. Eventually I shelved it altogether once my kids were born, and there those versions of the original draft sat for years.

When I pulled this book back out with the intention of finally bringing it to readers, first on Kindle Vella and now in paperback and ebook formats, I had a lot of challenges I needed to face and decisions I had to make. I had three completely different versions of this story. Which one was the best? I just wasn't sure. Plus, the technology was hopelessly—and often hilariously—out of date. John spent a lot of time searching for internet cafes and phone booths, for example, when he was hunting for a hotel room. And they encountered numerous problems that we'd now solve just by pulling out our phones. Here's an example from the first draft:

> *He pulled his address book and daily planner out of his suitcase and flipped to the right page, then sat down and read the hotel's directions for getting an outside line. Picking up the handset with his left hand, he started to dial the number...*

That reads like instructions for assembling furniture! I replaced that whole thing (which was from when he calls Charlie from Paris) with something like, "He pulled out his phone…."

So of course I eventually updated the technology. But first I had to figure out which draft to use, because there were some wild variations. In the original draft, John gets shot saving Olivia in a hold-up. The fact that he almost dies is what makes her realize she loves him. In another version, she sends him emails all year. He doesn't respond, but when she rushes to the airport to find him, he's racing to find her too, and they run into each other and reunite. In another version, they take a very formal approach to resolving their issues via a list. I can admit that one was a little dry and boring!

In the end, I stitched together versions two and three into a frankenversion. I changed the emails to letters. I made her realization that she loves him more organic. And I added a totally different prologue.

I think this long journey and struggle taught me a lot about persevering and never giving up on dreams. Even after all this time, and all those drafts, I absolutely love these characters, and I hope you enjoyed their journey!

Thank you to my family and friends for all their support and, of course, to my friend and editor Wil Mara, who's helped me turn dreams into reality.

About the Author

ANNE TROWBRIDGE loves writing romances that hit major emotional beats in swoony, angsty stories in which the couples really earn their HEAs. Expect banter, angst, and deeply emotional connections that resonate!

She lives in New Jersey with her husband, two kids, and two dogs. When she's not reading or writing, she's teaching language arts to seventh graders, which really should involve medals for bravery. She grew up all over the Midwest and somehow still loves to travel and see new places.

Join her and learn more about upcoming books at:

https://www.annetrowbridgebooks.com/

https://linktr.ee/annetrowbridgebooks